A Firm
Foundation

MYSTERY
and the
MINISTER'S
WIFE

A Firm Foundation

ANNE MARIE RODGERS

GUIDEPOSTS
NEW YORK, NEW YORK

In memory of my grandparents:
Lloyd and Phoebe McCleaf, who gave me
a sweet tooth and a love of music, and
Harold and Helen Bittner, from whom I inherited
my green thumb and, just possibly, the "bossy" gene.

Chapter One

The July heat enveloped the southern Appalachian region of Tennessee, pouring hot sunlight over the small town of Copper Mill.

Kate Hanlon sat with the choir in the tiny church of Faith Briar. Although her sky-blue paisley dress was both lightweight and sleeveless, she couldn't resist fanning herself with her bulletin.

Many others in the congregation were doing the same thing. The church's cooling system was no match for the sunlight streaming through the side windows, and the church felt like a sauna. Kate's shoulder-length strawberry-blonde hair was damp against her neck, and she suspected her soft curls were turning into a bird's nest around her face. Despite the heat, Kate's heart was filled with happiness as she listened to her husband, Paul, Faith Briar's pastor, conclude the Sunday service.

Oh, it was wonderful to be home!

Kate had gone away for nearly two weeks earlier that month. First, she had visited their former home church in

San Antonio. Afterward, she had flown east to see their youngest child, Rebecca, who was an actress in New York City.

She hadn't expected to miss Copper Mill and the unique residents of the little town so much. Kate had been born and raised in San Antonio, and after she and Paul married, they had lived there almost thirty years. So she thought she would feel a sense of homecoming when she returned for a visit.

But she hadn't, although she had enjoyed catching up with her extended family, as well as friends she had known through the years. Her life was here now, with her husband, her church family, and many dear friends.

Friends. She frowned as she scanned the congregation. Where was Livvy? There was a pretty good crowd, considering it was a hot Sunday in July right in the middle of vacation season. But Livvy's cheerful face wasn't visible.

Kate's best friend in Copper Mill was Olivia Jenner, the town librarian. Livvy had been one of the first people Kate had met when she and Paul had moved to town, and the two women quickly had become close. Livvy attended church as faithfully as Kate herself.

And yet today, she was missing. Livvy wasn't singing with the choir. And her husband, Danny, and two teenage sons, James and Justin, were sitting in their usual pew without her. Livvy rarely missed church, particularly when the rest of her family was present, and Kate worried that her friend might be sick.

The service ended, and the moment Kate was free, she rushed to catch Danny before he could leave.

"Danny!" she called.

He turned, a smile lighting his eyes. "Welcome home," he said as he gave her a brief hug. "How was your trip?"

"Delightful," she said. "But it's good to be home. I missed everyone."

"We missed you," Danny responded.

Kate smiled and said hello to James and Justin, then turned back to Danny. "Where's Livvy? Is she ill?"

Danny's smile vanished. "No," he said. "She's at the library."

Kate was shocked. "At the library? But it's Sunday morning."

"Yeah." Danny exhaled heavily. "She didn't have a very good week."

"Why?"

Concern shadowed Danny's eyes. "She hasn't said very much, except to tell me that she can't talk about it."

Can't talk about it? That sounded odd. Kate crossed her arms, thinking. Secrecy was unlike Livvy. "Why can't she talk about it?"

Danny shook his head. "I wish I knew. She's been as sad-eyed as a basset hound since Friday, and she worked late both Friday and Saturday nights. She's there again today."

That was strange. Livvy loved her job at the library, but it rarely required her to work late or on weekends. What could she possibly be doing that necessitated such long hours?

"What's she working on?" Kate asked.

Danny hesitated. He opened his mouth, then closed it again and sent Kate an apologetic glance. "You'll have to speak to her. She specifically asked me not to talk about it."

That wasn't like Livvy at all. What could be wrong? Kate's

level of concern soared even higher. "Maybe I'll run down there later. Do you think she'll be at the library all day?"

Danny nodded. "She told us not to expect her for lunch or dinner. She left meals for us in the fridge." His face grew even more mournful, and Kate's heart went out to him.

"I can try talking to her," Kate offered. "If she can't say much to you, I doubt she'll talk to me. But it won't hurt to try."

"Thank you." Danny's relief was palpable.

On the short drive home together in Kate's black Honda, Kate told Paul what Danny had said.

His reaction was very like hers. "Why can't Danny talk about it?"

Kate shook her head. "I don't know. Was Liv in church last Sunday?"

"Yes," Paul said. "And she seemed all right. I distinctly remember her laughing at one of my jokes."

Kate glanced at her husband, a smile on her face. Paul sometimes injected humor into his sermons, although the congregation didn't always find it as amusing as Paul did. "You remember her reaction to a joke?"

Paul chuckled. "It was a pretty feeble joke. She was the only one who laughed."

Kate smiled and then continued the conversation. "Danny said she was fine until Friday, so whatever happened must have occurred that day. And it must be related to her work. Why else would she be at the library on a Sunday morning?"

Paul shook his head. "I can't imagine, but you're right. It sounds as if something must have happened on Friday."

Kate made cucumber-and-tomato sandwiches for lunch,

served with a cantaloupe that one of the church members had given Paul. While they ate, she recounted to Paul more details from her trip, but in the back of her mind, she kept hearing Danny's words regarding Livvy. *She didn't have a very good week.*

As they finished their meal, Paul said, "You're worrying about Livvy, aren't you?"

Kate nodded, thanking God for this wonderful man who understood her so well. "I need to go down to the library."

"Go ahead," Paul told her. "I'll wash the dishes."

As she grabbed her handbag and keys, he called after her, "Keep an eye on the sky, honey. We've had severe thunderstorm warnings every day this week, and we've already had two wicked storms."

Kate nodded. "Thanks. I will."

IT TOOK KATE ONLY MINUTES to make the short drive into Copper Mill.

There were lights on inside the library as she approached. As she pulled open one of the heavy glass doors, Kate was surprised to find that the doors were unlocked. She noticed a large hand-lettered sign taped to the interior side of the glass: Closed Until Further Notice.

Closed until further notice?

A bolt of shock ran through Kate, stopping her momentarily. The library was closed—and not just for a day or two, but for quite a while, perhaps? It didn't say anything about when the library would reopen, a fact Kate found quite odd for a public facility. Something was very, very wrong.

Kate spotted Livvy the moment she entered the building.

There was a great deal of activity around the librarian but no buzz of excitement. Instead, barely anyone spoke. Despite the bright sunlight visible through the large windows, it felt like a funeral parlor without the music.

A woman Kate recognized as one of the Friends of the Library officers was using packing tape to reinforce sturdy, medium-sized moving boxes, which another woman was distributing. Several other people, some of whom Kate knew to be regular library volunteers, were removing books from the shelves and stacking them in the boxes.

Livvy wore a sleeveless blue-gingham blouse over a pair of white walking shorts. The shorts had been an unfortunate choice, since they were covered with dark streaks of dust and other unidentifiable stains. Livvy's reading glasses were shoved atop her head, pushing her tousled mop of auburn hair back from her face. She looked hot, harassed, and unhappy as she gestured with a clipboard and spoke to Morty Robertson, a retiree who often helped out at the library.

"Livvy?" Kate started forward.

"Kate!" Livvy's expression lightened momentarily, and she rushed forward. "Oh, I'm so glad you're back."

Kate caught her friend in a tight hug. "I'm glad to be back." She drew back and cupped Livvy's shoulders in her hands. "What on earth is going on here?"

Livvy's face crumpled. For a moment, Kate was sure her friend was going to break down. But after a tense moment while she fought for composure, Livvy said, "Exactly what it looks like. We're packing up the building."

"The whole building?"

Livvy nodded.

"Is the library moving?" Kate asked.

A flash of pain twisted Livvy's pretty features for a moment. "I don't have time to discuss it," she finally said.

Kate stared at her. "Why not?"

"It doesn't matter." Livvy pushed back a straggling lock of hair with the back of her wrist. Misery and apology were in her eyes. "I'm really sorry, Kate."

"It does matter," Kate said gently. "This is a community institution, Livvy. I can't be the only person who's upset about the library closing, temporary or not."

"I don't think a lot of people know about it yet," Livvy said. "I asked these folks"—she indicated the people working around her—"not to talk about it. But now that the weekend is passing, I'm sure word is getting around. I suspect there will be plenty of upset people in Copper Mill tomorrow." She glanced at her watch. "I have to get back to work."

"Livvy," Kate said quietly, "what's going on here? It's obvious you're not happy about it. How can I help?"

"You can't," Livvy told her. "There are things you don't understand, Kate. Things that I . . . that I can't share with you, as much as I'd like to. Please don't ask me any more questions."

"All right," said Kate. She suppressed a dozen more questions trembling on the tip of her tongue.

Livvy looked as if she was on the verge of tears, and Kate didn't want to distress her friend any further. She reached out to place a comforting hand on Livvy's arm.

Livvy backed away.

Kate froze. Livvy was her dearest friend in Copper Mill. What could be so wrong that Livvy would refuse Kate's comfort?

"I have to get back to work." Livvy broke the awkward silence between them. As she reached up to push her glasses higher on her head, Kate could see that her hand was shaking noticeably. "I'm sorry, I'm just really busy, and I don't have time to talk."

She sounded terribly upset, and Kate was positive she heard a note of fear in Livvy's voice.

Fear? What on earth could her friend be afraid of? The hurt Kate had felt a moment earlier when Livvy had retreated from her faded.

"What are you afraid of, Livvy?" Kate asked, but her friend shook her head.

"Nothing." Livvy gave a sunny, artificial smile. "Really, Kate. You see mysteries in every little thing that happens."

Little thing? Kate didn't consider the library closing a little thing in any way. "But—"

"Stop," Livvy begged in an undertone. Her expression looked frantic as she glanced around, then whispered, "I can't talk to you about this. I could lose my job."

"If the library's closing, haven't you already lost your job?" Kate asked.

Livvy shook her head. "No, I—Kate! I said I can't talk about this." And she turned away.

Chapter Two

There was little else Kate could do. It was clear that her presence was only upsetting her friend. It was equally clear that something terrible was happening at the library.

Slowly, she turned and headed back to her car.

Before she left the building, movement in the fiction stacks nearest to the door caught her eye, and Kate peeped around the corner. Morty Robertson was removing books from the tall shelves, wiping them off, and placing them in a box. Not far from him, a woman Kate didn't recognize was working at the same task.

"Hi, Morty," Kate said.

The older man straightened, and his gaze met Kate's. "Hi, Kate," he said without a trace of his usual lighthearted manner.

The other volunteer stood as well, rubbing her back. Morty tossed a hand in her general direction and said, "Kate, this is Louisa Pellman. Louisa, Kate Hanlon."

"Hello," said the woman. She had dirty-blonde hair and blue eyes that might have been pretty if not for the dark circles beneath them. In fact, for a woman who probably wasn't much more than thirty, she looked drawn and tired and older than her years.

Kate nodded. "It's nice to meet you, Louisa." Distracted by the strange goings-on, she turned back to Morty, who said, "Back from your trip, huh?"

She nodded. "It's good to be home. Except for this. Morty, what's going on?"

He shook his head. "Haven't got a clue. All I can tell you is Livvy's either getting ready to cry, crying or has just finished crying every time I set eyes on her."

"When did the trouble begin?" Kate asked.

"Friday morning," he said promptly. "Tosten Glass, that self-important windbag who's the president of the town council, came rushing in here right after we opened. He and Livvy went into her office, and when they came out again, she had less color than a faded bedsheet in the sun. And then she gathered all of us, employees and volunteers alike, and told us we had to begin packing everything."

"Tosten Glass." Kate had never met the man, although she had seen his picture in the *Copper Mill Chronicle*. Glass and the town council were the real power behind the more visible and ceremonial office of the mayor.

"Yeah. He bustled in here Saturday and again today and fusses at everybody to move faster." Morty snorted. "Like I'm going to take orders from him. Livvy's the only one he can boss around."

Kate lowered her voice. "And has he?"

Morty nodded. "They went into her office yesterday for a big, secret closed-door meeting, and when they came out, she looked even more upset than she already was."

"And you haven't heard why you're packing all these books?"

He shook his head. "Not a whisper."

The young woman Morty had just introduced her to drifted closer. "Are you talking about the library closing?" Her expression looked as dismayed as Kate felt.

Kate nodded. "Yes. I can't imagine how this could happen so quickly without anyone in town hearing about it."

Louisa clasped her hands tightly together. "It did seem to happen suddenly."

"So I see." Kate's mind was whirling, her thoughts touching on one possibility after another. "I think I'm going to ask a few questions," she told Morty and Louisa. "Maybe the mayor knows the reason behind this."

Louisa grimaced. "The mayor just got back from a month of service work in Mexico. I'll be surprised if he knows anything."

FEELING THAT SHE should be doing something but not knowing what that something might be, Kate went home.

Paul had left her a note on the counter telling her that he had things to do that afternoon and would be back by four. Glancing at the clock, she saw that the afternoon was passing quickly, and she had things to do too. Her flight had gotten in late the previous evening, and by the time Paul had driven her home from the airport in Chattanooga, she had been too tired to do more than fall into bed.

She spent the next several hours unpacking, cleaning, and catching up on all the dirty laundry she had brought home from her trip. She usually tried to reserve Sunday as a day off from housework, but she'd been gone two weeks, and even though Paul had done his best, it was clear his talents lay in areas other than keeping a clean and tidy home.

While she worked, she puzzled over what she should do next about the library. Livvy clearly didn't want her to do anything. So should she abide by her friend's wishes?

Maybe she *was* seeing a problem where there was none, Kate thought. Maybe the library was being renovated or repainted. That could explain all the packing.

But it didn't explain why Livvy was so upset. Or why she was afraid she would lose her job if she talked about it with Kate. Or why she had been so secretive, even with her own husband. And why would the head of the town council be coming in repeatedly to harass Livvy, as it sounded like he'd been doing?

Kate had a very bad feeling about the whole situation. She had learned to heed her intuition, and right now her intuition was shouting at her to figure out what was going on.

Paul came home as she was breading a couple of boneless chicken breasts dipped in honey-mustard sauce. She heard his truck pull into the driveway, and moments later, the door shut behind him. She looked up, smiling, as he came into the kitchen.

"Hi, honey. What's for dinner?"

Kate indicated the chicken, which she was just sliding into the oven. "Chick—" She stopped short, taking in her husband's appearance. "Paul Hanlon, what on earth have you been doing? You're *fried*!

And indeed he was. Paul was wearing a pair of his oldest jeans and a T-shirt. Both were filthy. His face, exposed arms, and neck all were so red, he nearly glowed.

"How did you get so sunburned?" she asked.

Paul lifted one hand to his neck for a moment. "I was working on a roof," he said in a nonchalant tone.

"A roof!"

He nodded. "Lucas Gregory called the day after you left. He asked if Faith Briar would like to be included in a multichurch building-repair effort. First Baptist and the Presbyterian church are also getting involved."

Kate smiled. Lucas was an Episcopalian priest and one of Paul's good friends. "What are you repairing?"

"There's a family named Pellman out in Skunk Hollow—"

"Where?" She couldn't hold back the laugh that bubbled up.

"Skunk Hollow. It's an area just past the Ash Grove Campground. In fact, the road that runs through there is called Skunk Hollow Trail."

Kate shook her head, chuckling. "Anyway, go on. You were telling me about the Pellman family. Wait!" She threw up a hand in a "stop" gesture. "I just met a woman named Louisa Pellman today at the library."

Paul nodded. "I heard she was volunteering there."

"So how do you know her?" As far as Kate could remember, she had never heard Paul mention the woman's name.

"I didn't. Lucas knew her, and she's the lady whose roof we're repairing."

"So this is the project you mentioned yesterday."

On the way home from the airport, Kate had done most of the talking, but Paul had told her that he was involved in a big project he would tell her about later.

Kate studied her husband. "That explains the sunburn."

"Mrs. Pellman's roof is in terrible condition," Paul said, "The house needed some structural repairs that she just couldn't afford." He raised a hand, index finger extended upward in a "hold on one minute" gesture, when Kate started to speak again. "St. Lucy's, First Baptist, the Presbyterians, and Faith Briar are all working together to reroof the home. We've organized four different teams that take turns working."

Kate didn't feel much better. "Don't all these people have to work?"

Paul shook his head. "We all agreed to take a week of our own vacation time."

"There are a lot of generous hearts in this little town." Kate was warmed by the story.

"Very generous," Paul agreed. "Several people at St. Lucy's chipped in to buy some insulated windows, which are also being installed. And Lucas has been thrilled with all the volunteers who've stepped up."

"So your sunburn is from working on Louisa Pellman's roof." Kate suddenly felt anxiety rise inside her. "Paul, what do you know about roofing? Thinking of you that high off the ground makes me a little nervous."

"I don't have to know a whole lot," he assured her. "Drew Mears from First Baptist works for a roofing contractor in Pine Ridge, so he's the crew chief. Ephraim Dresser from the Presbyterian church volunteered to take over the chairmanship. Between the two of them, they've got us and the materials organized."

"Who else is helping from our congregation?"

"Each church provided a five-man team. Ours includes Carl Wilson, Sam Gorman, Eli Weston—Eli was in construction, remember?—Joe Tucker, and me."

Kate reached into the fridge for the lettuce to make a salad. "Joe was also in construction when he was younger, wasn't he?"

"Yes. Both he and Sam worked for the same company. And even though Carl's a mechanic, he and I figured we can follow directions as well as the next guy."

"When did you start all this?" she asked while chopping tomatoes.

"Last week," Paul told her. "I spoke to the church about it last Sunday while you were away, and those fellows volunteered. We got organized and started later in the week."

Kate was impressed. "You've moved pretty quickly."

"Our goal is to get the roof done by next weekend."

"Is that reasonable?"

"Drew Mears thinks so, especially if we're working in four shifts."

"That's exciting. But you need to start wearing sunscreen," Kate told him.

"I know." Paul grimaced. "Before I picked you up in Chattanooga, I bought a big straw hat with a wide brim. That should help too." He stepped forward as if he intended to kiss her, then halted and looked down at himself. "I'd better go shower and change."

Kate chuckled. "You'd better."

OVER DINNER, Kate filled Paul in on the very little she had learned during her trip to the library. "So the library definitely is closed," she concluded. "But I have no idea why, and no one knows when—or if—it might open again."

"Are you going back?" Paul asked.

Kate's eyebrows rose as she looked up at her husband, who resembled a very large lobster at the moment. "Of course," she said simply. "Livvy's my best friend, and she's hurting. I have to help."

Paul put an arm around her and gave her a warm hug. "That's my Katie." He withdrew his keys from his pocket and jingled them. "Why don't we go over to Emma's and get an ice-cream cone? It can be sort of a 'welcome home' celebration."

Kate regarded him with amusement. "You just want an excuse to indulge that sweet tooth, honey."

"You caught me." Paul grinned.

"I always do," Kate said with a sassy smile as she grabbed her handbag and preceded him into the garage, where they climbed into Kate's Accord and set off for town.

As they drove, Paul turned on the radio and tuned in to a local station just in time to hear the weather forecast.

"There's a chance of severe thunderstorms again tonight, folks," the announcer said. "And until 10:00 PM, the National Weather Service has issued a tornado watch for Harrington County. So keep your eye on the sky and be careful out there."

With a sense of dread, Kate remembered some of the high winds and hail that had accompanied other storms that year. She did *not* want to be caught in a car during one of those. "Tornado season is supposed to be in the spring," she grumbled.

"That's true," Paul said, "but summer storms have spawned some pretty devastating tornadoes. The chance of a tornado coming through Copper Mill is pretty remote, though."

"Any chance at all makes me nervous," Kate told him. Neither of them had ever been close to a tornado, despite their years in Texas, and Kate was happy to keep it that way.

Chapter Three

Paul parked in front of the Mercantile on Main Street a short distance from the ice-cream shop. Kate looked down the street toward the library. "I wonder if she's sleeping at all," Kate said sadly.

"I hope so," Paul said in a sober tone, seeming to know exactly who "she" was.

They walked toward Emma's in silence. Kate was trying to make sense of what she'd seen and heard earlier that day. The sun was setting, although it was still so hot that she felt sticky and sweaty within moments.

Finally Paul broke the silence. "I can't believe Danny didn't tell me about the library closing. If I've seen him once, I've seen him ten times in the past week. We had a basketball game one night and a meeting of the church board. And I ran into him at the Elks' cookout . . ." His voice trailed off.

"No one knew anything was wrong until Friday," Kate reminded her husband. "Livvy has my cell-phone number, and I had the phone with me through my whole trip. I can't believe she didn't call me." But even as she spoke, she recalled Livvy's trembling voice and shaking hands. And the words she had whispered: *I can't talk to you about this. I could lose my job.*

Livvy had really looked afraid. Had Tosten Glass or someone else actually threatened her with the loss of her job? If so, Kate realized she had to be extremely cautious about what she said.

She felt a little odd not sharing her thoughts with Paul. They had been partners for nearly thirty years, and she rarely kept things from him, except perhaps for the occasional surprise birthday party or something she wasn't ready to discuss.

And yet until she knew more about Livvy's situation, Kate felt that it was Livvy's secret to keep.

"I just don't understand this. The library is a public building," Paul said. "It's paid for with our local taxes. Makes me wonder exactly why it's closed and how long it will stay that way."

Kate's mind was still on Livvy's dramatic statement. Was it really possible that someone had told her she could lose her job? Who would have the authority to fire her? The obvious answer, she realized, was the town council, which hired and terminated all public employees. Including the head librarian. She thought of what Morty had said about Tosten Glass's meetings with Livvy.

"Paul?" Kate spoke carefully. "Do you know Tosten Glass?"

"I've been introduced to him," Paul said. "But I've never had more than the most superficial contact with the man. Why?"

Kate sighed. "Oh, just something Morty mentioned when I was at the library."

Paul tapped his chin. "I do know that he's not running for

town council again, even though he's still eligible. I didn't hear a reason, though. I thought that was rather odd. He struck me as the sort of person who would . . . enjoy public office."

Reading between the lines, Kate surmised that Paul was trying to say that Tosten Glass liked the power that an elected office gave him.

Paul paused and opened the door for Kate as they reached Emma's. "Are you going to help pack up books tomorrow?"

Kate nodded. "Yes. I might learn more about this."

"Well, hello, Hanlons!" Emma called as they stepped into the air-conditioned ice-cream parlor. "Welcome home, Kate. Did you have a good trip?"

"Thanks, Emma," Kate said with a small wave. "It was terrific."

Emma Blount, the proprietor of Emma's Ice Cream Shop, wore a blouse covered in eye-popping yellow daisies. Kate sometimes wondered what it looked like inside Emma's closet. The gray-haired woman rarely wore other colors, and Kate had visions of an explosion of golden light blasting out of Emma's closet anytime the door was opened.

Glancing around, Kate noted that five of the six round ice-cream-parlor-style tables were occupied. Emma's was a popular place for families on a summer evening, and the teen population of Copper Mill also found it a good place to hang out. As they made their way to the marble counter, Kate and Paul exchanged greetings with several kids from Faith Briar's youth group.

"How are you two?" Emma asked as they neared her.

"Doing fine, Emma," Paul said when they reached the

counter. "How's your mother?" To Kate, he said, "Ada caught a cold last week."

"She's coming along," Emma said, her sallow face lighting up. "Thought she was starting a sinus infection, but antibiotics seem to be helping. Thanks for asking." Emma's mother, Ada, was ninety-two years old and suffered from Alzheimer's. Emma cared for her at home, and Kate often wondered how she juggled it along with managing the ice-cream parlor.

"Please tell her we'll keep her in our prayers," Kate said.

"I surely will." Emma pointed to a handwritten sign posted just below the list of ice-cream flavors. "What do you fancy tonight? Got a new house special. First time I've made it, but I think it's delicious."

"Chocolate-cherry marshmallow," Paul read out loud. "Hmm. I love chocolate-covered cherries. I think I'll try it, Emma."

"Cup or cone?" Emma didn't waste time getting Paul's treat ready.

Kate ordered a cone of lime sherbet. The cool fruity delight might just keep her from melting, she thought.

As Emma handed her the cone, she said, "Do y'all know what's going on at the library?"

"Your guess is as good as mine. I just saw the sign today." Kate took a quick lick to keep her sherbet from dripping.

Emma huffed out an annoyed breath. "Wonder how long it'll be closed? I got some books on tape for my mother, and she's finished with them. I need to get new ones."

Kate gave Emma a sympathetic smile.

Paul paid for their treats, then he and Kate said their good-byes as they exited the shop.

"At least we aren't the only ones in the dark," Paul commented.

"I almost wish we were," Kate said. "It really seems fishy to me that no one has heard anything about this."

"It does," Paul agreed.

Kate took another lick of her sherbet. "Is it just me, or has this heat gotten even worse? It feels like someone laid a wet blanket over me . . . after I got in a sauna."

"It *is* worse," Paul agreed. "Look over there." He pointed up at the surrounding mountains, visible even above the buildings of the town.

Kate looked just in time to see a jagged spear of lightning flash. After a significant pause, there was a faint, distant rumble. "That's not heat lightning."

"No," Paul said, "but it's nowhere near us."

Just then a voice called, "Hey, Paul. Kate. Hello!"

Kate turned at the same time Paul did.

The voice belonged to Sam Gorman, one of Paul's close friends and the owner of the Mercantile, which they were just approaching. Sam was the organist and choir director at Faith Briar, although watching his stocky figure plow toward them, Kate still found it incongruous that someone with hands the size of small hams could make such beautiful music.

"What are you doing at the store?" Paul asked after he had greeted his buddy. He consulted his watch. "It's almost seven o'clock on a Sunday evening."

"Just packing up a few nonperishables for my homebound folks," Sam replied. "Then I can make those deliveries first thing in the morning."

Kate thought it was incredibly sweet of Sam to take groceries to some of the people who were unable to come down to the store. *Only in a small town,* she thought.

"Hey, Kate, we missed your voice in the choir," Sam told her. "It was good to have you back this morning."

"It's good to be home," Kate responded.

Sam's smile faded. "Have you heard the news about the library closing?"

Kate nodded. "I have, although details seem to be sparse."

"It's big news," Sam said. "I just heard about it Friday. I was shocked out of my shoes when Livvy came in and bought all the moving boxes I had and then asked me to order about a million more."

"I bet," Kate said. "I was pretty shocked when I saw the notice about it being closed."

"It sure is going to feel different downtown without the library," Sam said. "I hope it doesn't take too long to do whatever it is they're doing." He shook his head again. "Well, I gotta get going. See you, Kate. Bye, Paul."

"Good-bye, Sam," they said together. Then they looked at each other and laughed.

They stopped to finish their treats before getting back into the car. Kate noticed that the lights were still on in the library. She worried that Livvy was going to make herself sick trying to keep up this pace.

Kate was about to open her car door when a movement caught her eye.

A boy was sprawled in the grass of the diminutive library lawn, one hand outstretched, holding out peanuts. About five feet away, a small squirrel hovered near the base of a black oak tree, eyeing the peanut and the boy.

Kate put out a hand to signal Paul. They walked on across the street and stopped to watch.

The squirrel crept halfway across the space between the tree and the boy. Then it stopped, its plumed tail twitching, and darted back to the tree. Twice more, it repeated the process, each time getting a little closer. Finally, on the fourth foray, the squirrel lunged forward, snagged the peanut, and raced back to the tree in a split second.

The boy giggled.

Kate caught her breath. "Are you okay?" she called to the boy. "Wild animals can carry rabies, you know."

He smiled as he sat up. "Squirrels rarely carry rabies. They're rodents, and rodents have never been known to cause a case of rabies in the United States. Also, the most common method of rabies transmission is a bite, and I've never been bitten by a squirrel."

Kate's mouth fell open as she and Paul both stared at the child. He sounded like an encyclopedia, yet he couldn't have been more than nine or ten.

Paul said, "You've done this before?"

The boy nodded. "I've been studying these while my mom's working in there." He jerked a thumb toward the library.

"You know your facts, son," Paul said. Then, as the boy rose from the ground, Paul added, "I'm Paul Hanlon, and this is my wife, Kate."

"It's nice to meet you. I'm Jeremy Pellman." The slightly built boy beamed. To Kate's surprise, he stepped forward and offered a hand.

Each of them shook his hand, then Paul said, "Your mom is Louisa?"

The boy nodded. "She's in the library. She just started volunteering there this weekend."

"I met her today," Kate told him.

"So you're spending your summer studying squirrels, are you?" Paul asked.

Jeremy grinned. "Just these squirrels. They're always around this tree, but they go in and out of a little hole over there. I think they might have a nest there."

"Don't squirrels nest in trees?" Kate had never heard of squirrels nesting anywhere other than in trees. Then again, she didn't know very much about squirrels.

"Mostly," Jeremy responded to her question. "But I think these squirrels are different from regular old red or gray squirrels."

"Different, how?" Paul asked.

"Well, first of all, I'm pretty sure they're flying squirrels. But even for flying squirrels, they're little," Jeremy told him. "And did you see how dark that one was? They're all that color. It's a whole lot darker than regular gray squirrels. Those aren't flying squirrels, either."

"Maybe these are the babies of the big ones," Kate said.

Jeremy shook his head. "I don't think so. The big gray ones chase them away when they come around."

"You're very observant," Paul said with a chuckle, patting the youngster's shoulder. "Good luck with your squirrel sightings."

"Thanks," Jeremy said.

Just then, a low rumble of thunder sounded.

"It's still rumbling around," Paul said. "Keep an eye on the weather, Jeremy, and go inside if that gets any closer."

"Okay," the boy said.

To Kate, Paul said, "Are you ready to go?"

She nodded. "Good-bye," they both said to Jeremy.

"'Bye, Mr. and Mrs. Hanlon. It was nice to meet you." Jeremy waved as Paul and Kate headed back to their car.

"What a polite child," Kate said. "Louisa Pellman is obviously doing something right."

Paul chuckled. "He was one smart little cookie, wasn't he?" He reached for her hand as he said, "I wanted to swing out by the Pellman place and show you our roofing project. But I'm not sure about this storm forecast. Maybe we'd better wait until tomorrow."

"Oh, let's go now," Kate said. She glanced at the sky, which was beginning to creep into pinks and lavenders as night approached, though it still was quite light outside. She hadn't seen any lightning in quite a while. "I don't think that storm's coming this way, do you?"

Paul scanned the sky. "It doesn't look like it," he agreed.

IT TOOK MORE THAN TWENTY MINUTES to leave Copper Mill and take the country roads out to Skunk Hollow Trail. The Pellman home was the first one they came to, and as Paul swung into the gravel driveway, Kate said, "Oh, it is run-down, isn't it?"

"It needs some work," Paul agreed. "But Mrs. Pellman says she can handle the mortgage, so she doesn't want to move unless she has to. She and her three children are staying with her parents until these repairs are done, but they'll be returning once all our mess is cleaned up."

He got out of the car and came around to help Kate out.

"They attend St. Lucy's," he went on, "and Lucas found out about the roof because Louisa got very ill with pneumonia last March. She almost lost her job—she's some kind of clerk over at the courthouse in Pine Ridge—and I guess there was concern that the children might be split up and placed in foster care. But their church stepped up and organized assistance for her until she was well again."

"I wonder why on earth she's volunteering at the library?" Kate mused. "And didn't you say she has three children?"

"I believe her parents live in town," Paul said. "Perhaps they're helping out. If I had to guess, I'd say Mrs. Pellman is trying to give back a little to the community in return for the assistance she's been given."

Kate nodded. "I suspect you're right."

"She's a good mother, according to Lucas. In addition to working, she does her best to keep the kids involved in church and school."

"If Jeremy is any indication, she's doing a fabulous job. What happened to her husband?"

"Lucas told me he has a serious alcohol problem, and there were some suspicions of abuse. She divorced him when the third child was a baby."

Kate shook her head sadly. "That's too bad."

"She's really trying. I feel like we're doing a good thing here, Katie."

"I feel like you're right." Kate squeezed Paul's hand as he led her toward the back of the house. "Just for the record, I am not climbing any ladders. I'll applaud your roofing efforts from down here on solid ground."

Paul laughed. "Come around here, and I'll show you where we're starting."

He spent several minutes explaining some of the tools and techniques to Kate, then pointed out the side where they had started. Although she could see nothing of consequence and most of his explanation went right over her head, Kate smiled and nodded as he spoke, delighted with his enthusiasm. He was in the middle of telling her something about "flashing" when a loud boom of thunder rattled the windows of the house.

"Yikes!" Paul said. "Where did that come from?"

"I don't know, but I think we were wrong about that storm not coming this way. Maybe we'd better go."

"Good idea." He took her hand, and they started around the corner of the house.

As soon as they stepped away from the shelter of the building, Kate noticed an ominous stillness. The air felt different in a way she couldn't really define. It was almost as if there was some invisible thing crouched in the atmosphere, waiting to pounce. Glancing at the sky, she was startled to see a huge bank of dark clouds. That hadn't been there ten minutes ago.

Paul stopped. "Whoa! Look at that." He scanned the purpling thunderheads on the horizon. "I'm sorry I dragged you out here. Let's go home."

"You didn't drag me anywhere," Kate told him as they hurried toward the Honda. "I didn't anticipate this any more than you did."

In moments, they were backing out of the driveway. Kate

looked out the window at the approaching wall of dark clouds. They had taken on a greenish cast, and she felt the first true pangs of fear. Like any Texan, she knew what those clouds meant. Tornadoes were a distinct possibility.

Soon, fat drops of rain began to fall. Paul switched on the radio as he started down the road.

"...is now a warning. Again, I repeat," the broadcaster said, "the tornado watch has now become a tornado warning. A funnel cloud was spotted to the northeast of Copper Mill just a short time ago. It has not touched down. We advise residents of Harrington County and surrounding areas to go to a safe area immediately. Get into a storm shelter if you have one, or take shelter in an interior room of your home with no windows. If you have a bathtub, lie down in it. If you have a basement, huddle in a corner. Use mattresses, pillows, and blankets to protect yourself from flying debris..."

"To the northeast? That's where we are," Paul said. Even as he spoke, the rain came faster, and in seconds, it was a torrential downpour. Lightning flashed and thunder boomed almost simultaneously, making Kate jump. "Maybe we'd better go back to the Pellmans' and get into the driveway so we're off the road. We'll have to ride out the storm there, Katie. It would be foolish to try to drive back to town in this."

"Sounds like the best option." Kate could barely force out the words because her throat felt so tight. She took deep breaths, determined to stay calm. They had experienced tornado scares when they lived in San Antonio, although neither of them had ever seen any kind of funnel cloud.

Paul whipped the Honda into reverse and made a three-point turn on the narrow country road. Slowly he began driving back the way they had come. He leaned forward over the steering wheel as if that would help him see through the curtain of rain in front of them. "Don't let me miss the driveway."

"I'm looking." Her words were cut off by loud pinging sounds, and she realized that hail was hitting the car.

Within seconds, it was impossible to hear anything but the cacophony of ice hitting metal. Kate twisted her hands together and began to pray silently, not wanting to distract Paul from his driving. Some of the pieces of hail were the size of golf balls. She didn't even think about the damage being done to her car; she just wanted them both to be safe.

After what seemed like hours but probably was barely minutes, the hail sounds began to die away. Paul turned off the windshield wipers because it was no longer raining. Kate took a deep breath and forced herself to relax as silence fell. That had been some kind of experience, but she hoped the storm had moved on.

Then another huge flash of lightning, combined with a clap of thunder, lit up the world like a nuclear explosion.

For one brief instant, she could see everything around them. To her surprise, they were nearly back to the Pellmans' home. She could see the house clearly for an instant, only a couple hundred yards down the road, before blackness claimed the world around them again.

She turned to Paul. "I think—"

"Listen!" he shouted, grabbing her arm to emphasize his words. He hit the brakes so hard, she was thrown against her seat belt for an instant.

Kate listened.

The stillness was replaced by another sound now. A roaring sound, which she instantly recognized as high wind. *Very* high wind. As it got louder and louder, it began to sound like a train approaching.

"We have to get out of the car!" Paul leaned across Kate and threw open her door. Then he unbuckled her seat belt and practically shoved her out of the car, yelling again, "Get out of the car!"

In an instant, she was soaked to the skin. Paul must have climbed right over the console and passenger seat because he followed her out, leaving the car door ajar behind him. "In the ditch!" he shouted. "We need to get down!"

Kate stumbled forward, her hair whipping wildly around her head. As she did so, another extended series of lightning flashes and simultaneous thunderclaps illuminated the world around them a second time.

Not the length of a football field away was an enormous black thunderhead with a funnel cloud descending from it.

Chapter Four

The funnel undulated as its height and girth grew and shrank repeatedly.

A surge of paralyzing terror rushed through Kate. Her mouth went cotton dry. Her lungs felt compressed; she was unable to take a deep breath. *Dear Lord, we are yours. We give ourselves into your care. Shield us, save us. Keep us from harm.*

She continued to pray as Paul reached her. He placed one strong arm around her waist, propelling her forward. The ground was sloping down.

"Lie down here," he shouted in her ear, gripping her forearm and dragging her down with him.

Kate didn't even question him. She knew one of the worst places a person could be was in a car during a tornado. She knew the drill: if you get caught outdoors, go to the lowest ground you can find. The bottom of a ditch was good, unless the area was prone to flash flooding.

The ditch along the side of the road had been dry before the storm.

Paul pushed her down the bank into the ditch, and she sucked in her breath as muddy water splashed into her face. There was water in the ditch now, although perhaps only two inches or so, and she held her head up high enough to avoid drinking the muddy brew. She realized she was lying on a mattress of large balls of hail.

Paul threw himself down half beside her, half on her, pressing her into the hail and muddy earth. Around them, the roar continued. Interspersed with it, she could hear occasional odd noises that sounded like pistol shots, clanking, and ripping—presumably debris in the funnel as it hit other pieces of debris. In her mind's eye, she could see again the funnel cloud in that one bright instant of light. It hadn't been on the ground, she thought. *Dear Lord, please don't let that thing touch down. Please.*

She lifted her head as far as she could, straining to see through the darkness that had descended. Yet another lightning strike showed the tornado moving past the Pellmans' home without a direct hit, but Kate watched as a corner of the roof lifted off and was instantly whipped away. She lowered her head again, instinctively pressing herself against her husband.

Paul's larger body protected her. Once or twice she felt him jerk and hiss in a breath, and she realized debris of some sort was hitting him. His mouth was buried in her hair, close to her right ear, and he was praying the Twenty-third Psalm, using the traditional King James language that both of them had learned in childhood. With the noise around them, she could barely hear him, but she took up the verses as well.

". . . He maketh me to lie down in green pastures: he leadeth me beside the still waters. He restoreth my soul: he leadeth me in the paths of righteousness for his name's sake. Yea, though I walk through the valley of the shadow of death . . ."

Paul and Kate repeated the familiar comforting prayer as the sounds of the tornado assaulted their ears. While they prayed, the wind died down and the roaring sound faded away.

As quiet fell, Paul raised his head cautiously. A moment later, he gathered up Kate like a rag doll and laid her on the grassy bank before flopping down beside her on his back.

She looked at the sky for a few moments as she tried to process everything that had just happened. Finally she turned her head and looked at Paul. He was covered from head to toe in mud. Even his hair was muddy. The whites of his eyes looked startling peering out of his mud-covered face.

She must have looked the same, she realized. Slowly she sat up. Then she began to laugh. "All those years in Texas, and we never even saw a tornado. We move to Tennessee, and what do we get? A close encounter."

Paul had gotten to his knees and then pushed himself to his feet. "A *very* close encounter," he said soberly.

She couldn't stop laughing. Paul extended a hand, hauling her to her feet. As he enfolded her in his arms, the laughter turned to hitching breaths and then to sobs. A part of Kate's brain registered the fact that she was becoming hysterical, but she felt completely unable to control her reaction.

Paul hugged her tightly, rocking slightly back and forth.

"*Shh-shh-shh,*" he said. "We're okay. You're okay, Katie." He repeated it over and over again, hushing her until she began to take deep gulping breaths. Slowly she calmed herself.

She shivered involuntarily. "*Br-r-r-r,*" she said. "I'm freezing." It was raining again, hard enough that the worst of the mud on Paul's face began to melt away.

A smile flickered across his lips as his grim expression lightened. "All day you complained about the heat, and now you're cold."

"I was lying in a ditch filled with balls of ice," she reminded him with a chuckle as she regained some of her spirit.

"And the storm blew the heat away." He held out his arms. "Feel how much cooler it is?"

The levity she felt suddenly fled. Kate whispered, "Oh, Paul, you shielded me from the worst of it. Are you all right?"

He nodded. "I think so. A couple of times, I felt some little stings, but nothing big hit me."

She walked around behind him and tugged up the sport shirt he'd been wearing. There were several red welts on the skin of his back, but no blood, for which she was grateful.

"Let's go home and clean up," she suggested, sliding her hand into his.

"Good idea." He glanced up at the road. "Except for one little problem," he added slowly, looking over her head.

Kate turned to see what he was looking at. "Dear heavens! Where's the car?" Their car was gone. *Gone?*

Even as she spoke the words, she saw the Honda. It had been pushed down the road about a hundred feet and was now pointed in the opposite direction.

"There." She pointed.

They walked down the road toward the car. The door that Paul had left open was shut. To Kate's shock, the engine was still running, and when Paul opened her door, the radio blared out at them.

"Unbelievable," Paul murmured.

"Miraculous," Kate corrected. "I was praying that the tornado wouldn't touch down."

"Me too," Paul said, "and it looks like our prayers were answered. He pointed across the land in the direction the tornado had gone. Kate could see debris, the occasional downed tree, broken branches . . . but the wholesale destruction that would have accompanied a direct strike was absent.

Paul took her hands. "Let's take one more moment in prayer before we go," he said quietly.

IT WAS FULLY DARK and much later than Kate had expected when they finally arrived home. A downed tree and power lines blocked the road right at the edge of town, and Paul had been forced to take a roundabout route to get back to the parsonage.

"You go ahead and take your shower first," Paul told Kate as they got out of the car, which he had pulled into the garage. "I'm going to call the power company and alert them to those downed lines. Then I need to call the roofing committee chairman and tell him the Pellmans' roof may have sustained some damage."

On the ride home, Kate had shared what she had seen when the funnel cloud raced past them. "No 'may have' about it," Kate told him. "I saw part of the roof lift right up in the air, and then a section of it was torn away." She shook her head. "It looked as easy as tearing paper."

She handed him some newspaper from the stack she kept to recycle. "Here. Try to dry off as much of the mud and mess as you can before you go into the house. Why don't you shower first? I can wait. And whatever you do, leave your shoes and socks out here. It's going to be hard enough to clean the upholstery in the car. I don't want to have to clean mud from inside the house too!"

A small smile touched Paul's lips, lightening the grim expression he had worn since she had mentioned the roof. "All right. I'll go first. After I shower, I'll make my calls and then we'll make some cocoa. I don't know about you, but I could use a hot drink."

He paused and ran a hand across the hood of the Honda, then grimaced at the feel of the pitted surface. "I can't do anything about this tonight. Tomorrow will be time enough to call an insurance adjustor to look at the car."

They took turns showering, and Kate threw their muddy clothes into the washer. After she was clean and dry, she made the hot cocoa and shared it with Paul. Then she attacked the interior of the Honda with soap and water. Even though they had found some old blankets in the trunk and spread them over the seats, there was mud on the steering wheel, the pedal, the door handles, and even the dashboard knobs where Paul had turned on the heat.

As she worked, her mind kept rehashing the terror she had felt lying in that ditch. Several times, she had to stop, sit back, and simply take deep breaths until she stopped shaking.

Finally she felt satisfied that the car was clean again. As

she put away the cleaning items, she thought of Livvy and the library, and she realized she hadn't even given a thought to how the town had fared.

Hurrying inside, she grabbed the phone and dialed Livvy's number, waiting impatiently while the phone rang.

"Hello?" Livvy finally answered on the third ring.

"Livvy! Are you okay?"

There was a cautious pause. Kate had forgotten completely about the strained manner in which they had parted.

"Kate, is that you?"

"Yes, it's me. Are you okay? And how about the library? We drove out to Louisa Pellman's house and—"

"What? During the storm? Are you all right?" Livvy sounded very concerned.

Kate realized that she had been babbling and was on the verge of hysteria. "Sorry." She stopped and took several deep, calming breaths. "Paul and I were caught in the storm, and we saw a tornado. Paul and I got out of the car and laid in a ditch, and the car got blown down the road. Do you know if anything in town was hit?"

"You saw a tornado! I haven't heard about any damage, and I think the gossip train would already have stopped at this station if something major had happened. Kate, just how close were you to this tornado?"

"How long is a football field?" As soon as she asked the question, Kate realized how ridiculous it was. She knew the answer already. It seemed as if all her brain cells had been shaken up and rearranged in patterns that weren't fitting together quite right.

"A hundred yards," Livvy said automatically. "Fifty and fifty, remember? *That's close!*" Her voice rose as Kate's words sank in. "Did anything hit you? Do you have a concussion?"

This was one of the more bizarre conversations Kate ever remembered having with her friend. She didn't blame Livvy for thinking she'd been hit in the head. She chuckled. "No. Nothing hit me. Except Paul when he dragged me into the ditch and fell on me."

"Dragged you . . . ? Tell. Me. Everything. In order, from the beginning."

Kate complied, and when she finished, there was a long moment of silence.

"Oh, Kate," Livvy whispered. "What a near miss." Her voice caught. "I would never forgive myself if . . . if anything had happened . . . I'm sorry." The words poured out. "When you wanted to talk earlier, I brushed you off. I'm sorry for that. I'm just so afraid . . ."

Thinking about the library helped take Kate's mind off her recent terror. "Afraid of what?"

There was a silence. "I know it sounds paranoid, but I don't want to talk on the phone," Livvy said quietly. "Plus, the boys don't know the details, and I don't want them to find out what's really going on. Can you meet me at the library tomorrow morning? We'll find someplace private to talk."

"Of course," Kate said instantly. "I'll be there first thing."

"I promise I'll explain then." Livvy paused. "I'm going to go thank God for keeping you safe now."

"Good idea," Kate said. "Paul and I did that once, but I think it bears repeating."

SHORTLY AFTER EIGHT on Monday morning, Paul left for the Pellmans' house. Unfortunately, the power lines were still down. The power company had been by, though, because orange cones and a sign cautioned drivers that high-voltage lines were blocking the road. He was forced to take the same detour that he had used the night before.

Daylight revealed more damage than he and Kate had noticed before. Trees had lost large branches, a shed on a farm had collapsed, and the Pellmans' mailbox lay about three feet away from the post on which it had been fastened. Although it was the middle of summer, leaves were everywhere, casualties of the high wind that had stripped them from the trees.

There were three cars already parked in the lane outside the Pellman place when he arrived. Getting out of his truck, Paul walked around the side of the house.

"Hey, Paul." Pete MacKenzie waved. Pete was the pastor of the Copper Mill Presbyterian Church. He stood with Ephraim Dresser and Drew Mears. All three men had their hands on their hips as they looked up at the roof.

Paul walked over to join them. It was apparent, even from the ground, that the roof had taken quite a beating. Splintered edges of beams stood out jaggedly against the sky, and the ground was littered with shingles and pieces of asphalt paper.

"How are you doing?" Ephraim asked. He was a big bear of a man with a bushy brown mustache and a gleaming bald pate. "Heard from Sam Gorman at the Mercantile that you got caught out here last night. He heard it from Danny Jenner's oldest kid."

Paul knew by now how efficiently news was disseminated in Copper Mill. He'd bet phones had been ringing off the hook the previous night and this morning. "We're fine," he said. "Kate and I drove out here so I could show her the project. The tornado came right by us."

"I bet that was some kind of scary," Drew Mears said.

As slight as Ephraim was burly, Drew looked as if a good puff of breeze would blow him away. Paul had seen him scrambling around on the roof, though, and he knew Drew's looks were deceiving. The little man was all muscle, as agile as a monkey.

Paul nodded in response to Drew's comment. "I don't recommend it." He gave the men a brief accounting of the tornado, pointing out the ditch in the distance where he and Kate had taken refuge. "Kate said she saw a corner of the roof get torn off," he reported.

Drew sighed. "More than a corner from the way it looks down here. Why don't I go up and take a look? Then we can assess our options. Somebody want to help me get the ladder off my truck?"

After a brief inspection, Drew came back down the ladder, shaking his head. "We're going to need roughly twice as many bundles of shingles as I estimated before." He pulled his features into a dejected expression. "We're also going to need beams to replace supports. Some of the rafters went flying along with the roof. I guess I'll work up an estimate, and we can meet tonight to talk about what to do next."

"Sounds good. I'll let everyone know." Pete's voice was sober.

Ephraim cleared his throat. "This looks like it's going to take more than a week." He glanced at Drew, who nodded.

"Yeah," said the roofer, "I suspect we'll be working at least two more weeks. It's a mess up there. We're going to have to do some additional structural repairs before we can shingle."

"Two more weeks?" Pete sounded worried. "We're going to have to talk to our volunteers and see if they're willing to commit that much time. I know a lot of them were using personal days and vacation time to cover this."

"If not, perhaps we can get a second volunteer group together, either to work a second shift or to take over for a second week," Paul said.

"I'm afraid I'm in the can't-give-more-time category," Ephraim said. "I can help this week, but next week I have to travel out of town on business. It's not something I can reschedule. Maybe I need to step down from chairing the committee and let someone who can be there from start to finish take over."

There was a short silence.

Pete finally said, "Any idea who might consider it?"

Each of them shook their heads.

Ephraim sighed. "I'll mention it when we all meet this evening. Perhaps someone's heart will be moved to take on the project."

"Why don't we pray before we leave?" Paul suggested. The words were a familiar echo to the ones he had uttered in almost that exact place the night before.

Chapter Five

After Paul left for the Pellmans', Kate dressed in a yellow-and-white-striped seersucker camp shirt and khaki shorts in deference to the heat. She tied a sheer yellow chiffon scarf around her head to keep her hair out of the way, since she planned to work at the library for at least part of the morning.

On the short drive from home, evidence of the previous night's storm was everywhere.

Even though the tornado hadn't come through Copper Mill, the hail and powerful thunderstorm had done significant damage. Leaves and twigs littered streets and yards. On Main Street, a huge branch had broken from one of the big old trees. It had blocked the road at one point, although a crew with gas-powered chain saws had made progress on reducing it to movable sections.

There were signs and cars with paint damage and pockmarks, indicating that the hail had come through town as well. Outside Betty's Beauty Parlor, a sign hung at a crooked angle where the metal had torn away from the wall on one side.

Kate pulled into the lot behind the library, parked right next to Livvy's SUV, and got out of her car. Then she stopped short. Morty was perched at the top of a tall aluminum ladder, nailing plastic over one of the library's second-floor windows.

"Morning, Morty. Is that storm damage?" Kate called up to him.

"Mornin', Kate," he returned. "Sure is." He paused and twisted to look down at her. "I heard you and the mister had a little excitement last evening out at Skunk Hollow."

In the bright sunlight, with Morty grinning down at her, Kate found that she was able to laugh. "We did. I could live a hundred years without ever having that much 'excitement' again, let me tell you!"

Morty was still shaking his head when she walked to the door after giving him a few details of her experience.

To Kate's surprise, she could see a dozen or more people scurrying around inside the library. Tugging open one of the heavy glass doors, Kate headed for the main office, where she could see Livvy standing with several other people.

As she headed for them, a voice hailed her. It was Jeremy Pellman's mother.

As Louisa Pellman approached Kate, she scanned Kate's face. "I heard about the tornado. Thank heavens you weren't hurt. I would have felt terrible."

"Why?" Kate smiled. "Were you the one who chose the path of that storm?"

Louisa could barely smile at the small joke. "It's my house your husband is fixing. He's doing me a kindness I can never repay."

"Around here," Kate said, "we don't repay. We pay it forward."

Louisa looked troubled. "If only it were that simple."

Kate opened her mouth to ask the young mother if there was something she could help her with, but just then Livvy approached.

"Good morning, Kate." Livvy looked as exhausted as she sounded. She gave Kate a warm hug, pulling her away from Louisa.

"Good morning." Kate hugged her back, instantly focused on her friend.

"I'm so happy to see you unscathed." As Livvy stepped back and glanced at her, Kate saw her friend's eyes open wide. "Relatively unscathed," she amended. Livvy winced. "How did you get that scratch on your cheek? That must have hurt."

Kate sent her friend a wry smile. "I never even noticed it."

Livvy briefly closed her eyes. "It's a miracle neither of you was hurt badly." She brushed a tender finger over Kate's cheek.

Kate nodded. "God was watching over us, I'm certain. I'd happily live the rest of my life without experiencing another terrifying event like that."

"I imagine so. I heard that a tornado touched down near Pine Ridge and destroyed a barn. I wonder if it was the same funnel cloud you saw."

"It could have been. As I can now attest, tornadoes can travel large distances very quickly. Although, thankfully, the one we saw wasn't on the ground."

"We have a broken window upstairs," Livvy told her. "I suppose it was the hail. Either that or something the wind slammed against it."

Kate grimaced in sympathy. "I saw Morty covering it. Anything damaged?"

Livvy nodded. "Several of our historical publications got wet. I'm going to have to ask the town council to authorize funds for an expert to look at anything that needs serious recovery work." She paused, taking in Kate's clothes. "Did you come to help?"

Kate nodded. "Among other things," she said, subtly reminding her friend that she had promised to talk.

"Great. You could go upstairs first and begin picking up the wet books. I already picked up the valuable ones I'm worried about, but there are others. I think if we lay them on some tables to partially dry, press them overnight, and then dry them again the next day, they'll sustain the least damage until I can get them to a specialist. The pages could get very brittle if we aren't careful."

Kate nodded. "All right. I'll make that my first task." She indicated all the people working in the stacks. "I thought I'd be right on time at nine, but I feel as if I've arrived late for the party. What time did everyone start?"

"Eight," Livvy said. "I've been working longer hours trying to get everything done before next Monday."

"What's next Monday?"

Livvy's eyes began to tear up, and she took Kate's arm, pulling her into the office. She closed the door behind them, turned and leaned against it, then said, "I received notice Friday morning from Tosten Glass, the president of the town council, that we have to be moved out of this building a week from today. Next Monday," she added for clarification.

"A week! Do the others know?" Kate asked.

Livvy shook her head. "They know we need to move fast, but I haven't told anyone how soon it's supposed to happen."

"Why not?"

"Mr. Glass told me I had to keep it quiet through the weekend. I think the council wants to make this happen quickly before there's a big fuss when people find out. I need to announce it today, though, so everyone knows what kind of time constraints we're up against."

Which meant it would be all over town by nightfall, given the speed with which news traveled in their tiny community.

"There's going to be a huge public outcry when people hear," Kate predicted. She knew her face must have reflected the shock she felt. Even looking at the buzz of activity in the room beyond them, she could hardly take it in. "Something funny is going on here," she said.

"I don't know what it could be." Livvy's voice trembled. "As far as I know, there's nothing exciting or unusual about the library. Our budget is reasonable, our attendance is excellent. The computers are in use a high percentage of the time . . ." She trailed off, apparently unable to come up with anything negative to say about her beloved library.

"Where are you moving to?" Kate asked. She couldn't imagine a location better suited to the library than this one, right in the heart of the downtown area.

Livvy shook her head. "I don't know yet. I don't think they've chosen a new place yet."

Kate was almost too stunned to respond. "They don't have a new location? That's insane!" She paused. "This must seem like a bad, bad dream to you, Liv. Do you really think you can pack up this entire library in one week?"

Livvy shrugged. "I have no choice." There was a hopeless, resigned quality to her response.

"No choice?" Kate tilted her head. "Why do you say that? What would happen if you refused?"

Livvy's face lost every ounce of color. "I can't do that!" Her tone was so vehement that Kate nearly stepped back a pace.

"Why not? Yesterday you said you could lose your job. Is that what you mean?"

Livvy clamped her lips shut and stared at Kate. "I can't tell you," she finally said. A tear escaped and ran down her cheek.

"Livvy," said Kate gently. "I can't help if you don't tell me what's going on."

"There's nothing you can do to stop it, Kate." The librarian shook her head. There was an almost frightened expression on her face.

"I can try," Kate said with determination. "With or without knowing everything you know, I have to try to find out why this is happening."

"No!" Livvy burst out, her face flushing. "Someone threatened to fire me if I told anyone what was going on. I only received permission to talk to the volunteers today because the library can't be packed and moved without them. Kate, you *cannot* let it get out that I told you any of this. I could lose my severance package if it gets out that I'm trying to stop the closing or even talking about it other than to announce the closing to the volunteers."

Kate was appalled at the threat. It certainly was an effective way to frighten someone into compliance. "Who's responsible?" There had to be some way to stop them without letting on that Livvy had spoken to Kate.

"I don't know." Livvy bit her lip. "Tosten Glass is the one who told me about the closing and gave me the deadlines, but he never threatened to fire me. Not openly, at least."

"So you didn't see the person? Was it a phone call?"

Livvy shook her head. "It was an unsigned note left on my desk. Done on plain, old copy paper, so there'd be no way to trace it even if I wanted to."

"And it said . . . ?"

"It said I'd be fired if I didn't cooperate with the council. Heaven knows, we can't afford to lose my income with two kids starting college soon, and if I should be fired without any severance . . ." Her expression looked so helpless that it tore at Kate's heart.

"But it wasn't just aimed at me. The note also said that Danny could be removed from his teaching position. Whoever is behind this threatened to make up some story about Danny behaving inappropriately with his students. Kate, Danny would be devastated if something ruined his reputation. Teaching is his life, not just a job to him. And we need his insurance, not to mention his salary."

"Those are significant threats. Not like someone saying 'You'll be sorry' or egging your house." Kate was infuriated by the pure meanness of the anonymous note. "Why do you think it was Tosten Glass?"

Livvy shuddered. "He's a horrible, horrible man. He comes in here asking me for details about how quickly we're getting things packed up. He seems as if he can't wait to close down the library." She paused. "In all fairness, I may just *want* him to be the bad guy because he's so slimy. He might have had nothing to do with that note."

"Yes, but for someone to be able to back up those threats, it would have to be someone with a fair amount of power in this town. You couldn't be fired easily, nor could your contract be broken and a severance package withheld, and rumors about Danny probably could be debunked quickly unless someone in a position of authority embraced them. Would Tosten have had the opportunity to plant the note?"

Livvy shook her head. "I don't see how. On Saturday, when the note showed up, I went to the diner for lunch, and he was there too."

Another thought struck Kate. "Livvy, if the library closes, will you even have a job?"

Livvy nodded. "I asked about that. Mr. Glass told me I'll stay on salary while they find a new location for the library." Livvy's eyes grew moist as she held up a hand in a "stop" gesture. "I'll be too upset to do my job if I try to talk about this any more." She clasped her hands tightly together. "Please, Kate, whatever you do, don't let anyone know I talked to you. There can't be even a whisper that you know these things."

"I promise I'll be careful." Kate gave Livvy a hug, patting her friend's back when Livvy clutched her tightly. "I'll go on upstairs and get started."

Livvy moved aside, and Kate opened the office door. Right on the other side of the door was Louisa Pellman. She held a clipboard against her chest and took a startled step backward, deep color sweeping into her face as she nearly tripped and fell. "H-hello," she stammered, clutching at the desk.

Kate hastily grabbed her elbow. "I've got you, Louisa." To take the young woman's mind off her clumsiness and set her at ease, Kate said, "You're giving this project a lot of time. That's nice of you."

"Everyone's doing so much for me that I wanted to do something for the community." Louisa rushed through the words, confirming Paul's guess about her motives.

"You know," Kate said, "I'm really glad you and your children are staying with your parents right now. Last night would have been a terrifying experience for all of you."

Louisa shuddered, and Kate, seeing her distress, changed the subject.

"Oh, I met your son Jeremy last evening," Kate recalled, smiling. "He's quite the budding biologist, isn't he?"

Louisa's tense expression relaxed. "He loves animals," she said. "He knows more than I do about a lot of them. Right now, he's convinced himself that there's something special about those squirrels outside the library." She shook her head, as if that couldn't possibly be true.

But Kate had thought the young man's observations sounded extremely plausible. "He's very knowledgeable," she said diplomatically. "Is he out there again today?"

Louisa nodded. "He always asks to come with me when he knows I'm coming to the library." She glanced at her watch. "Although I have to work at noon, so we're only here for a few hours."

"Oh yes. I heard you work at the courthouse," Kate said. She grinned. "Not many secrets in this town, are there?"

Instead of smiling, Louisa's brows drew together. "No,"

she said soberly. "There aren't. I should get back to packing."
And she turned away.

Kate thought about Livvy as she climbed the stairs to the
second floor. Had Tosten Glass really written that nasty note?
Why would the president of the town council threaten Livvy
and Danny? As Kate entered the room where the historical
collection was kept, she decided that although she didn't
know the man, she needed to meet him very soon.

Chapter Six

A s Kate looked around the room she saw that Morty
Robertson had finished covering the window and was
working inside. Armed with a dustpan and a broom, he
was sweeping shattered glass into small piles and placing
the piles into a bucket.

"Hello again," she said.

"Hello, Kate. Isn't this something?"

"Something awful," she agreed. "Livvy sent me to help.
Shall I begin laying the books on tables?"

Morty nodded. "That'll be fine. I'll help as soon as I'm
done cleaning up this glass."

Kate noted that he had already stapled heavy plastic over
the window frame from the inside as well.

Kate began picking up many of the wet books and laid
them on tables. They had been on a bookcase beneath the
window that must have fallen over after the window broke.
Kate got a roll of paper towels and began to wipe them off,
one by one, careful to brush off any shards of glass that might
still be clinging to them.

When she had a stack of five or six, she and Morty carried them downstairs and laid them on tables hastily placed against one wall.

While Kate worked, she considered the implications of what Livvy had told her. Once, as she passed Morty on the stairs, she said, "When Livvy is away from the library, how easy is it for someone to gain access to her office?"

Morty didn't even have to think about it. "She doesn't lock the door. Anybody that needs something can go in."

After the fifth trip, Morty declared that they needed to take a break. Since her bad knee was throbbing, Kate thought that sounded like a fine idea. She wondered if her face was as flushed as his as she sank into a chair in the historical room with a bottle of water.

On the table in front of her lay a copy of the *Copper Mill Chronicle*. Pulling it toward her, she noted that this was the edition from two weeks ago, the first of the two Thursdays she had been out of town.

She scanned the headlines. To her amusement, the lead story was about the roofing project at Louisa Pellman's home. There was a nice shot of Louisa and her children standing in front of the house. Jeremy stood on one side of his mother, and on her other side, she held the hand of a little girl who looked to be about kindergarten age. In her free arm, Louisa held a toddler. Goodness. She really had her hands full, Kate thought. The article went on to mention that Louisa worked part-time in the records office at the courthouse but hoped to find full-time employment. No wonder the poor woman had those circles beneath her eyes.

Flipping through the thin newspaper, Kate's eye caught

another headline: NO REELECTION BID FOR GLASS. Tosten Glass again! Kate had seen and heard the man's name more in the past twenty-four hours than she had since she'd moved to town.

She read the article. It said that three members of the seven-member council were up for reelection. Two were running for a second term. Tosten Glass also was eligible to do so, as Paul had mentioned, but apparently he had decided just two weeks ago not to seek office again, citing personal reasons. Of course. That was the catch-all phrase used when someone didn't want to share their future plans with the press.

Still, Kate had to wonder why Tosten decided not to run again. He would have every expectation of being reelected, since all the candidates were running unopposed. And he probably would have been elected president again. Why wouldn't he want that? It could be something as simple as family problems, she supposed.

"Ready to start up again?" Morty interrupted her thoughts. "It's been about ten minutes."

Kate groaned as they rose together. "That went by awfully fast. Are you sure your watch didn't skip some time?"

Back to work. Up and down the steps she trudged. Each time she brought down several more books, she gently opened the volumes that were already drying to new sections in order to dry the pages somewhat equally. It was apparent that several of them were going to need expert attention, and she purposely didn't try to pry apart any pages that appeared stuck. None of the books could be sent away until they were completely dry, she realized, because they would be risking mold, not to mention ink stains, on adjacent pages.

Not long after she and Morty had resumed their rescue operations, a moving van emblazoned with the logo of a Pine Ridge company pulled up. One man hopped out and walked inside, presumably to talk to Livvy, while three others busied themselves opening a sliding side door on the large van.

When Kate brought down the next load of books, the men were carrying out the first of the chairs and tables and stowing them in the big van.

She held the door open for a man with a dolly before she walked up the steps again. Smiling at the gray-haired fellow, she asked, "Where will you be taking these?"

"They're going into storage," the man told her. "Some warehouse in Pine Ridge."

The man's words were confirmation of what Livvy had told her earlier. Kate's chest felt tight, and a lump rose in her throat. How were the town's longtime residents going to feel as this news got out? The signs on the doors might have gone relatively unnoticed over the weekend, but with all the downtown businesses open and passersby seeing the moving truck, news would spread now.

The sheer sneakiness of the whole maneuver felt sinister to Kate. She was more determined than ever to meet Tosten Glass.

"Hey, Mrs. Hanlon!"

As Kate came downstairs again, a childish voice hailed her.

Looking around, she saw Jeremy Pellman waving at her from the back door. "Hi, Jeremy. I need a break. Want to sit down with me for a minute?" She walked outside with the boy and sat down in the grass beside him. "It's awfully hot out here, isn't it?"

The boy nodded. "Yeah, but it's okay in the shade."

"What are you doing today?"

He grinned. "Guess."

"Squirrels," Kate said in a dry tone.

He giggled. "Yep. I was inside reading, but I got tired of that, so I came out here," he said.

"Where are your sisters?"

"With Grammy. Hey, how did you know I have two sisters?"

"I'm a mind reader," Kate said in a deep dramatic tone that made him giggle again.

"I get to come along because I'm quiet and I like to read," the child informed her. "And Mom knows I like to watch the squirrels."

"Does she know you're touching them?"

He rolled his eyes. "You sound just like her. She said the same thing you did about rabies. But if you want to be exact, I haven't touched one yet."

"By all means, let's be exact," Kate said with a grin.

"Mom says I notice all kinds of details," Jeremy said.

"Oh?" Kate was amused.

"I notice lots of details about the squirrels," he said, clearly proud of this feat.

Kate laughed. She reached out to ruffle the boy's hair before getting to her feet. "I imagine you do."

She had just started back inside when two strangers entered the library right behind her.

Kate grew curious. She knew almost everyone else in the

library, but who were these men? The pair had walked right past the movers without any indication that they knew the men carrying out furniture, so she didn't think they were associated with the move. In addition, the men seemed to be dressed too nicely to be movers. One wore a pair of khaki slacks with a blue dress shirt, while the other had on an expensive-looking pair of shiny leather loafers. Both of them wore no-nonsense expressions that practically shouted, "We have a schedule to keep, so don't waste our time." Something told her these men were people that bore watching.

Quietly, she moved toward them as the men sought out Livvy. Although she strained to hear, Kate couldn't quite catch their names. Livvy's voice carried a little more clearly, though.

"Building and Zoning?" she said. "You need to inspect the building now? We're going to be out in one week. It might be easier if—"

"No," said one of the men. "We need to do it today, Mrs. Jenner. I'm sorry if it causes any inconvenience. We'd like to start in the basement, if you'll show us the way."

"I'll do it," Kate said.

The men swung around. Livvy looked a bit startled, but after a moment's hesitation, she recovered quickly. "Thank you, Kate."

"If you'll follow me?" Kate beckoned to the men and set off at a brisk pace.

She led the pair to the basement door, then switched on the lights and headed down the unadorned wooden steps. "They use some of this for storage," she told them over her shoulder. "Is there something in particular you need to see down here?"

The shorter of the two men shook his head. "We need to take some general measurements. Thank you. We can find our way back upstairs when we're done."

"All right." Instead of heeding the man's unspoken dismissal, Kate headed farther into the basement and switched on light after light. As she had hoped, the men followed. "If you don't mind, just turn off the lights when you're finished."

"Thank you." The taller man smiled absently at her. He turned to the other fellow and pulled out a notebook. "All right, let's get started."

Kate turned and left the two men to their measurements. But she didn't go back upstairs. Instead, she quietly slipped behind a large stack of book boxes near the foot of the stairs. The basement was so quiet that Kate could hear the men's voices easily, even when they were in the room beyond where she was hiding.

"We've got to look at everything on this checklist," the first man said.

"All right, where do you want to start?"

"How about asbestos abatement? The preliminary survey I have doesn't show any, but we have to inspect for it. While we're at it, look for signs of rodent or insect infestation. Somebody told me they have a lot of squirrels here. That will have to be dealt with too."

Kate's attention sharpened. What did that mean? She hoped it meant something perfectly harmless, but from the man's tone of voice, she suspected that wasn't the case.

"Then we'll make sure we know where all the utilities are so they can be disconnected," the man was saying. "Once all that is documented and the radon testing is done, we can see about getting the municipal permit."

Asbestos abatement, rodent infestation, and radon testing. Kate mouthed the phrases to herself. She could see why the building would need to be inspected for those things if there was going to be any type of construction work done, which was what she inferred might be happening, especially since the utilities were going to be disconnected.

She wondered what the municipal permit was for. Did zoning laws require permits for renovation? Was someone planning to buy the library property? She hadn't heard that the town needed money, but perhaps that was the reason. It still didn't explain the need for the library's hasty closing, though.

"Take this to that far corner," she heard one of the men say to the other. "We need square-footage measurements too."

Fearing she'd be caught eavesdropping, Kate left the cover of the boxes. She moved as quietly as possible as she tiptoed to the stairs. The old wooden steps creaked a bit when her weight settled onto them, but the men were moving around in the other room, and she was pretty certain they didn't hear her.

Still, it was a relief to slip through the door into the hallway and carefully close the door behind her without a sound.

AT LUNCHTIME, Kate was surprised to see Paul's truck pull into their driveway right behind her. He often visited members of the congregation and joined them for lunch if he wasn't meeting someone at the Country Diner.

"Hello," she called as she unlocked the front door. "What are you doing home?" She laughed. "Not that I don't enjoy your company."

Paul grinned. "You were gone for two weeks. I missed sharing meals with you, so I thought I'd join you today. After all, you are one of my parishioners."

"So I am," Kate agreed. She hung her purse on the coat tree in the entryway and turned to hug her husband. "How was your morning? You went back out to the job site, didn't you?"

Paul nodded, and Kate felt the weight of the previous night's experience depressing the pleasant interlude. He kept his arms around her and rested his chin atop her head. "I can't tell you how many times this morning I flashed back to lying in that ditch. I shudder every time I think about how differently our evening could have ended."

"I know. I kept my brain so busy this morning that I didn't think about it much unless someone else brought it up. I think it was my subconscious protecting me from post-traumatic stress."

"It'll get better," Paul said in a firm tone.

She wasn't sure whether Paul was reassuring her or himself more.

With a kiss on the forehead, he released her. "You were right. Part of the roof came off. In fact, one whole corner of it is gone or damaged. It's going to take even more work to get it repaired now."

"I'm so sorry," she said. Together, they walked into the kitchen. "How much do you estimate it will take?"

"We won't know until after we meet with all the volunteers

this evening. We have to see if we still have enough people to complete the project."

"I'll say a prayer for you this afternoon," Kate promised. "I'm sure this setback is temporary." She paused. "Are turkey-and-swiss sandwiches on whole wheat okay?"

"Sounds great. How did your morning go at the library?"

Kate opened her mouth to tell him what Livvy had said. Then her conscience reared its head. She had promised not to tell anyone, and as difficult as it was, she thought she'd better not confide even in Paul. All it would take was one accidental reference, and Livvy and Danny could find them-selves in desperate straits—if the author of that anonymous note was serious about the threats.

"There's something odd about the circumstances of the closing," she said cautiously, "and I want to find out what it is."

"Uh-oh. Detective Hanlon is on the prowl again. Look out, America."

She grinned at him. Then she remembered her most recent discovery. "Oh! I almost forgot. What is asbestos abatement?"

Paul stopped in the act of pulling a carton of milk from the refrigerator. "I don't know. Sounds as if it has something to do with asbestos removal. Where did you hear that?"

"I overheard two men talking at the library."

"Why didn't you ask them?"

Kate smiled slightly as she spread mayonnaise on wheat-bread slices. "They didn't know I was there."

"Aha." Paul chuckled. "What else did you detect?"

Kate frowned as she thought for a moment. She could legitimately tell Paul about the library closing this way without endangering Livvy's secret. "A moving van came this morning and started loading furniture. When I asked where they were taking it, one of the men said the things were going to be stored at a warehouse in Pine Ridge. So the library isn't just closing for a few days, Paul. The library is going to be closed for some time."

Paul shook his head. "I don't understand why no one knows the reason for the closing."

"I don't either. I know it wouldn't be a popular plan, but keeping the entire community in the dark until the day of the move seems excessive. It makes me wonder if this was planned to occur when the mayor was going to be out of town. Lawton Briddle would have had a few dozen questions for them. It's as if someone needs it to happen before people can organize to stop it." Kate built the sandwiches as she spoke. "Which could be exactly what's going on. It was kept secret as long as possible, but once they started packing, it would only be a matter of time before word got around town. So there's some urgent reason to get the stuff moved."

Kate sliced each sandwich in half and slid them onto luncheon-sized plates. "Those men I overheard were inspecting the building for several different things. I think it's possible the town council has sold or is selling it. Hence, the library has to move."

"But why aren't they just moving to a new location?"

Kate opened her mouth, then closed it. "Livvy swore me to secrecy regarding certain aspects of this. But I don't think she'd mind if I tell you this part, as long as neither you nor I tell anyone else."

Paul nodded. "I understand. I won't breathe a word."

Kate set the knife in the sink. "There is no new location."

"What?" He sounded genuinely shocked.

"The town council hasn't found a new site for the library yet."

"I guess that explains the storage," he mused. "But are they really going to store the entire contents of the library? It's going to cost the town council a fortune. In addition to the books, there are thousands of dollars' worth of furniture, electronic equipment, and who knows what else. They'll have to insure it too, I imagine, and that won't come cheap."

"The town council doesn't have a fortune to spend," Kate said. "And they're never going to find a better location than the one we have now. So if they did sell the property, the town of Copper Mill must need money desperately."

"I'm not the detective in this family, but again," Paul said, "why must the fact that the library is closing indefinitely be kept secret? Because of the community's outrage? Which would be perfectly justified, I have to say."

"The only reason I can think of for keeping it a secret," Kate said, "is if the sale of the library land benefits someone financially."

But who?

Chapter Seven

After lunch, Paul went to his office at the church while Kate decided to look into both asbestos and radon. When she had been upstairs in the library the day before, she'd noticed that several of the computers were still up and running, and she hoped to be able to use one of them.

She was just about to leave the pleasant coolness of the house when the telephone rang. Closing the door on the heat that waited beyond, she quickly went back to the phone in the kitchen. "Hello?"

"Hey." It was Livvy.

Kate set her handbag down. "Hi. What's up?"

"I just heard something really interesting."

"What's that?"

Livvy paused. "The town council has called a meeting at two o'clock this afternoon."

"This afternoon?" Kate was surprised. "But it's Monday. Don't some of those people work?"

"If they do, they're taking time off."

"What's it about?" she asked.

Livvy sighed. "I tried to call Tosten this morning to ask about getting funding to have these damaged books assessed. It's imperative that we move quickly before they're permanently damaged. I couldn't contact him, so I called the vice president of the town council, Chalmers Petersen, and explained my concerns. He said he'd track down Tosten and get back to me. Next thing I know, Chalmers is calling me back to say they're calling a meeting at two, and he'll get me an answer as soon as he can."

"Okay," Kate said slowly, thinking through the new information. "Should one of us go to this meeting?"

"I can't," Livvy said. "I need to be here to supervise the packing. Can you fit it in?"

"Of course." Kate changed her plans without batting an eyelash. This was a heaven-sent opportunity to get a good look at the major players involved in this mess. "But am I allowed?"

"Unless specifically mentioned as a private or closed-door session, the general public can attend."

It already was nearly one thirty, so Kate quickly freshened up and went straight over to the Town Hall. Town-council meetings were held in the multipurpose room, as were any other public meetings that needed space.

She parked on Main Street, across from the row of pretty Victorian homes that lined the street, and walked to the town hall.

When she entered the building, Kate reveled in the immediate blast of cooler air that hit her as she made her way to the multipurpose room. She paused for a moment in the open doorway. All the members of the council were present, it appeared, standing in small clumps chatting before the meeting began. She knew all of them, by sight if not personally. As she started forward, seven heads swiveled in her direction.

Tosten Glass was not difficult to miss. Not particularly tall, he was exceedingly portly. His suit vest and jacket stretched tightly across his round belly, straining the buttons. He had a thick, bushy gray mustache that all but covered his top lip. His hair was pitch black and contrasted so sharply with the gray of his mustache that Kate suspected he either used shoe polish or a hair dye of some sort on it. It was thick and frizzy and a little long and equally thick and bushy sideburns curled down in muttonchops nearly to his jawline. She would dearly love to have a chat with his hairdresser, she thought, suppressing a smile.

He hustled over to her as she crossed to a line of chairs against the wall and took a seat.

"I'm Tosten Glass," he said, extending a hand. He wore an insincere politician's smile. Kate suspected he was incapable of *not* campaigning, even though he reportedly wasn't running for office again. "And you are . . . ?"

"Kate Hanlon," she said.

"Ah. You're the new pastor's wife."

Kate had discovered that "new" was a relative term in Copper Mill. Becoming identified as a local was as tough as being called a native Texan if you hadn't had an ancestor at the Alamo. Smiling, she simply said, "Yes."

"It's nice to meet you. How can I help you?" His handshake was disturbingly limp, and his hands were cold and clammy despite the heat of the day. He had a rather officious manner that could set a person's teeth on edge after very limited exposure, she suspected.

"Oh, I'd just like to watch the meeting," she said. "I was in town, and someone mentioned it. I've never seen a town-council meeting."

Tosten looked taken aback. "Well, er—"

"Of course you can watch the meeting, Kate." A second man walked up. "It's a public meeting."

"Hello, Floyd," Kate said, shaking his hand as well. "Thank you."

Floyd Jenkins owned a local nursery. He wore his usual summer uniform, long khaki shorts with a deep green shirt emblazoned with the logo of his business. He was deeply tanned from his many hours of outdoor work.

"If you're expecting excitement, you've come to the wrong place," he said, offering Kate a laid-back, friendly smile. A network of wrinkles carved lines at the corners of his eyes as he added, "Council meetings are about as thrilling as watching paint dry."

Kate chuckled. "That's all right. It's a cool place to sit and escape the heat, which is mighty important to me right now." Which was true, to an extent.

"You and me both," Floyd said.

As he drifted away, Kate turned back to Tosten Glass. Recalling the article in the paper, she said, "I'm sorry to hear about your personal difficulties."

Tosten's forehead furrowed as he swung his head around to stare at her. With a chuckle that sounded more manufactured than genuine, he said, "I have no difficulties, little lady. My life is just fine . . . and getting better by the day."

"Oh, my mistake," Kate said. "I saw that you weren't running for office for personal reasons, and I assumed those reasons had to do with personal difficulties of some kind. It's nice to hear that it's the opposite."

Tosten didn't appear to know what to say in response to that. He lowered his head and eyed Kate with a frown. Finally his defensive posture relaxed a bit, and he made a visible effort to offer her a strained smile again. "That's right. It's just the opposite."

He left her shortly afterward, to Kate's relief. Standing close to Tosten Glass made her feel as if something slimy had touched her skin.

She took a seat along the wall as the council members moved to the center of the room and seated themselves at a large round table. From her vantage point, Kate could see almost everyone. Floyd had his back directly to her, but everyone else offered her at least a profile view.

Tosten opened the meeting by calling the roll. He welcomed Kate, and she got the impression that it wasn't usual to have visitors observing council meetings, even the open ones.

Seated next to Floyd was Chalmers Petersen, a retired school superintendent with iron-gray hair and the ramrod bearing of a military man. He was the vice president to whom Livvy had spoken, and Kate had the impression that Livvy liked and respected the man. He said little, but when he did speak, the others paid attention.

To Chalmers' left was Tosten, and on the other side of Tosten sat Ben Dean. Kate only knew Ben by sight. He was a huge man with heavily muscled arms that befitted his work as a local carpenter and handyman. His hair was dark, his eyes small and close set, and he sported a thick black beard that nearly obscured his mouth entirely. Like Chalmers Petersen, Dean said little, but his silence held a surly quality, and his tone was disagreeable nearly every single time he opened his mouth.

In sharp contrast was Eva Mountjoy, the only woman on the board. Eva had been the commercial loan officer at Mid-Cumberland Bank and Trust until her retirement, and despite the fact that Kate knew that her husband had left her the previous year for a much younger woman, Eva's expression seemed to be permanently fixed in a cheerful smile that practically guaranteed approachability. Her voice was light and sweet, but Kate had heard she had a mind like a steel trap when it came to numbers. Eva handed around minutes from the last meeting, and Kate surmised that she was the group's secretary.

Malcolm Dekker, the funeral-home director, sat to Eva's left. He peered at the others through glasses with unbelievably thick lenses. His slightly prominent teeth were an unfortunate shade of yellow, and his face was long and thin, giving him the appearance of a myopic rodent. Malcolm hated to waste time, Kate noticed, and when someone—usually Tosten—began to natter on too long, he had no qualms about paraphrasing the person's comments and rushing the meeting forward. The few times Kate observed a faint expression of amusement on Chalmers' impassive face occurred whenever Malcolm broke into one of Tosten's monologues. She got the impression that neither Chalmers nor Malcolm cared much for Tosten.

The final member of the town council was Carey Carver, who owned the local feed store. He was a tall, thin man with a prominent Adam's apple and a shock of red hair that matched his milky pale, freckled skin.

Then Tosten announced that the reason for gathering at this unusual time was because of the impact of the previous night's storm on the library. The storm had been only the second in fifty years to spawn a tornado that did damage in the county, the hail that had fallen was the largest on record, and so forth and so on.

"What, exactly, was the impact?" Chalmers asked when Tosten stopped to take a breath.

"Some of the books in the historical collection received water damage when a window broke," Eva said, her explanation as concise as Tosten's had been verbose. "I spoke with Mrs. Jenner a short time ago, after Chalmers alerted us to the need for this meeting. She has asked us to authorize funds for the evaluation and repair of damaged historical books. Time is a critical factor because the volumes got wet."

"What kind of money are we talking?" Floyd asked.

"We don't know." Tosten took back control of the meeting. "If we decide to fund this, which I am not at all sure is prudent, we will have to set some financial parameters."

"Then how can we authorize it?" Malcolm squeaked.

"I'm against spendin' any money on old books," Ben Dean announced.

There was a general moment of incredulity evidenced by several people rolling their eyes at this spectacularly plebian point of view. Chalmers Petersen actually snorted out loud. Kate noticed Tosten's expression was curiously blank and unreadable. The others went on just as if Ben had never spoken.

"Mrs. Jenner spoke with a restoration expert who will assess the books for us and stabilize them." Eva named a figure that Kate didn't consider out of bounds in any way. It was greeted with varying expressions of interest or approval, except, of course, from Ben Dean, who Kate was beginning to believe shared a common ancestor with the Grinch.

There was a pause. "So what do we do?" asked Carey.

Kate doubted he ever willingly made a decision without someone else leading the way.

"Someone needs to make a motion," Malcolm informed him. "Another person seconds it, we discuss it, and then we call for a vote." Apparently Malcolm was the parliamentarian of the group.

"I move that we authorize the aforementioned amount to be used by the librarian for the assessment of books damaged by the storm," Chalmers said promptly.

"Second." Floyd leaped on the chance to move things along.

"I think it's a waste of money," Ben Dean groused. "The library's closing anyway—"

"Ben!" Tosten's voice was sharp and overly loud. He immediately dialed down his volume, and his words were restrained, although Kate could tell he wasn't pleased with the change of subject. "That is a separate issue with which we've already dealt. There is no need to go into it again." He appeared to realize that the entire council was staring at him, and his shoulders hunched forward as he assumed a placatory tone. "It's over and done with."

"Yes, but you said we'd make finding a new place to house the library a priority," Eva reminded him, "and we haven't talked about it at all."

"We just met on Thursday." Tosten shrugged. "It's only been four days."

"Somebody at the post office said the library's got to be closed by next Monday," Floyd said. "I guess I didn't realize when we voted last Thursday that all this was going to happen so fast. If that's true, don't we need to find a place for the library pretty quickly?"

"People." Tosten's face was a flaming, furious red, although he still made an attempt to modulate his tone. "May I remind you that Thursday's meeting was closed and confidential?" He looked pointedly at Kate. "Today's is not, and we should *not* be discussing that meeting at this time."

"I thought his lawyer was just blowing smoke. Do you really think he'll sue us if word gets out?" Eva didn't appear to care about the lack of privacy of the meeting.

"I know I would," Ben said in an aggressive tone. "I told you we were dealing with fools." He glared at Tosten.

"People! Stop!" Tosten bellowed.

Silence fell. The council president exhaled heavily and placed both hands on the surface of the table, looking down until he had regained control.

When he raised his head, he turned to Kate. "Mrs. Hanlon," he said in a cheery, patient tone in stark contrast to the contentious notes of a moment earlier. "I'm sorry for wasting your time this afternoon. It appears that we are going to need to go into closed session, so we'll have to ask you to leave."

Kate smiled at the council members as she gathered her

handbag and rose. "Certainly," she said. "This has been quite interesting. Thank you for letting me observe our democratic processes in action."

Was it her imagination, or was there alarm in Tosten's eyes? Certainly, a gleam of amusement lit Eva's gaze, and Chalmers Petersen even offered her a small smile. Floyd said, "Thanks for coming, Kate," as she slipped from the room.

Kate could hardly contain herself as she closed the door of the multipurpose room behind her.

Several things were clear. First, the entire council was not in agreement with the exact conditions of the library closing, as witnessed by Eva's concern and Floyd's confusion.

Second, Eva's comment about Thursday's meeting indicated that there had been at least one other person present, a lawyer representing someone else—a man from Eva's use of the pronoun *he*. And it was possible that the other person in question had also been in attendance.

Third, Ben Dean didn't seem to be interested in looking any further than the closing of the library on Monday. *And* it had appeared that Ben and Tosten had been discussing the situation privately without including some or all of the rest of the council.

Mentally, Kate divided the council into groups. In one group were Tosten Glass and Ben Dean, who both seemed to want the library closed and weren't too worried about its future. Why else would they be against restoring the historical documents?

In the second group were those who had assumed that the library closing was a short-term measure until a new location was found. Eva and Carey definitely fell into that category. Kate thought she could infer from their reactions that neither of them had spoken privately with Tosten about anything to do with the library.

Third were the people whom she couldn't read yet. She wanted to like Chalmers Petersen, if only because he hadn't seemed to be a fan of Tosten Glass. He also had been the one to call the meeting so quickly after Livvy voiced her concern. Malcolm's question about authorizing the funding would seem to indicate that he was in the second category with Carey and Eva, but she really didn't have enough evidence to merit that yet. And Floyd Jenkins hadn't expressed any particular opinion during the meeting, so she wasn't sure where he stood either.

So who was this mysterious "he," and what did he have to do with closing the library? Who was his lawyer?

And perhaps the most ominous question of all: why did both Tosten and Ben Dean seem so unconcerned about what was going to happen after the move on Monday?

Chapter Eight

Returning to update Livvy on what she had learned about the book restoration, which wasn't much, Kate saw Jeremy Pellman curled in an armchair in a quiet corner. The boy was engrossed in a thick book, his lips moving as he read, but he glanced up and smiled when he saw her.

"Hi, Jeremy. Any squirrel sightings today?" she called as she followed Livvy to her office.

The child shook his head and grinned. "No, but I'm not giving up yet. Mom made me come in out of the heat for a while, though."

When Livvy gave Kate a quizzical look, Kate told her about seeing Jeremy hand-feeding a squirrel.

Livvy smiled. "Recently, he's spent a lot of time here. He's always checking out books about animals and natural phenomena. Very inquisitive mind. I bet his teachers love him."

"He's a sweet child," Kate said. Then in a few sentences, she told Livvy what had transpired during her brief visit to the town-council meeting.

"So do you think we'll get the money?" Livvy asked with a worried frown. "Those books are going to be terribly damaged if we don't."

Kate thought for a moment, mentally counting heads. She nodded. "I can't be sure, of course, but I think there's support for it. The cost wasn't outrageous."

Livvy closed her eyes. "I hope so. I have plenty of other things to worry about without letting some of our most valuable historical items be ruined."

"I can stay until suppertime," Kate told her friend. "Got a job for me?"

Livvy did, and within minutes, Kate found herself involved in another packing assignment. This time she was taping together boxes and taking them to the volunteers who were removing books from the shelves.

For the next two hours, Kate was glad for the mindless task. It gave her time to reflect on everything she had learned that day. At five o'clock, she put down the tape and walked to Livvy's office, where her friend was going through files and folders.

"I've got to head home," she said. "But I'll come back tomorrow if you like."

"We'll be here at eight," Livvy told her. She gave her friend a wan smile. "Thanks for your help, Kate."

But before Kate could answer, she heard a child shouting. "Mom! Mom!"

Kate stepped out of the office to see Jeremy Pellman calling for his mother.

Kate rushed toward the boy, who had stopped near the

front desk and was looking around wildly. "Jeremy! What's wrong? Are you hurt?"

The child shook his head. "No, not me." His lip was quivering, and his entire face radiated distress. "I was lying in the grass again, trying to get a squirrel to come to me. One of them's friendlier than the others. But just as he came out of a hole in the wall, a cat jumped out and grabbed him!"

Jeremy's mother arrived in time to hear most of his explanation. She knelt before her son and placed gentle hands on his thin shoulders.

"Oh, Jeremy, I'm so sorry. But you know cats are predators. It's natural for them to go after small, fast-moving creatures. That poor little squirrel probably never knew what hit him."

"Yes, he did." Jeremy looked up at his mother as if she was a bit dense. "I jumped on the cat, and he ran away. The squirrel's right here in my pocket." He pulled open the chest pocket of the knit shirt he wore. Kate leaned in for a closer look. Sure enough, a small gray squirrel lay curled in the bottom.

"Jeremy Pellman! That squirrel could bite you. Take it outside right now." Louisa looked horrified.

Kate was taken aback too. Squirrels were cute at a distance, but she had never had any urge to get up close and personal. They were rodents, after all.

"Is he, uh, still alive?" she asked.

"Yes." Jeremy turned to her, ignoring his mother's command. "But his leg is hurt. We have to take him to a doctor."

"Jeremy . . ." Kate hesitated. "I don't think there are doctors for squirrels. Veterinarians don't usually treat wild animals."

"There's a wildlife rehab place outside Pine Ridge. You

could take it there," Livvy offered. She had followed Kate out of the office to see what was going on when Jeremy yelled, and now she offered the boy a small box with a lid. "You could put it in here, if we put holes in the lid so he gets plenty of air."

"Thanks!" Jeremy's face lit up as he accepted the box.

Louisa said, "Jeremy, we have to pick up your sisters from Grammy soon. We don't have time to babysit this squirrel." She took a deep breath. Clearly, it wasn't easy for her to refuse her son's pleading gaze. "It's a wild thing. You're going to have to let it take its chances outside."

Undeterred, Jeremy immediately turned and looked up at Kate pleadingly. "Will you take me? We have to save him, Mrs. Hanlon."

Kate hesitated. She wanted to go home. It was growing late in the day, and her energy level was flagging fast. But still . . . a squirrel was one of God's creatures. And what kind of Christian would she be if she refused to help it? Besides, the pleading look in Jeremy's hopeful gaze was impossible to resist.

"All right," she said, "but you can go only if your mother gives her permission."

Louisa looked stricken. "I can't put you out like this."

Kate smiled. "You're not. I'm going to take it to the wildlife center even if Jeremy doesn't go along."

"Pleeeease, Mom?"

Louisa finally nodded. "All right." She looked at Kate. "Do you mind dropping him off at my parents' afterward? She lives on the east end of Hamilton."

"That's not far from our house," Kate told her. "I'd be happy to."

"Yay!" Jeremy put the squirrel in the box and covered it

with the lid, complete with airholes. He was dancing from foot to foot by the time Kate copied down Louise's cell number in case of an emergency and retrieved her car keys.

Kate called Paul on her cell phone as they walked to the car. He sounded a bit groggy when he answered the phone.

"'Lo?"

"Hi, honey." Kate paused. "Did I catch you napping?"

"Forty winks," he confessed, chuckling. "I just got home."

"It's going to be a while before I get there," she told him. "Jeremy Pellman found an injured squirrel, and he's talked me into taking him to the wildlife center."

"Softy." Paul chuckled.

Kate snorted. "Oh, like you would have turned him down."

"You've got my number." Paul laughed harder. "Love you. Good luck saving the squirrel."

"Love you too. Bye."

Kate put away the cell phone and turned to Jeremy. "Let's go."

They'd been driving less than ten minutes when her eagle-eyed navigator pointed to a sign. "There it is!"

The sign read HCWC, and in smaller script below, Harrington County Wildlife Center. Kate turned left onto a gravel drive and followed it through several twists and turns up a rise, into a forest, and partway up a steep hill.

"Good heavens," she said. "This place is really remote."

She wasn't sure she liked being so far out of town. What if another storm blew up? Kate could feel her pulse speed up and her tension level rise at the mere thought, and she forced herself to stop imagining the worst.

As they came around a bend, the drive ended in a circle in front of a small prefabricated home. A riot of bright flowers with lots of reds and oranges among them filled the grass circle, and a merrily bubbling fountain occupied the center. In the trees around the edges of the small swath of green lawn, Kate noted a number of birdfeeders and birdhouses of differing sizes and styles. To the side and behind the house were several smaller wooden buildings with outdoor runs and pens, and one extremely long wire cage.

"They must like hummingbirds," Jeremy observed. "That's a butterfly and hummingbird garden."

As she braked and halted the car, Kate smiled at him. "You know a lot about animals, don't you?"

He grinned and ducked his head. "I like animals. For my birthday, I want a puppy."

"When's your birthday?"

"A week from tomorrow."

"Oh! Next Tuesday?" Kate said. "And how old will you be? Twelve?" She was pretty certain the child wasn't that old, but she didn't want him to think she underestimated his age.

Jeremy shook his head. "No. I'll be ten."

"Wow! Double digits," Kate said. "Pretty exciting, *hmm*?"

"A puppy would be more exciting," he said, making her laugh out loud.

They walked to the front door, where another sign welcomed them to the HCWC. Kate tugged open the screen door and stepped inside with Jeremy just a pace behind her.

Almost simultaneously, a woman with long, curly brown hair twinkling with silver strands walked through the same door. "Hi. I'm Elspeth Getty. How can I help you?"

"We have a squirrel that needs help," Kate said. "I'm Kate Hanlon, and this is Jeremy Pellman." Each of them shook hands with the woman. "Jeremy has been watching a group of squirrels right outside the Copper Mill Public Library, and one of them was attacked by a cat today. Jeremy managed to get it away from the cat, but it appears to be injured."

"All right." Elspeth turned to the counter behind her and picked up a clipboard with a sheet of paper attached. "This is an intake sheet." She took the box from Jeremy and cautiously opened a corner of the lid. Then, when no squirrel popped out, she opened it wider.

"Oh! A baby. *Hmm*. Maybe not a baby." Her brow furrowed briefly, then she said, "Let me do a quick look-see and get it set up in a cage while you fill that out. I'll be right back."

Kate sat down on a love seat beside Jeremy as he filled out the information requested. The paper asked a number of questions: where the animal had been found, the names of all who had handled it, whether anyone had touched it with bare hands, what injuries had been observed, and what had happened to the animal, in addition to the usual contact information. Kate hesitated over that for a moment, then told Jeremy to put her name and phone number in the space. Jeremy was too young, and his mother was too busy.

"This would be a fun place to work," Jeremy observed.

Kate grinned at him. "For you, certainly."

Elspeth came back into the room then. She held out her hand for the clipboard and glanced over the information. "So it looks like your squirrel has some leg wounds from that cat."

"Do you think he'll live?" Jeremy asked anxiously.

Elspeth hesitated. "I hope so, but I won't make you any

promises. Cats often do internal damage to little creatures that doesn't show on the outside. Still, he looks pretty good, so keep your fingers crossed. You're a hero," she said to Jeremy. "You must have been pretty quick to get him away from the cat with so little damage. Usually they're badly injured or killed when cats get them." She glanced again at the information they had provided, then continued. "And you're the only person who touched him, right?"

Jeremy nodded.

Immediately alert, Kate said, "Is that a problem? Could it have rabies?"

Elspeth shook her head. "Squirrels aren't known to be a rabies virus carrier. Unless he was bitten, just washing his hands thoroughly is all he needs to do. If you want to give me a call in a day or so, I can let you know how the squirrel's doing. And if he recovers and is releasable, we can take him back to the same place you found him."

Kate hesitated. "That may not be possible. The library is being closed. I don't know what the plans are for the building, but they may not welcome a colony of squirrels."

Elspeth looked alarmed. "You mean you think they might exterminate them?"

"I don't know what to think," Kate admitted.

"Could you please let me know the moment you hear about the disposition of the building?" Elspeth asked. "I need to get some more information about this squirrel. There's something unusual about him."

Chapter Nine

Jeremy was a delightful child, but by the time Kate drove him to his grandparents' house, she was almost too tired to respond to his questions and conversation.

Two days before, she had finished her vacation and come home. The previous day, she'd found out the library was closing and had been pinned down in a ditch while a tornado roared over her head. And today she'd climbed and descended the library stairs countless times during the morning, attended the town-council meeting and worked in the library again in the afternoon, and then helped Jeremy save his squirrel. And throughout the day, she'd been actively engaged in seeking out more information about why the library was closing. When she thought back over all she'd accomplished in just a few hours, she had to laugh at herself. It had been an insane schedule, albeit one of her own making.

When she turned onto Hamilton Road, Jeremy directed her to a home right across from Copper Mill Park. "That one right there, with the green shutters," he said, pointing.

There was a car in the attached carport and a second one, a somewhat battered-looking, aging compact that Kate suspected belonged to Louisa, parked behind it. Kate pulled over along the curb behind a third car. Kate whistled as she braked. "What a car!"

It was a beautifully restored or maintained old Cadillac, probably from around the time she was born. The roof was white, and the body was a pretty robin's-egg blue. The tires had spotless, wide whitewalls with shiny chrome hubcap covers. All in all, a marvelous classic car.

"It's okay, I guess. It belongs to my mom's friend." Jeremy sounded distinctly unenthusiastic, particularly when Kate compared his tone to his vivacious chatter during the ride home. She could only surmise that Jeremy didn't care much for whoever owned the Cadillac.

The front door opened, and Louisa stepped onto the porch. She turned and spoke to someone inside, shaking her head vigorously. When she turned back again, Kate thought she appeared upset or agitated. But when she spoke, both her tone and her words were calm and cordial.

"Hi, Kate," she called, waving. "Thank you very much."

Kate smiled and lifted her hand in return. "No problem." To Jeremy, she said, "See you tomorrow. I'll say a prayer that your little squirrel gets better."

"Me too," the boy said as he climbed out of the car. "Thank you."

As she drove away, Kate decided that Louisa Pellman certainly was doing a great job as a solo parent. Jeremy was a terrific little boy.

FEELING TIRED TO THE BONE, Kate walked into her home after dropping off Jeremy. She found Paul in his office. When she paused in the doorway and said, "Hey," he set down a sheaf of papers and came out to the living room.

"Would you like a glass of sweet tea?" he asked.

Kate nodded as she collapsed into one of the overstuffed chairs. "Yes. I made decaf earlier, so the caffeine won't be a problem."

"Sweet tea on the way." Paul veered into the kitchen, then returned shortly with glasses for them both.

"I started dinner," he went on. "I wasn't feeling ambitious, but I preheated the oven so we can put in some fish sticks. And I cut up watermelon and got a mess of lima beans ready to steam."

"Thank you," she said with a sigh. "I'm so tired."

Paul took his own seat, smiling. "What did you do this afternoon?"

Kate recounted her afternoon, detailing the council meeting, her work at the library, and helping Jeremy's squirrel.

Paul chuckled. "That kid really is something. If he doesn't grow up to be a vet or some kind of animal trainer, he's missing his calling."

"He does love animals," Kate agreed. "I believe Louisa must understand him pretty well, since she lets him come along with her to the library." She paused, struck by a new idea. "What would you say to inviting Louisa and her children to dinner one evening?"

Paul smiled. "I'd say it sounds like a great idea. Do you have a day in mind?"

Kate thought for a moment. "Tomorrow evening? There's nothing on our calendar."

"Works for me," Paul said. "I wonder if she works tomorrow? That might be a complication. I don't know who keeps the children while she's working."

"Her mother does. That's where I dropped off Jeremy today."

"Well it can't hurt to ask," Paul said. "Why don't you give her a call?"

"I don't have— Wait, yes, I do have her cell-phone number," Kate said. "She gave it to me before Jeremy and I left for the wildlife center."

Kate got the slip of paper from her handbag and padded into the kitchen to make the call. When Louisa answered, she said, "Hello, Louisa, this is Kate Hanlon."

There was a long silence. "Kate? What . . . why are you calling?"

A bit taken aback by the lack of welcome, Kate cleared her throat. "Paul and I wanted to invite you and the children to dinner tomorrow evening if you're free."

"Oh. Oh!" Louisa's voice warmed considerably. "That's very thoughtful."

"We were discussing you, and we thought it would be nice to have a chance to get better acquainted."

"You were . . . discussing me?" The younger woman's voice sounded hesitant again.

Suddenly Kate thought she understood. She'd forgotten that Louisa had lived with an abusive husband. It made perfect sense for her to be cautious.

"We'd like to get to know you and your family better," Kate

told her. "Paul got a kick out of my story about Jeremy and the squirrel."

"I just bet." Louisa's voice sounded more confident again.

Kate waited, uncertain about what to say next. But then Louisa chuckled and seemed friendly.

"Are you sure you want three lively children barging into your home?"

Kate laughed. "We have three lively grandchildren. They won't do anything that hasn't been done before."

Still Louisa hesitated. "*Um*, I suppose it wouldn't hurt. All right, yes. We can come to dinner. Thank you."

In the background, Kate could hear Jeremy's high voice. "Is that Mrs. Hanlon? She invited us to her house? Hurray!"

"All right, then," Kate said. "Why don't we say six o'clock?"

"Six would be fine," Louisa said. "Thank you again. I'll see you then."

Kate returned to the living room and shared the plan with Paul. "I hope I make more progress tomorrow than I did today getting information on the library closing," she said, collapsing again into her chair. "I felt like I did a lot of wheel spinning today."

He frowned. "So you didn't make a lot of progress in your quest to find out what's going on?"

Kate shook her head. "Not nearly as much as I need to." Then she smiled. "But I did have a wonderful experience a little while ago at the wildlife center. I met this amazing lady named Elspeth, who devotes herself to healing wild animals. She has a ministry saving the lives of God's creatures."

"All God's critters got a place in the choir," Paul quoted

with a grin. The words were a line from a catchy children's folk song. Kate recognized it immediately because her own children had sung it in the children's choir at their old church when they were small.

Kate groaned. "Now I'll have that song stuck in my head for days." Already, the chorus was tripping through her mind.

"I love that song," Paul said. "I'm sure I saw a copy of that music somewhere in the filing cabinets. I'm going to suggest to Sam that we get a children's choir together to sing it."

Copy . . . A light snapped on in Kate's head, and she sat up straight. "That's it!"

"What's it?" Paul looked startled by her sudden burst of energy.

"You mentioned a copy. This afternoon at the meeting, Eva handed around copies of the last meeting's minutes. I'm sure there must be files of all town-council matters."

"I would assume so," Paul said. "I know the town council doesn't have an office at Town Hall like the mayor does, but I'm sure any official documents would be kept there."

"Official documents like meeting minutes," she said. "I saw Eva taking minutes at the meeting this afternoon. I wonder if there are copies of minutes of all the town-council meetings available to the public."

"There should be," Paul said.

"Although," Kate said, "I presume the minutes from closed meetings aren't available to the public, and the meeting last Thursday was a private session. Those are the minutes I believe I'd find most useful."

"Do you think you might find something helpful in any of the other minutes?"

"I don't know," Kate said, "but it surely can't hurt to read them." She made a mental note to stop by Town Hall in the morning before heading to the library to help Livvy. Then the rest of the discussion at the meeting came back to her. "Paul," she said slowly, "I forgot something. I think it's important. Carey Carver didn't appear to know that the library was officially moving out next Monday. Why wouldn't a member of the council who made the decision know the dates?"

"Maybe there was a subcommittee responsible for the details," Paul suggested.

Kate shook her head. "Over something as important as closing a building that offers such a great service to the community? I can't imagine that."

"I can't either," he confessed. "I was just throwing it out there."

"The meeting deteriorated right before they asked me to leave so they could go into closed session. But while the meeting was melting down, Eva asked a question that led me to believe there is someone else involved in the library closing. She mentioned a lawyer who might sue them for talking about it. How is that possible? And who could he be representing?"

Paul ran his fingers through his hair. "You've got me. The only way that makes sense is if someone else owns the library and doesn't want folks to know. But how could someone else own a public library that's been administered by the town for so many years?"

"There's a lot about this that doesn't make sense." Kate

took another sip of her tea, and they both fell silent, contemplating the situation.

Remembering where Paul had been when she arrived, Kate made a vague gesture toward the office. "What's with all the paperwork?"

Paul shifted in his chair. "It's all the project paperwork."

"I thought someone else was handling that."

"Ephraim Dresser was, but he has to go out of town next week."

"So you're doing it?" Kate smiled. Her compassionate husband was unable to resist when someone asked for his help.

"So I'm doing it," he agreed.

Kate relaxed again, smothering a yawn. "I'm sorry," she said.

"You look like you're ready for bed right this minute, and I have a meeting in an hour," Paul observed. He glanced at his watch. "We'd better eat."

"I just packed too many things into too short a window of time," Kate said ruefully.

"Maybe you'll feel more like yourself tomorrow," Paul said.

"I sure hope so," she replied as she got slowly to her feet. "Until I figure out how to stop the library from closing for good, I need every hour I can get."

THE ROOFING VOLUNTEERS met at St. Lucy's Episcopal Church at seven that evening. Despite her exhaustion, Kate had offered to clean up the supper dishes while Paul hurried off to his meeting. He suspected she would be sound asleep by the time he got home.

St. Lucy's was a graceful white structure located just a block down from the Presbyterian church on Smoky Mountain Road. The building sat on a slight bank, with a pair of matching staircases curving up from either side of the front driveway to meet at the porticoed front porch.

Tall, single, and sandy-haired, Father Lucas Gregory, the parish priest, was a fit man in his midthirties with a tanned face and twinkling blue eyes. Although he wasn't on the committee of volunteers working on the roof, he attended the meeting to support the men from his congregation.

"Hey, Lucas," Paul said, extending his hand as he strode up the steps. "Good to see you."

"Back at you, my friend," Lucas said as they shook. "I understand you had a close call with that tornado the other night."

Paul nodded. "Close enough."

"I bet." Lucas' expression sobered. He raised his free hand and clapped it over Paul's hand, which he was still holding. "I thanked God for keeping an eye on you. I can't imagine our pastoral community without you."

Paul was touched. "Thank you," he said to his friend. "I appreciate both the prayer and the compliment." He released her hand and went on down the carpeted hall to the choir room, where the meeting was being held.

He found a good many men already seated. Most of them had heard about his near escape from serious harm the previous evening. They were full of questions, which he fielded until Pete MacKenzie and Lucas entered the room.

Just as they prepared to open the meeting, another man walked into the room. He was average height, and he looked to be about fifty. He had dark hair shot with silver and worn

in a severe fifties-style flattop. He smiled confidently at Pete
and took a seat.

Pete called the meeting to order. He turned to the newcomer. "This is Jerry Cox," he said. "Jerry's coming onto the
project to replace Ephraim, who can't stay with us."

Then Pete turned matters over to Drew Mears, who
explained the damage to the roof and told everyone about the
extended time line. Paul noticed a number of concerned
faces, but when Pete asked for a show of hands of men who
were willing to stick with the project for two more weeks,
provided they adjusted to suit people's schedules, every hand
in the room went up, except for Ephraim Dresser.

Ephraim took the floor then to explain about his business
trip and tell the group that Paul would be taking over the
paperwork.

Paul rose. "I know nothing about roofing or construction,"
he said, "but I have the time to coordinate the project, and
I'm willing to give it a shot if you guys are willing to be patient
with me. I'm sure Louisa Pellman is anxious to get back into
her house."

After a few more minutes, the meeting concluded. The
mood as the group dispersed was optimistic. Paul walked over
to Jerry Cox and extended his hand. "Thank you for volunteering. Do you have experience with roofing?"

Jerry shook his head. "No, but I'm smart. I'll figure it out
as we go."

The answer troubled Paul a bit. "Drew knows what he's
doing," Paul told Jerry. "He's the one to talk to about what
we'll be doing."

"Thanks." Jerry smiled. "I can handle it." He was willing

to work, no question, but his attitude seemed a little cavalier. Paul could only hope that Jerry would prove to be a team player who could follow directions when they were twenty feet off the ground.

Ephraim joined them then and extended his hand to Paul. "I really appreciate you stepping up. I'll give you my cell-phone number in case you have any questions after I leave town."

Chapter Ten

On Tuesday morning, Kate followed her usual routine, albeit a bit stiffly. Between lying in a ditch, packing innumerable boxes, and trekking up and down the stairs repeatedly, her body was protesting the unaccustomed activities.

During her morning Bible study, she was assailed by another of those moments when the what-ifs from the tornado experience overwhelmed her. What if one of them had been hit by flying debris? What if the tornado had touched down? What if they hadn't known to seek the low ground? Or, heaven forbid, what if they'd been sucked up into the vortex and dropped again some distance away?

Deluged by the possibilities, even though none of that had occurred, she clasped her hands and simply began to pray. *Dear Lord, replace my fears with thankfulness. Your hand surely was over us during that tornado.* She continued to pray until she felt her racing heart slow to a normal rhythm, until she felt flooded with peace and grace and was ready to begin her day.

Before she dressed, Kate called the wildlife rehabilitation center. Paul left for the day while she was waiting for someone to answer, and as he went out the door, he sent her a long-distance kiss and mouthed, "See you tonight."

The director Kate had met yesterday answered the telephone. "Good morning. Harrington County Wildlife Center. This is Elspeth."

"Good morning, Elspeth. This is Kate Hanlon. Did our little squirrel survive?"

"Hi, Kate. Yes, he made it through the night. It doesn't look as if he has injuries other than the leg, which I treated. I put him on a course of antibiotics, and if all goes well, he can be released in a week or so."

"Oh, that's terrific news," Kate said. "I'll tell Jeremy."

"He seemed like a sweet kid," Elspeth remarked.

"He is. That squirrel owes its life to him. I've never seen a child so patient. He spends hours watching those squirrels."

"He does?" Elspeth sounded extremely interested. "Could you call me today or tomorrow if he's at the library watching them? I'd like to talk to him a little more."

"Sure. Although he's too young to hire," Kate cautioned with a laugh.

Elspeth chuckled. "Too bad. I bet he'd be a great intern. The thing is, Kate, I spent a good bit of time last night trying to figure out exactly what type of squirrel this is. It doesn't look like a familiar species. Did you realize it's a flying squirrel?"

"Really? I guess I hadn't looked that closely." She laughed. "Jeremy told me it was, but I suppose I doubted his assessment. Although heaven only knows why," she said, grinning. "That boy already knows more about animals than I ever will."

"It's not one of the two species commonly found in Tennessee. In fact, I can't find anything quite like it in any of my reference materials. I already put in a call to a friend of mine who's an expert on flying squirrels."

"How is it different?" Kate knew Jeremy would bombard her with questions when she reported Elspeth's findings to the inquisitive child.

"The color and size are wrong. I'm pretty sure this is an adult, but it's even smaller than the Southern flying squirrel, and the fur is really dark gray, almost black. The feet and face *are* black, in fact. Are there others like this?"

"I don't know," Kate said with regret. "I saw my first and only one Sunday evening, and it could have been this one. But Jeremy studies them for hours, so I'm sure he could tell you more."

"So there's more than one."

"I'm not even sure of that. I did get that impression from him, though."

"Could you find out and call me?" Elspeth asked.

It seemed like a small thing in return for the assistance the wildlife center had rendered to them, but Kate still had to suppress a sigh. It was a squirrel, for heaven's sake. She needed to be spending her time trying to figure out how to save the library, not identify a rodent.

"Sure," she finally said. "I'll call you when I've talked to Jeremy. I'll be seeing him this evening."

"Thanks. It's a cute little critter." Elspeth hung up, apparently content with that.

All God's critters got a place in the choir . . . The familiar melody played in her head as she donned a slim denim skirt and a pale mint weskit-style blouse with short sleeves and tiny buttons running down the front. *Oh, great.* Now she was going to have that silly song running through her head all day. Just wait until she saw Paul, she thought as she slipped her feet into green espadrilles and switched her handbag to a denim one with silver Western accents.

As she drove to town, she remembered Jeremy telling her about his upcoming birthday. He was a special child, Kate thought, and she wondered what she could do to recognize his special day.

The answer came to her as she braked at a four-way stop: a sun catcher. She would create a sketch of Jeremy's squirrel and reproduce it in stained glass so that any time he looked out the window, he would be reminded of his act of kindness. She couldn't make it as dark as the real squirrel, of course. The real thing was very dark, and she did want the color to show up when sunlight penetrated it. But she began to get excited as she thought about the specifics of the sketch. Oh, she couldn't wait to begin! Perhaps that afternoon she would have some time to get started.

Before she quite realized it, she was pulling into a parking spot near the library. She'd intended to stop by Town Hall first to read through the town-council minutes, but her automatic pilot had taken her straight to the library when she wasn't paying attention. She laughed at herself. Well, since she was there, she might as well go in and say hello to Livvy. And if the computers were still up, she could do a search to see what she could learn about Jeremy's squirrel.

As soon as she walked through the doors, she noticed the same morose atmosphere from the day before. Many of the same faces glanced Kate's way when she entered, although she didn't see Louisa Pellman among them.

But before Kate could even move around the horseshoe-shaped circulation desk into Livvy's office, the front door opened, and Jeremy Pellman rushed in. "Mrs. Hanlon! Did you talk to the wildlife lady?"

His volume was quite a bit higher than one normally preferred in a library, but since it no longer mattered, no one fussed at him.

"Hi, Jeremy," Kate said as the child skidded to a halt in front of her. "I sure did. Your squirrel was still alive this morning, and the wildlife lady thought he was doing fine. She said you may be able to release him here once he's healed."

"Really?" The boy's eyes were shining.

"Really," Kate confirmed. She gestured toward the steps. "I'm going upstairs to look up some information on squirrels. I know you're eager to get outside and watch them, but I would appreciate your help for a little bit."

"Okay." Jeremy looked delighted, and his walk as they made their way to the second floor carried just a hint of a swagger, Kate thought with amusement. Oh, to be so easily thrilled!

"What are we looking up?" Jeremy asked as they drew two full boxes up to one of the computers. "Flying squirrels in Tennessee." Kate pushed the keyboard toward him. "Here. You're probably light-years faster on this than I am."

Sure enough, the boy's fingers flew. Kate smiled ruefully at his youthful speed. Technology today was a little overwhelming, she thought, when you could still remember watching *The Wizard of Oz* on black-and-white rabbit-eared television and using a party-line telephone in your home growing up.

"Here," Jeremy said. "I did a search for that, and we got all these links. Which one should I click on?"

Kate scanned down the list. "Try that one."

A moment later, an encyclopedic-looking entry came up. Kate and Jeremy read it and examined the photographs of flying squirrels. "So there are Northern flying squirrels and Southern flying squirrels in Tennessee," Kate summarized.

"There's some other kind too," Jeremy said, pointing at the screen, "because ours doesn't look like any of those."

"Sure doesn't." Kate grinned at him. "You never know, you could have a new subspecies of squirrel named after you. Pellman's flying squirrel," she said.

Jeremy laughed out loud as they closed the browser window and walked back downstairs. "That would be way cool."

"Way cool," Kate agreed. Her comment had been tongue-in-cheek, but it went right over Jeremy's head. "Since we just looked at those other squirrels, why don't we go outside and observe yours for a little while. We could write down the differences for Miss Getty."

"Miss who?"

"The wildlife lady."

Kate and Jeremy sat beneath a tree for almost thirty minutes, but not a squirrel was in sight.

"They're probably all inside the air-conditioned library," Kate said, "where we should be."

Jeremy shrugged. "They hardly ever come out in the morning. It's like their rest time or something."

Kate stared at him in mock menace. "And it didn't occur

to you to tell me this *before* we came out here and sweated ourselves to death?"

Jeremy giggled, falling onto his back on the soft grass as he did so.

Kate watched him, smiling fondly. "I almost forgot," she said. "The lady from the wildlife center wanted to know if you have ever seen more than one of these squirrels."

Jeremy sat up, nodding vigorously. "Sure I have. Two of them chase each other around sometimes, and one day when I had a whole bag of peanuts, four or five came out."

Kate nodded with satisfaction. "Thank you. I'm going to let her know that right now." And she got up and walked back into the library to call Elspeth Getty.

She used the phone at the front desk to make the call. Then she looked for Livvy.

Her friend wasn't among the busy workers scattered here and there around the building. Then Kate noticed that the door to the office was closed. She passed the counter and walked toward the office, hoping to catch Livvy. She was in luck, she realized, when she knocked softly on the door, then peeked inside. Livvy was sitting at her desk, unmoving.

"Hey, lazybones," Kate teased. "You don't have time for lollygagging around. You've got troops out here that need orders."

Livvy slowly turned her head and looked at Kate. Her hazel eyes were dark pools of despair, and her face looked pale against the bright pink of the flowered top she wore. "Close the door," she said in a monotone.

Shocked and concerned, Kate did exactly that. "What's wrong?" she demanded. She rounded the desk and laid a hand on her friend's shoulder. "Livvy, what is it?"

Livvy flicked a finger at a piece of paper lying on her desk. It was letter-sized and had been folded in thirds; a matching envelope lay beneath it. "I got another note," she said.

Kate sucked in a breath of dismay. She bent over the desk and picked up the paper.

The note was on plain white copy paper like the last one, printed in a standard font. It read:

This is your last warning. Keep your nosy friend out of the library's business, or you and your husband will be unemployed AND UNEMPLOYABLE.

"Oh, Livvy, I'm so sorry. I know this is frightening, but—"

"Stop."

"Pardon?" Kate stared at her friend.

"I said stop," Livvy repeated. There was both sorrow and fear in the gaze she turned on Kate. "You have to stop asking questions, Kate. Danny and I can't afford to lose our jobs or our reputations."

"But, Livvy, I'm learning things. I know I'm on the trail of the real reason behind the library closing."

"No!" Livvy wasn't a person to raise her voice, and Kate jumped, shocked at her friend's tone. "I'm not asking you. I'm telling you. *You have to stop.*"

There was a moment of silence between the two friends. Livvy's words hung in the air, a divider between them as solid as a wall. Kate understood Livvy's fear. But she was also certain that ignoring the situation wasn't going to help. The only way to save the library was to find and stop the people behind it.

"I'm sorry," she said quietly as she turned and left the office. She couldn't stop, but she was going to have to be extremely cautious with the rest of her investigation.

Although Town Hall wasn't far, she moved her car from the library to a spot right in front of one of the gorgeous old Victorians that lined the street across from the Town Hall. This one had been lovingly restored with what looked like classic Victorian colors. It was a deep indigo blue accented by trim work in a soft crimson with paler ivory accents.

Getting out of the Honda, she considered the best place to start her sleuthing. Obviously, she couldn't go to Tosten Glass. If he was behind the closing, as it appeared could be the case, she couldn't afford for him to know she still was digging for information.

She would go to the mayor, she decided, and if he couldn't help her, perhaps she'd try the *Chronicle's* reporter, Jennifer McCarthy. The trick would be getting information out of Jennifer without letting on that it had anything to do with closing the library.

Surely one of the two of them would have what she was after. The town-council minutes were one thing she wanted to check, but she also decided to take a look at the annual budget while she was there. She recalled her discussion with Livvy, and the final question that had remained in her mind. Could there have been a budget shortfall large enough to warrant the council having to sell off some of its assets? As important as the library was, it wasn't a necessity.

Crossing the street, she walked along the tree-lined path and up the concrete steps to the double-glass doors. It was hot and humid again today. She was thoroughly sick of this weather, she decided, and she'd only been home three days! But after Sunday evening's experience, the memory of which still could make her shudder, she concluded that she'd be more than happy with a few nice cool days when there was zero percent chance of any kind of storms.

She waved at Skip Spencer, the local deputy, as she passed his office on her way back to the mayor's office at the end of the hall.

The door was closed, so she knocked.

"Yes?"

It wasn't exactly an invitation to enter, but she opened the door and stepped in anyway. "Hello, Lawton."

"Well, hello, Kate." Lawton Briddle rose to his feet and extended a hand across his desk to Kate. After they shook, he gestured toward one of the two armchairs for guests that were set a discreet distance from his desk. "Would you like to sit down?"

"Thank you." Kate chose a chair. "Do you have time to answer a couple of questions for me?"

"Certainly," he said, gesturing expansively. "Ask away."

Kate smiled. The mayor seemed to be in exceptionally fine humor. It was an auspicious start. "I was wondering if you have a copy of the town's annual budget. I'd like to take a brief look at it. Also, can you tell me where the minutes of town-council meetings are kept and if it might be possible for me to see them?"

Lawton nodded. "The budget is right here on my computer. Meantime—"

The telephone rang. Lawton didn't have a regular secretary.

"Just let me answer this," he said to Kate, holding up one finger. He pushed a button and said "Hello?"

"I'd like to speak to Tosten Glass, please," a shrill female voice said.

When she heard the request, Kate sat forward, realizing that Lawton had hit the speakerphone button. She knew the mayor could be . . . showy at times, and she suspected this display was for her benefit more than for any real need to use the speakerphone. But she was interested in hearing who was trying to contact Tosten.

"This is the *mayor's* office," Lawton said, a trace of irritability in his tone. "You'll have to call him at home or on his cell phone."

"Well, could you just give him a message?" The woman must not have been listening because she kept right on going. "This is Lillian with Skyler and Clark Properties. Could you please tell him to stop by today? I have the preliminary plans for his new building ready."

"Ma'am, you have the wrong number," Lawton said. "This is *not* the office of the town council."

There was a small silence. "Oh," said the woman. "Why didn't you tell me that in the first place?"

Lawton looked at Kate. He held out both hands in exasperation, shrugging his shoulders while she struggled not to laugh. He shook his head as he hit the Off button. "You cannot imagine how often that happens," he told her. "I get tired of taking personal messages for Tosten."

"What does Skyler and Clark Properties do?" Kate asked. She'd seen the name around town, but she'd never paid much attention to it before.

Lawton frowned. "They build and manage apartment buildings. I believe they have about five properties under their belt now."

"Apartment buildings," Kate repeated. What was Tosten Glass doing talking to someone about apartment buildings? It probably had nothing to do with the library situation, she reminded herself. Still, she couldn't shake an uneasy feeling, and she filed the information away to review later.

"As we were discussing before we were interrupted," Lawton said, "you were asking about the town-council's meeting minutes. Most of them are public record, so I don't see why you couldn't take a look."

He swiveled his desk chair around to face a large filing cabinet and bookshelf behind him. Reaching up, he tugged a hefty dark blue notebook off the shelf and turned back to Kate. He laid the heavy volume on the desk with a *thunk*. "These only go back to 1985," he said. "There's another notebook from before that, but you won't need it if you just want this year."

He pulled his keyboard toward him and hit a few keys. "I'll print you out a copy of the budget, and you can take that with you."

He rose and came around the desk, picking up the notebook and carrying it to a coffee table on a small rug in front of a love seat along one wall. "You can sit here and read the minutes."

"Thanks." Kate sat and opened the notebook.

Lawton said, "These are just the regular meeting minutes."

Kate nodded. She'd been expecting that. "So the minutes from the closed-door sessions aren't public?"

"Nope," he said. "Those are confidential."

"Oh." Kate hadn't expected to get a lot of information, but she'd been hoping there might be something available from those private meetings. If something big concerning the library had happened at a regular session of the council, she was certain the entire town would have known about it. After all, Jennifer McCarthy got the agenda for every public meeting, and she attended if there appeared to be any controversial issue brewing. Still, there might be some clue that had been overlooked, so she intended to read the previous months' minutes.

Kate decided to start with the first meeting in January. Surely something of the magnitude of the library closing and moving would have taken some time to develop. But she found nothing in January's minutes.

February . . . March . . . clear up through May, there was no indication of any sort of issue regarding the library other than approving a request from the Friends of the Library to put up a tent in the library's yard during the downtown summer flea market held at the end of August. Kate supposed that wouldn't be happening now, but she found it interesting that in June everyone appeared to assume that the library would be there in August. The event was still two weeks away.

Reading on, she still didn't see anything odd in June. In fact, that month, the council had set a date for the annual Christmas Open House. How could no one have heard of the closing yet?

On the heels of those realizations, Kate hit pay dirt. Of a very modest sort, but pay dirt nonetheless, she thought.

The previous Thursday, while Kate was away, a special meeting of the town council had been called. The public minutes were very short and to the point. The meeting had been called because a lawyer from McMinnville over in neighboring Warren County had asked to address the council immediately. According to the single page of information, the lawyer presented "previously unknown information" to the council, after which they went into private session. Previously unknown information? Kate tapped the page with a finger. If she were a betting woman, she'd bet that information had something to do with the closing of the library. It seemed too coincidental to be unrelated.

The lawyer's name wasn't mentioned until the end of the document. Then the name "Ellis Hayer, Esquire" appeared one single time. It looked as if the council secretary had intended to keep Hayer's identity anonymous but had slipped up and recorded it once. Kate thought about Eva Mountjoy, who had signed these minutes as well as the others Kate had read. Eva was no fool. Could she possibly have left the name accessible on purpose? Regardless of how it got there, Kate was relieved to have a new lead to follow.

Chapter Eleven

Kate quickly pulled a pen and a small notebook from her handbag and wrote "Ellis Hayer" on the paper. Reading on, she saw the meeting notes for the previous day's special session approving Livvy's funding request. Eva had faithfully documented the brief discussion about the library closing before Tosten called a closed-door session. What Kate wouldn't give to read those private meeting minutes!

Oh well. Kate was a firm believer in the old adage, "Where there's a will, there's a way." And she certainly had the will—namely her determination to prevent the library from closing—to find out all the facts she needed to keep it open.

Kate flipped the meeting-minutes notebook closed and rose from her chair. Shouldering her handbag, she walked to the desk and laid the notebook atop it.

"Thank you," she said to Lawton. "I need a favor. Could you not mention to anyone that I was here this morning?"

He looked at her quizzically. "Because?"

"I'd rather not say," Kate told him. "I'm doing a little research for a friend, but it's a secret, and I'd really love to keep it a surprise." Which technically was true.

Lawton eyed her for another minute, but finally, he said, "All right."

"Thank you!" she said. "One more thing. Have you heard anything about new construction or development planned for the downtown area over the past few months?"

Lawton frowned. "No, I would know . . . Oh, wait. A couple of months ago, someone told me they heard there were going to be some new apartments coming in downtown. But nothing formal has been done, and I haven't heard about it from any of the council members. Also, there would have to be building permits, and I'd be aware of those. I dismissed it as a rumor." He extended a set of stapled pages to Kate. "Here's that copy of the budget."

"Thanks." As she accepted it, Kate's smile turned to a frown. "I've read the council minutes—the public ones, at least—back to the beginning of the year. I don't remember anything like that being discussed or even brought up and tabled. I'm sure I'd remember it. Where on earth would they put them, anyway? There aren't any suitable vacant lots that I can think of."

Then an ugly thought struck her as she remembered the phone call he'd taken earlier. "You don't suppose they're planning to renovate the library for apartments, do you?"

Lawton looked disturbed. "I guess I'd better find out. I assumed that real estate call was personal business, but maybe it wasn't."

"Was Tosten Glass in charge while you were gone?"

"Yes," he said, and he didn't sound happy about it. "But I certainly never thought the council would make a major decision like closing the library without my input."

"Why might they have done that?"

"I can't imagine," the mayor said. He was silent for a moment. Then he mumbled, "I don't know what happened to Tosten."

"What do you mean?" Kate asked.

He shrugged. "We were classmates. He lived down the street from me when we were growing up. We used to be close friends." He gestured to the far wall, which was covered with framed photographs, plaques, certificates, and all manner of memorabilia celebrating Mayor Lawton Briddle. "See the pictures on the far left in the double frame?"

Kate walked over to examine the photos. Both were stills from the *Copper Mill Chronicle* of yesteryear. The top one showed three young boys, perhaps Jeremy's age, holding large flat pans, standing in a stream in pants wet to the knees. The caption below read, "Tosten Glass, Gerald Foxfield and Lawton Briddle panned for gold during a Boy Scout camping trip."

Kate grinned. "Since you're not living in a mansion, I suspect no gold was found."

Lawton chuckled and shook his head. "No, but Tosten was convinced we were close. He'd have stayed out there for weeks if his mother had allowed it."

The bottom photograph showed two older teens wearing baseball uniforms. One leaned on a bat, the other wore a mitt and held a ball loosely. The caption read, "Lawton Briddle and Tosten Glass, both seniors, are tied for the state record RBI average."

"He beat me," Lawton recalled, walking over to join her. "By two-tenths of a point."

"I bet that was tough," Kate said sympathetically. She looked more closely at the two photographs, trying to discern which one was Lawton and which one was Tosten, but no luck. The pictures were grainy black and whites, and both men had . . . prospered since then.

"Didn't matter much. We both got full rides at the University of Tennessee. And the record was broken the very next year. Anyway," he said with a shrug, "he's changed. Hard to be real friendly with the man these days. I never saw anybody so obsessed with making money."

"What does he do?" Kate asked. "For a job, I mean." She didn't think she'd ever heard.

"He's part owner of a manufacturing business."

Kate glanced at the photos again. "Who's Gerald Foxfield?"

"He was a friend of Tosten's from his church," Lawton said. "He lives in McMinnville, and even though it's not exactly on the other side of the country, I lost touch with him." He paused a moment. "Haven't thought of Gerald in years. I wonder if he's still in McMinnville."

McMinnville! Ellis Hayer, the lawyer who'd addressed the council, was from McMinnville. Now wasn't that a coincidence, Kate thought. It looked as if a trip to McMinnville was on her agenda.

THERE WAS ONLY ONE COMPANY in the county that advertised asbestos abatement and removal, according to the phone book Kate had consulted before leaving home. Radon detection, testing, and mitigation apparently weren't quite as specialized, because Kate had found three companies that advertised their services. All four of the companies were in or near Pine Ridge, so after her visit to the mayor concluded, Kate turned the Honda northwest toward the county seat.

She had written down the addresses of the four places she wanted to stop. All of them were on main streets with which she was familiar, but she decided to go to the asbestos place first.

She parked and walked into the building.

"Hi, there." A receptionist greeted her with a smile. "How can I help you?"

"My name is Kate Hanlon. I'd like to speak to someone about an asbestos project," Kate told the woman.

"Then you want to speak to the owner," the receptionist replied. "She's in the office this morning. Have a seat, and I'll see if she can talk to you now."

The woman reappeared moments after she had vanished down a hallway. Beckoning to Kate, she directed her through a door on the right. "This is Kate Hanlon, Lynn."

"Hello, Kate." A pretty blonde, who looked somewhat younger than Kate, rose from behind a desk stacked with files. She walked toward Kate with her hand extended, and when Kate took it, shook as firmly as any man. "I'm Lynn Flasher. How can I help you?" Quickly, she added, "I'm not hiring right now."

Kate smiled. She perched on the edge of a visitor's chair in front of the desk as Lynn returned to her seat. "I'm not here about a job," she said. "I'm hoping you can give me some information."

Lynn's eyebrows rose. "I will if I can. What are you looking for?"

"I need information about asbestos abatement and radon testing. Can you tell me what's involved in asbestos abatement and why it's done?"

"I know a little bit about radon too, so I'll give you both," Lynn said with a smile. "Asbestos abatement is nothing more than removing asbestos from a building. People have to be licensed to handle it, and any building being considered for construction, renovation, or demolition has to be inspected to see if asbestos is present and create a management plan for removal, if necessary," Lynn said.

The word *demolition* shocked Kate a bit. It certainly wasn't something she'd considered until her conversation with Lawton.

Lynn went on. "Harrington County property-transfer laws require that if the building is being sold, you have to have those kinds of inspections done, along with a survey of the property and some other things. Asbestos and radon are both known causes of cancer. Radon is an odorless, colorless gas released from underground sources. It can build up in a structure. No federal regulations require the testing, but there are federal guidelines in place. Most contractors follow those guidelines because not doing so is just an invitation for a lawsuit, you know?" The phone on her desk rang then, and she glanced at it. "Oops, I have to take this. Sorry."

"Just one more thing," Kate said as she rose, tucking her handbag beneath her arm. "Have you been contacted by anyone in Copper Mill or contracted for any work at the Copper Mill Public Library?"

The businesswoman shook her head. "No."

"Thanks for your time," Kate said as she headed for the door. "I appreciate the information."

Back in her car, Kate headed for the first of the radon-mitigation companies. But to her chagrin, she received the same response from all three of them. No one from Copper Mill had contacted them or contracted any work at the library. No one had even heard any rumors about it.

Yet. Had she jumped the gun? She had heard the two building inspectors speaking only the previous morning. The town council probably hadn't contacted the companies yet. Kate made herself a mental note to call each company later in the week. Now that the owners had met her, a telephone call would probably net the information she needed. She knew she was taking a risk that word might get back to Tosten Glass that she'd been asking questions about contracted work, but she couldn't see a way around it.

She drove home, puzzling over the new information. If the library was being sold as she'd suspected, maybe the deal just hadn't been completed yet. Then preliminary inspections would make sense. They'd also make sense if the building was going to be renovated for apartments.

AT HOME AGAIN, Kate had an early lunch and decided to bake a strawberry-rhubarb pie. The strawberry season in Tennessee was long over for the summer, but she'd been given some hothouse strawberries that really needed to be used.

Before she began, she checked the telephone book for Ellis Hayer's listing. She'd forgotten that the lawyer lived in McMinnville, a small town on the other side of Pine Ridge.

It was the second time that day that McMinnville had come up. Could it be a coincidence that the lawyer who addressed the council and Tosten Glass' childhood buddy were both from McMinnville? Kate wondered if she was overly suspicious, because she really didn't believe it was a coincidence.

She wrote down the address for Ellis Hayer, Esquire. Then she looked for Gerald Foxfield, but there was no listing for that name in the entire directory for Harrington County. Kate felt her certainty that she was onto something deflate. She realized that his number could just have been unlisted.

On the other hand, if the man had moved away, maybe there really was no connection. Maybe she was overthinking the whole thing.

She needed to talk to Hayer today, if possible, but it would have to wait until her pie was done.

She assembled her ingredients as the conversation she had with the asbestos-company owner kept rolling around in her brain. What had Lynn Flasher said? The first reason for asbestos abatement was construction. Not a possibility, since the library already existed.

Reason two: renovation . . . a possibility, if she considered her theory that the building was being sold.

Reason three: demolition. It was a horrible thought, and Kate hated even considering it. But Lynn Flasher had mentioned demolition. What if . . . surely the town council wouldn't . . . would they? Who could help her? Who would know something about the process involved in demolishing a building?

Maybe Eli Weston, she thought, as she suddenly remembered that Eli had worked in construction before opening his antique shop. A back injury had forced his change of career. She'd try to talk to him this afternoon as well.

She put the pie in the oven, then she went into the office and got on the Internet to see if she could track down Gerald Foxfield. Their home computer had a slow-as-molasses connection, but she'd have to try it, because she couldn't go to the library. Livvy knew Kate well enough to recognize that it would be nearly impossible for her to stop sleuthing now, but Kate didn't want to upset her friend any more than she already was.

Kate washed up her dishes and cleaned the counters while she waited for the computer to complete a search. When she checked back, the search was done, but it hadn't come up with anything. Either Gerald Foxfield really had moved from McMinnville, or he was really good at keeping his personal information private.

The moment the pie came out of the oven, she set it atop a cooling rack and rushed to the coat tree, where she grabbed her handbag and dug for her keys. Moments later, she was zipping into town again. Eli's shop was on Smith Street, tucked between Smith Street Gifts and the Country Diner. Kate parked along the street and walked into the store.

She stopped just inside the door, letting her eyes adjust to the dimmer light. The store was well lit, but the bright summer sun was enough to blind anyone temporarily.

Eli was ringing up a customer as he turned to Kate, his brown eyes pleasant behind the lenses of his thick tortoiseshell glasses. "I'll be with you in a minute, Kate."

Eli completed the transaction a few moments later. As soon as the customer left, he turned to her with raised eyebrows. "Hey, there. What can I do for you, Kate?"

Kate smiled. "You used to be in construction. I'm hoping you can enlighten me a bit on something."

"I'll do my best," Eli said.

"Tell me everything you know about asbestos abatement and radon mitigation."

Eli nodded. He told her much the same thing Lynn Flasher had. Then he asked, "What's this about?"

Kate shrugged. "I recently overheard two men discussing asbestos and radon. They were also talking about rodent and insect infestations, disconnecting utilities, and getting some kind of municipal permit. Could they have been talking about doing those things in preparation for selling a building?"

Eli pushed his glasses up on his nose. "I guess the rodent and insect inspections might also be done before a sale, but I can't imagine why they'd need to disconnect the utilities if all they're doing is selling a building."

"What about renovation?" Kate nearly asked him about the possibility of demolition, but she wasn't ready to voice it yet. It was just too incredible. Surely no one would tear down the library.

Eli hesitated. "If significant renovations are done, yes, utilities might be turned off, but that's usually done on-site for very short periods of time."

Kate's concern increased. She had a very bad feeling about where this was going. "I wondered about that. Is a municipal permit needed to sell a property?"

"Not in Copper Mill," he said slowly, "although regulations might differ in other places. It's not needed for renovations, either. All renovations are approved by the zoning commission, but that's the only approval the town requires."

"Any other reasons a municipal permit would be required?" Kate pressed.

Eli nodded. "I can only think of one. Municipal permits are always required for demolition."

Kate nodded and thanked Eli, trying to conceal her dismay. She didn't want to say or do anything that might infer anything other than a passing interest, even to Eli. There was too much at stake. She clasped her hands tightly together. It sounded very much as if the town council was planning to tear down the library. And the secrecy surrounding the whole thing looked very, very suspicious. Why would the council hide something like that?

Maybe, she thought, the council wanted to present it as a done deal, because people in Copper Mill would have a fit when they found out.

Kate's brain was racing. She could hardly bear to think of the word *demolition* in connection with the library. It couldn't be, could it? Would the town council members do that?

Not all of them, she was certain. But who else could be involved besides Tosten Glass and Ellis Hayer's mystery client? And how could she find out for sure?

As an idea occurred to her, she began to nod to herself. She couldn't go barging into the library and tell Livvy the building was being torn down without getting solid proof first. Even though something in her heart told her she was right, she needed evidence, and she had to get it without anyone suspecting that Livvy had told her anything, or that she was continuing to investigate.

Evidence. She might not be able to prove anything—yet. But there might be a way to get some confirmation.

Chapter Twelve

Paul tried to remind himself of the good they were doing as he sat back on his heels and wiped sweat from his eyes with the arm of his T-shirt. He laid down his hammer and reached for his water bottle. Drew had lectured them over and over again about staying hydrated. One story he'd told about a guy passing out and falling from a roof had impressed them all enough that they were being extracautious.

To Paul's left, the new guy mirrored his actions. Catching Paul's eye as he screwed the cap back on his water bottle, Jerry winked. "Hot enough for you?"

Paul smiled. "It's a scorcher, isn't it?"

Jerry laughed. "Yeah."

He had been a good addition to the crew, Paul had to admit, even if the man's somewhat cocky manner rubbed Paul the wrong way. He suspected he wasn't the only one who felt that way, but the fact that Jerry had volunteered showed that his heart was in the right place, regardless of his attitude.

"Which church do you go to, Jerry?" Paul asked.

Jerry shrugged his shoulders. "I don't have a church. Never saw much use for it."

"I assumed you were affiliated with one of the churches in our work crew," Paul said. "How did you find out about the project?"

"I saw the article in the *Chronicle*," Jerry told him. "I know Louisa, and I thought it might be nice to help out."

"That's great," Paul said, impressed. "We really needed someone with your skills on the crew." Jerry had turned out to be a fairly skillful carpenter whose capabilities had made the job of repairing the rafters go much faster than Paul had anticipated.

"Yeah, the rest of you guys sure aren't any great shakes as construction workers," Jerry said, laughing.

Paul laughed too, but inside he felt bad for Jerry. It was those types of comments that made the others dislike him.

"Jerry, if you don't have a church home," Paul said, "I'd like to invite you to visit us at Faith Briar Church. We're a small, welcoming congregation, and I'd be glad to introduce you around."

Jerry hefted his hammer and picked up one of the large roofing nails they were using. "Thanks, Rev, but I don't think so. Church just isn't my thing."

Paul made himself smile. "If you change your mind, don't forget my invitation. Do you have any concerns you would like me to pray about for you?"

Jerry snorted. "Nah. Pray away, Rev. I got no problems."

AN IDEA OCCURRED TO KATE. She needed a way to get information from Tosten Glass, but she needed to speak with him in person when she did it. After driving to a local gas station that still had a working pay telephone, Kate opened the phone book. Tosten's number, along with all the council member's personal numbers, was listed in the front of the book, and she quickly placed a call to the council president. Disguising her voice took little effort, since the booth was along a busy road with traffic roaring in the background. She asked him to explain the local noise ordinance to her.

When Tosten had described the ordinance, Kate said, "I got a complaint. I wanna put it in writing and deliver it to you personally. Where you gonna be today?"

Tosten chuckled in a tolerant manner, still not recognizing her voice. "I'm leaving the library now and I need to stop by the Mercantile, so I should be home in about half an hour."

Bingo! thought Kate. She intended to meet him at the store.

The Mercantile was only half a block from Weston's Antiques, so she decided to park near the antiques store again.

Kate drove back to town and found, to her delight, that the same space in front of Eli's that she'd vacated just minutes before was still available. Parking there, she got out of the car and headed toward the Mercantile, forcing herself to walk at a sedate pace as she neared the corner of Smith and Main Streets. She crossed to the library side of Main before crossing again to the opposite side, where the Mercantile was located. Tosten had been at the library when she had called him. It was possible she would beat him to the Mercantile.

She pulled open the door of the Mercantile and entered

the cool interior, blessing Sam for installing central air in the old brick building. The bell above the door tinkled in greeting, and Sam looked up from the front counter, where he was tallying something on a clipboard.

"Hi, Kate. How are you?"

"Hot." Her response was succinct. "Is there any chance of a cooldown coming our way?"

"Next week I think it's supposed to be a little better," Sam said. "At least the ten-day forecast says so."

"Oh, I hope that forecaster knows what he's talking about." Kate grinned at Sam as she grabbed a basket and headed for the aisles. It was impossible to see who might be in the store because the shelves were too tall. And she was afraid to ask Sam if Tosten Glass was in the store for fear she might be overheard, so she listened carefully to see if she could hear him.

He wasn't in the first aisle or the second. She didn't want to get too far from the front of the store in case he came in and then made a quick exit, so she took a quick peek down the third aisle, grabbing some snack crackers for her dinner guests. She also couldn't resist grabbing a small bag of colored Goldfish, which she knew would be a big hit with the Pellman children.

As she picked up the Goldfish, she spotted Tosten coming around the corner in her direction. Her pulse leaped, and her stomach felt jittery. She hoped she was a good enough actress to pull this off.

"Hello, Tosten," she said.

"Why, hello, Kate." He smiled widely, immediately slipping

into politician persona. "Having crackers for dinner?" He chuckled as he indicated the contents of her basket.

Kate forced herself to smile too. "Dinner guests," she told him, "including children."

"Ah. Children." Tosten didn't sound as if he was familiar with the concept.

"Do you have a family?" Kate inquired. "We have three children. Two of them are married and have given us grandchildren. Grandchildren are such a blessing."

"I'm not married," Tosten said. His tone was a bit stiff.

Oops. The last thing she wanted to do was make the man uncomfortable. She took a deep breath and adopted a sympathetic tone. "How are you doing? I imagine it's been a difficult day."

His eyebrows rose. "Difficult?"

"Well, yes," she said. "People all over town are talking about the library closing. I bet you're fielding questions left and right." She barely paused for a breath. "And I'd venture to say that a number of them aren't exactly calm and friendly."

"That's certainly true," Tosten said. His tone was warmer now, and he nodded.

"If I've heard one idea about what's going to happen to that building," she told him, "I've heard twenty. The most popular rumor is that it's going to be turned into an apartment complex. I was also told it might just be torn down to make way for condominiums. My personal favorite is the movie-theater rumor." She chuckled.

Tosten chuckled too. "People do have vivid imaginations."

"Do you mind if I run something by you?"

"Of course not." He looked pleased to be consulted. If he was a bantam rooster, he'd have been strutting.

"I had an idea," she said. She smiled at him. "You're the perfect person to consult."

"Consult away." He beamed and stood straighter.

"I was thinking of bricks," she said, choosing her words carefully. Timing was everything, and she didn't want him to see what was coming. "Have you ever seen painted bricks from a building sold as mementos or historical memorabilia?"

He nodded. "Of course."

"Well, I thought that if the library really did get torn down, it might be smart to save some bricks. We could have them hand painted with a picture of the old library and perhaps a blurb about the years it existed on the back. It could be a fabulous fund-raiser." She paused expectantly, plastering a wide smile on her face.

"I'm sure we can arrange to salvage some—" Tosten stopped abruptly. "I mean, in the event that were to happen, that's an excellent idea. But as you said, the rumors are flying thick and fast. I imagine we'll hear some that will make a movie theater seem conservative."

Kate forced herself to laugh heartily at his attempt at humor, ignoring his first response. Finally she said, "I'd better get going. Dinner doesn't make itself, unfortunately. It was nice to see you again, Tosten."

After Tosten said good-bye and walked away, Kate stood where she was, her whole body trembling as she placed a hand against one of the sturdy shelves for support. Her scheme had worked, but she wasn't happy with the results. Although he hadn't come right out and said it, she was nearly certain that Tosten had all but confirmed her worst fear: the library was going to be torn down. He *had* told her, she thought. The beginning of his response to her idea about the bricks was probably the most honest thing the man had said all day.

She debated about what to do next. The time for caution had passed, she feared. Her first inclination was to rush to the library and tell Livvy about the demolition. Her second thought was that she needed to contact some of the other council members and find out if they were aware that the library might be demolished. The third thing she needed to do was try to talk with the lawyer in McMinnville.

She paid Sam for her items and left the Mercantile, heading for her car. She quickly decided that she wasn't going to tell Livvy just yet. The news was going to be a devastating blow. The more information Kate could gather first, the better. For the first time, she realized what a monumental task she could be facing. How did one stop a demolition?

But that was exactly what she was determined to do.

As she walked up Smith Street to her car, a man came out of the Country Diner and walked toward her. His size was the first thing Kate noticed; the man was huge.

Then she realized she knew him. It was Ben Dean, the man she had likened to the Grinch at the town-council meeting. As he stomped toward her, she drew in a deep breath. This was the perfect opportunity to find out what—if anything—he knew about the demolition.

"Mr. Dean?" she called. "Good afternoon."

Ben Dean's head came up. He looked around until he had

focused on her, and the motion reminded her of a bull trying to decide whether or not to charge.

As he drew closer, he grunted. "You're the lady from the meeting."

She nodded. "Kate Hanlon."

"Whaddaya want?" Ben Dean was never going to win any awards for his social graces.

"As a member of the town council," she began, "you might be able to help me." She watched him closely, choosing her words. She might be using the same scheme, but she was going to have to vary her approach a bit. "I was just speaking with Tosten Glass a few moments ago about an idea I had."

He just looked at her. "Huh?"

She wondered how in the name of heaven this man had been elected to the town council. "I was thinking," Kate said, "that perhaps we could salvage some bricks from the original library, paint and date them, and then sell them. People love historical memorabilia."

"Salvage bricks? You can't just take bricks out of a wall willy-nilly." His tone was scornful.

Kate kept her voice light. "Oh, I know. I've just been hearing rumors all day about what's going to happen with the library, and at least one of them has the library being torn down completely. I thought if that's going to happen, perhaps we could save some of the bricks for a fund-raiser." She warmed to her theme, even though she intended for it to remain nothing more than an idea. "You know, we could give the proceeds to the library, wherever the new location will be."

"Where'd you hear the library might get torn down? From that feller, that lawyer?"

"Ellis Hayer?"

"Yeah, him." Ben didn't appear to remember, or perhaps care, that he wasn't supposed to give out confidential information from the closed meetings.

"Was there anyone at the meeting with Mr. Hayer?" she asked, wondering how much she could get out of him.

His eyes narrowed, and Kate realized this man wasn't as dense as he appeared to be. "I'm not going to talk about that with you. Tell me how you know the library's gonna be torn down."

"Oh, I don't," she said. "I heard the rumors, and I just was what-iffing, trying to think of ways to capitalize on it if that ever happened."

"What-iffing? Huh." He gave her one brusque nod and brushed by her without another word, leaving Kate standing there staring after him. Was he involved? Did he know about the possibility of a demolition? Reviewing the conversation in her head, she realized it was impossible to tell for certain from Dean's reactions whether or not he already knew— although his first scornful response indicated that he wasn't thinking about the building coming down.

Should she pursue ambushing other council members with the same technique? Kate thought about them. Carey Carver, with his seeming inability to make an independent decision; Eva Mountjoy, who seemed like a smiling pixie until one realized she had held a demanding job in banking for many years; Malcolm Dekker and Floyd Jenkins; and Chalmers Petersen. No, she decided. Unless the opportunity presented itself, she wouldn't seek them out. Ben Dean was the one she deemed most likely to have been involved in shady activities . . . and now she wasn't even sure about him.

She dug for her car keys and unlocked the Honda, leaning inside and turning the air-conditioning on high as she started the engine. Then she opened the windows and waited a few minutes. It might be hot on the sidewalk, but it was an oven inside the black Accord when it was parked and closed up on days like this.

After a minute or so, she slid behind the wheel. Ellis Hayer, Esquire, in McMinnville was going to be her next stop.

KATE MADE THE DRIVE to McMinnville to search out Ellis Hayer, the lawyer whose name had been mentioned in the minutes she had read earlier.

Ellis Hayer wasn't hard to find. She had the address, which was right on Main Street. As she drove into town, on the right she saw a large green and gold sign reading, "Hayer and Strate, Attorneys-at-Law."

Kate swung into the parking lot. Apparently Hayer and his partner did all right for themselves. The practice was a small building of attractive gray limestone with a flagstone walkway from the parking lot to the front door. It was beautifully land-scaped with holly interspersed with petite dogwood trees and shrubs, such as summer-flowering pink clethra and hydrangea.

When Kate stepped into the office, the impression of quiet luxury was even more pronounced. An oriental rug created a small seating area surrounded by elegant cherry chairs and a love seat. Another rug led back a short hallway.

A receptionist behind an L-shaped counter looked up and smiled. "May I help you?"

"Is Mr. Hayer available?"

The girl glanced down. "Do you have an appointment?"

Kate shook her head. "No, but I'd like to speak with him if I may. My name is Kate Hanlon."

"May I tell him what this is in reference to?"

Kate smiled and shook her head. "I'd rather discuss that with Mr. Hayer, if you don't mind."

"All right." The woman smiled as she rose and walked down the hallway. "Give me a moment."

Assuming that a moment could mean fifteen minutes or more, Kate took a seat and picked up a copy of *Southern Living*.

Before she could even finish the first article on theme elements to give a home a Southern flair, Kate heard a masculine voice say her name. She glanced up.

A good-looking younger man approached with his hand extended. His blond hair was cut in a youthful style that gave him disordered curls on top paired with close-cropped sides. He wore dark pants with a white shirt, a gleaming black leather belt and black dress loafers, and a floral-patterned tie of lavender, black, and pale gray.

Kate rose and took his hand. "Hello. I'm Kate Hanlon."

"Ellis Hayer." He sent her a sparkling smile, and she saw that his eyes were an arresting shade of light brown, almost amber. "How can I help you today?"

"I'd like to ask you a few questions. Before I do, I have to ask that you keep this conversation in confidence."

Hayer's face was inscrutable. "I can't promise that unless you are a client," he said.

Kate was silent for a moment. "It's about the Copper Mill Public Library," she finally said.

Hayer's expression froze.

Thinking quickly, she dug into her handbag and pulled a quarter from her wallet. "Here," she said, placing it in his hand. "If I pay you, may I be considered a client?"

Hayer looked startled. Then he laughed, his expression warming. "I'm intrigued." He pulled a yellow notepad toward him and scribbled across a sheet, tearing it off and handing it toward her. "Here's a receipt," he said. "Consider yourself a client."

Chapter Thirteen

Ellis Hayer's brows drew together as he absorbed Kate's statement. "The closing of the library?" His voice was quiet, but Kate thought she detected an element of anxiety.

Kate nodded. "I know that you addressed the Copper Mill town council last Thursday, after which the council went into private session. The following morning, the Copper Mill librarian was told the library would be closing next Monday."

Ellis blinked rapidly. He crossed his arms in a classic defensive gesture. "I can't confirm any of that, Ms. Hanlon." He smiled. "Even if you are a client, any information I might have about a previous client would have to remain confidential."

"It's Mrs. Hanlon, but you can call me Kate." She smiled at him as she went on. "Yesterday afternoon, I attended an emergency session of the town council, and something that was said led me to believe that the council is worried about a lawsuit if some information becomes public. I presume you have a client who is involved in the closing in some way."

Ellis took a deep breath. She could almost see his thoughts racing around inside his head. "I'm not permitted to talk to you about this. It would violate the hypothetical client's privacy, not to mention client-attorney privilege."

"I understand," Kate said in a reassuring tone. "But Mr. Hayer, please listen. This library has served Copper Mill faithfully for years. Has it been sold, or are there other plans for it? Is there a new owner to whom I could speak?"

"The building hasn't been sold. It was never owned by the town in the first place," Ellis said. A moment later, he looked horrified with himself. "You didn't hear that from me," he mumbled, his face growing red.

Kate patted his arm. "Hear what?"

But Ellis continued to look upset.

"Who holds the deed?" she pressed. "Is it still the original owner? Or at least a descendant of the original family?"

Ellis straightened. He held out his hand very formally and said, "I'm afraid I can't represent you anymore in this matter, Mrs. Hanlon. I can refer you to someone else if you wish."

"No thank you." Kate smiled. "I appreciate your time."

"Good-bye." Hayer paused just long enough to shake her hand briefly before striding away and vanishing into an office near the end of the hallway.

As Kate left the comfort of the air-conditioned office and braved the heat once more, she felt pleased that her trip had not been in vain. She may not have gotten a name, but she'd learned another vital piece of information. According to Ellis, the town of Copper Mill had never owned the library. It was exactly what Paul had proposed.

Could that possibly be true? The Harrington County Historical Society was housed in an early twentieth-century schoolhouse in Pine Ridge. She'd have to visit and see what they could tell her about the library's history. Glancing at her watch, she realized she would have to stop in Pine Ridge the next day. For now, she needed to head home and get ready for her dinner guests.

The Harrington County Courthouse could be another important stop, she thought as she drove back to Copper Mill. She wanted to get a look at the deed to the library. Did a deed show who all the owners of a property had been, going back to the very beginning? And if not, was there any way to get that information? She didn't even know, but she was determined to find out.

It felt as if the drive back to Copper Mill took much longer than the same drive had taken a short time ago. Of course, she reminded herself, she'd stopped a couple of times then. And she hadn't been nearly so tired.

As she drew close to Copper Mill, she saw a modest white house with a wide front porch and a steeply pitched roof on her right. Glancing at the time, Kate went with an impulse and put on her turn signal. She pulled into the gravel driveway that led to the little house, which was on a slight rise a bit back from the road, and parked beside the house.

Joshua Parsons, who lived in the house, was ninety-three years young, as he liked to tell folks. His beloved wife, Alma, had passed on before Kate moved to Copper Mill, but Kate knew they had lived in the little white house since the day they had married decades earlier. Joshua had shown Kate a small black-and-white snapshot of Alma and him on their wedding day once, and Kate had been tickled to see what an attractive young man he had been.

As she got out of the car, a movement at the front door caught her eye.

"Howdy there, Kate." The old man stood just inside his screen door, grinning at her. "No pie?" he asked when he saw that her hands were empty.

"Hello, Joshua. I'm sorry, I didn't bring any pie today." As she came up the short cracked concrete of his walk, she noticed a galvanized bucket next to a flower bed. Kate knew that Joshua still planted and tended a small garden out back, and on previous visits, she'd also seen the old-fashioned pump he drew water from to take care of his flowers and vegetables.

"Joshua Parsons, I hope you're being careful in this heat," she told him. "I see that bucket, and I know you've been out here watering."

"Gotta keep my garden goin'," he responded. "Dusk and dawn, Kate, dusk and dawn. I ain't goin' out there when the sun's out. It's just too hot for me."

"It's too hot for everyone." Kate reached for the handle of the flimsy screen door.

"I can't stay long," she said as he led her into the living room and cleared a pile of newspapers off a chair for her. "I'm on my way home from McMinnville, but I have a question for you."

"Shoot," he said, pointing his index finger at her with his gnarled thumb cocked like the hammer on a pistol. Then he cleared off another chair, setting its pile of newspapers atop yet another stack heaped on a side table.

Having been to Joshua Parsons' home several times, Kate

was aware of his habit of stockpiling large quantities of newspapers and books all over the house. It was still a sight to
behold. "Do you remember if the Copper Mill Public Library
is or has ever been owned by anybody other than the town?"
she asked.

The old man shook his head slowly. "I can't recall. Seems
like there mighta been somethin' once." He cackled. "It just
ain't in these old memory banks no more."

Kate chuckled along with him. "That's all right. I know
what you mean about the memory banks. Mine seem to
short-circuit more than they used to."

"Land sakes, girl, you're just a young thing," Joshua
declared. "You get to be my age, you won't be able to remember your own name!"

"It wouldn't surprise me," Kate said ruefully.

She stayed for a little while longer, visiting with her
friend. He was in high spirits and seemed quite well, despite
the heat. Before she left, he managed to extract a promise
from her to bring him a pie the next time she was out his way.

As she finally took her leave and headed home, something
was bobbing around in her brain, almost within reach. But
she wasn't quite able to catch the stray thought. There was
something about Joshua's house that she thought could aid in
her investigation—

She snapped her fingers. The newspapers! That was it.
There was another old-timer in town who might be a good
source of information: Earl Pennyweather, the former owner
and editor of the *Chronicle*. Earl lived in a retirement home
now. Tomorrow, she promised herself, she'd stop by there and

ask him what he remembered about the library's history. The simplest thing, of course, would have been to ask Livvy. But Kate didn't dare go to her friend after Livvy's fearful reaction that morning.

As she let herself into the house a short while later, the unmistakable smell of chicken casserole wafted from the kitchen, and she realized that Paul must have arrived home before she did.

"Bless you," she called to Paul, whom she could hear rattling something around in the kitchen. "The chicken casserole smells delicious."

"Thanks to you," Paul said, coming into the living room. "All I did was throw it in the oven. You're the one who created it."

The casserole was one of Kate's old standby recipes that her family loved. Consisting of chopped chicken, Stove Top Stuffing, and several kinds of cream soup, it froze easily and had the added benefit of being tasty enough that even most children liked it.

"What else have you planned to serve?" he asked.

"There's honeydew and cantaloupe to cut up," she told him. "I already have a tray of cold vegetables with dip in the refrigerator. And I bought some Goldfish crackers for the children. Could you put them in a basket?"

"I'll do that, and then start on the melon," he told her.

"Thanks. We make a good team." She gave him a quick kiss and hurried into the bedroom, where she changed her clothes and tidied herself before heading to the kitchen.

When she entered the room, she was thankful to see that Paul had already set the table.

"Louisa and her children should be here any minute," Kate said. "I appreciate you doing all this. I know you had a busy day too. Are you tired?"

Paul's face was red despite the sunscreen he'd applied and the hat he'd worn all day. "I'm a little worn out," he admitted. "But nothing I can't handle."

The doorbell rang, and he glanced toward the entryway. "Sounds like our guests have arrived."

Chapter Fourteen

The Pellman children were all delightful. Jeremy and the middle child, six-year-old Addyson, chattered throughout the meal, saving them from any awkward moments. The youngest child, Julianne, was barely three, but she showed the same engaging personality that her siblings did.

Louisa was more reserved, barely meeting Kate's eyes when she first arrived. As she relaxed, she was friendly, yet she seemed hesitant to talk about herself very much. Kate attributed that to the sad experiences she undoubtedly had during her marriage and tried to keep the conversation from getting personal.

As the meal concluded, Paul took the two older children into the living room to find a game to play while Kate and Louisa lingered at the table with Julianne.

"So I understand you work at the courthouse," Kate said. "Have you found it interesting?"

Louisa smiled. "Not so much at the moment. I'm helping out in the deeds office while the lady who usually works there is recuperating from minor surgery. She's working two days a week right now. It's not the most interesting work in the world."

"Have you worked other places?" Kate asked.

Louisa shook her head. "I was always a stay-at-home mother, so I don't have many skills."

"Raising children requires quite a bit of skill," Kate said. "Don't sell yourself short."

"That's what my mother says." Without even pausing, the young woman deftly snagged a cup that her youngest had knocked over. Not a single drop spilled. "I applied for a job as an assistant in the school system, but I haven't heard anything yet. That would be nice, because the full-time position offers insurance."

"Yes, that would be nice," Kate agreed. "Do you have any coverage now?"

Louisa hesitated, and Kate instantly regretted the question. It was too personal, just what she had hoped to avoid.

"I'm sorry," Kate began.

"No, it's all right." Louisa nodded. "My ex-husband's insurance covers the children to some degree, although he has tried several times to take them off his policy. If I can get a job and put them on my policy, I'd love to stop relying on him."

Kate didn't know what to say, but apparently Louisa wasn't finished.

"I have full custody," she confided. "My husband has supervised visitation with the kids twice a month if he wants it. I got a restraining order after he put me in the hospital two years ago. I initiated divorce proceedings after that, and he has fought me on every penny of child support I ask for. Thankfully, he moved away from Copper Mill. I should be sorry that he doesn't want to see the children very much, but I'm not. The children's lives are better without him around, as much as it saddens me to admit that. If I can just find a way to support us without his money, things will be even better."

"How do the children feel?" Kate asked when Louisa fell silent. It was the most she'd talked all night.

The young mother shrugged. "The girls don't really remember him, so they don't say anything. Jeremy, unfortunately, remembers the shouting and physical confrontations. He worries that his father might come back someday."

Kate winced.

"I know," Louisa said sadly. "You've been so kind to Jeremy, Kate, and I appreciate that." Suddenly she stopped talking. She seemed to withdraw into herself, and Kate realized the time for confidences had passed.

Kate stood and began to clear the table. "Since you work in the deeds office," she began, "perhaps you can tell me how to go about getting a look at a deed."

Louisa accepted a damp paper towel from Kate and began to wipe Julianne's face and hands. "The parsonage deed?"

Kate shook her head as she added soap to her dishpan. "No. I'd like to look at the deed to the library."

"The library?" Louisa sounded taken aback. "What for?"

Kate weighed her words. She hadn't even told Paul about the demolition yet. "I'm just curious about how long it's been a library, that sort of thing. Since it's not going to be a library anymore, I want to document its history."

Louisa appeared to accept the explanation. After a long moment's hesitation, she said, "I can't take the deed away from the courthouse, but I could look at it and tell you what it says."

"Really?" Kate turned to her, touched by the offer. She'd looked at deeds before, and she knew the process took time. It was a trade-off: she'd have to wait until Friday, but the time it would have taken her certainly could be better spent investigating other things. "That would be wonderful." Mentally, she struck one task off tomorrow's list.

"What information are you interested in?" Louisa asked.

"I'd like to find out who all the building's prior owners have been," Kate told her.

Louisa nodded. "A title search. That should be no problem. People come in and do title searches all the time. I work again on Thursday, and I could bring you the information on Friday, if that's all right."

"That would be fine." Kate wished she didn't have to wait two days, but she knew that Louisa would save her some time.

Kate cleaned up the dishes while Louisa took Julianne into the living room with Paul and the other children. It was very thoughtful of Louisa to help her, and it would free her up so she could visit Earl Pennyweather and look into some other things. And, she thought, her spirits falling, tell Livvy about the demolition.

When she was finally finished with the dishes, Kate dried her hands and walked into the living room. To her surprise, Paul and the children were nowhere to be seen.

Louisa stood near the coat tree. For one instant, Kate saw an expression of panic or guilt cross her attractive features, but then she smiled, and Kate thought she must have been mistaken.

The telephone rang, disrupting her train of thought. Returning to the kitchen, she picked up the receiver. "Hello?"

"Is this Kate?" It was a woman's voice that sounded familiar, but Kate couldn't place it.

"It is. How can I help you?"

"This is Elspeth Getty from the Harrington County Wildlife Center."

"Oh yes. Hello, Elspeth."

"Good evening. I have a huge favor to ask of you, Kate."

"Ask away," she replied cheerfully.

"Would it be possible for you to get some photographs of some of the other squirrels at the library, if there are any? I've photographed this one so I can send information to some colleagues, but it would be a lot more compelling if they could see that there's a population and not just one lone animal."

"Oh, I'm so sorry I forgot to get back to you," Kate said. "There definitely are others. No promises. It's so hot that I don't think they're out a whole lot. But I'll do my best."

"That's all I ask. Thanks."

When Kate hung up and returned to the living room, Louisa was waiting by the door. "Paul took the, uh, the children out for a short walk. I was just about to ask if you wanted help in the kitchen," Louisa said.

"I'm finished in there." Kate walked over to the young woman and opened the front door. "Let's join them."

The two women left the house. Paul had found a large ball in the garage, something they kept around for the occasions when their grandchildren visited. He and Jeremy had both little girls in the grassy yard, taking turns gently kicking it to each of them.

Kate watched for a moment, noting how solicitous Jeremy

was when Julianne, the smallest one, fell. "He's so good with his sisters," she murmured. "You must be very proud of him."

"I am," Louisa said, equally quietly. "But sometimes I worry that he takes on too much responsibility. It's hard for him to relax and just act his age, you know?"

Kate nodded. "He does relax, though. Have you seen him when he's watching the squirrels?"

Louisa rolled her eyes. "When he's got squirrels on the brain, he doesn't even hear me when I call him." The women chuckled together.

As they walked across the grass, Kate told Louisa about the request for photographs.

Louisa said, "I'll bring Jeremy with me when I come to the library tomorrow afternoon."

"That would be great," Kate said. "I was trying to imagine myself lying on the library lawn taking pictures of squirrels. It won't seem nearly so, so *eccentric* if Jeremy helps me."

Both women laughed again.

Paul saw them and waved. "Hey, there. Want to join us?" As Kate and their guest walked across the grass toward him, he said to Louisa, "I met someone who knows you. A new fellow joined our roofing team after one man had to leave us. His name is Jerry Cox."

Louisa looked blank. "Jerry Cox? I don't know anyone— *oh.*" Kate was amazed to see the color drain from Louisa's face. A moment later, she began to blush furiously as she said, "Oh, *that* Jerry. Right. I forgot all about him."

Paul sent her an odd look. "I got the impression he knew you pretty well."

Louisa looked away. "He was a friend of my ex-husband."

Paul looked pained. "He's a good carpenter, and he's doing a great job on the team," he said, clearly attempting to repair his gaffe.

"Why don't we go in and have some dessert now," Kate said into the awkward silence that fell. "I have strawberry-rhubarb pie and brownies. Who's ready for something sweet?"

KATE DREAMED ABOUT the library that night. She couldn't remember much of the dream the next morning, but she had one very vivid memory of watching a wrecking ball swing toward the library while huge black thunderheads spawned a frightening storm that was heading right for her. No wonder it had left her feeling anxious and afraid. She was still reliving Sunday evening's scare.

She'd been unable to shake the feelings even during her morning Bible study and meditation. One of the morning's Bible verses had included a well-known Proverb: "Trust in the Lord with all your heart and lean not on your own understanding."

She did trust in the Lord, she mused, but she often struggled with discerning his plan. She prayed that he would reveal the reasons behind the library's closure and demolition and would prevent those events from happening. But was she right to pray that the Lord would stop those involved from carrying out their scheme? What if something much bigger and better was supposed to come of all this? Shouldn't she simply be praying for the fortitude to deal with the changes and to help others do the same?

No, she decided. She had to trust that the feelings in her heart were God-given. It wasn't simply her *desire*; something deep inside was telling her to fight for the library.

She dressed for the heat again, pulling on an elastic-waisted, tiered skirt in a light, crinkly fabric. It was a gorgeous teal, gold, and copper pattern. She paired it with a simple teal T-shirt with a modest scoop neck. Around her neck, she clasped a large ceramic starfish on a gold chain.

When Kate walked into the library a short time later, she felt as if she had displaced time somewhere. A great amount of material on the first floor had been removed from the bookshelves and trucked away to some storage facility in Pine Ridge. Although some of the furniture remained and volunteers still bustled about, the library had a sad, empty quality to it already.

Livvy, wearing denim capri pants, practical sneakers, and a simple tank top, was giving directions to a pair of young women.

Kate started toward her friend.

"Oh, excuse me!" Kate was solidly rammed by someone carrying a box. She staggered forward a step, dropping her handbag, and the box holder backed up a pace.

"I'm so sorry," the person said as a few items from Kate's bag scattered over the floor.

It was a woman's voice, and as she set down the box that had impeded her line of sight, Kate saw it was Eva Mountjoy, the sole woman on the town council.

"Hello, Mrs. Mountjoy," Kate said, kneeling and gathering up her lipstick.

The other woman looked flustered. "Kate Hanlon! Are you hurt? I'm the clumsiest mover ever." She took a breath as she bent to pick up Kate's handbag and a few other items. "Please call me Eva," she added, holding the items out to Kate.

Kate smiled as she slipped the straps of her handbag over

her shoulder. Here was another opportunity to test her approach. Of course, if Ben Dean had called around and told the whole council she'd spoken to him the previous afternoon, it might be time wasted. Still . . .

"Let me help, Eva," Kate said. She picked up a second box and headed for the door in the direction Eva had been moving. "May I get your reaction to an idea I had?"

Once again, she went through her story about hearing rumors and thinking of using bricks as historical mementos for a fund-raiser.

Eva appeared taken aback by the idea. "It's a lovely idea, dear, but I can't imagine that the library is going to be torn down."

"I don't know." Kate shook her head and recounted the conversation she'd overheard between the two inspectors. Once again, she was extremely careful never to use Livvy's name or even mention the librarian.

Eva shook her head as her face filled with distress. "Oh no, this is terrible." She peered at Kate. "Do you really think that could happen?"

Kate nodded. "Based on the things I've heard, I'd have to say it's within the realm of possibility. Maybe Tosten could tell you more about it."

"Tosten." Eva said his name as if she had a bad taste in her mouth. "If I know Tosten Glass, he's probably getting some kind of kickback from this thing somehow."

"Kickback?" If that was true, it would confirm one of Kate's first theories about the library closing: financial gain. "You think Tosten could be involved in closing the library for money?"

"It wouldn't surprise me one bit. But I'm not going to go

around saying that. Knowing that man, he'd sue me." After another moment's conversation, the small woman went back to work.

Gathering herself, Kate headed toward Livvy again. She halted while Livvy finished speaking. As the volunteers walked away, Kate stepped closer to her friend.

"Hey. How are you doing?"

Livvy cast Kate a glance that combined sadness, bitterness, and a certain amount of anger. It wasn't an expression Kate was accustomed to seeing. "How do you think?" Then her shoulders slumped. "At least I still have my job. Thanks for not making waves."

Kate shifted, feeling momentarily guilty. Then she thought of what she had learned. She took Livvy's elbow in a gentle grip and turned her toward the office. "I need to talk to you."

"Kate! I've got things to do." Livvy made a mild attempt to shake free.

"Please?" Kate asked quietly. Something in her voice must have communicated the gravity of her need, because Livvy immediately led her into the office. Kate closed the door as Livvy sank down into the chair behind the desk with a weary sigh.

"The day has barely started, and I'm tired already," she said. "What's going on?"

Kate heaved a sigh of her own. This was going to be hard. "I have some bad news."

Apprehension settled on Livvy's face. "What now? I thought being forced to move the library was as awful as it could get."

Kate took a deep breath. "Livvy . . . I'm fairly certain this building is going to be demolished."

Chapter Fifteen

Livvy's face went white as a sheet of copy paper. "Demolished? *Torn down?*"

Kate nodded.

"You must be wrong. Why would you say that?" Livvy looked so stricken, Kate could hardly bear it. "They can't tear down this building. It's the *library!*"

Kate shook her head. "I hope I'm wrong," she said, "but it's looking more and more as if I'm on the right track."

"Why didn't Tosten tell me?" Livvy was crying openly. She reached for a tissue from a box on her desk and blotted her eyes. "Is he just going to wait until the wrecking ball shows up and let me find out that way?"

"I think Tosten Glass doesn't want you talking about it because he's involved. I think he's going to benefit from it in some way. Maybe he's afraid folks in town will find some way to stop the demolition if word gets out."

"But why would Tosten—or anyone on the council—want this building torn down? I don't understand!"

"I don't either," Kate said. "But we're going to find out."

"Kate," Livvy said, looking even more troubled, "I already told you how I feel about you pursuing this. I can't afford to lose my job or have Danny's reputation ruined." She looked miserable. "But you're not going to stop investigating, are you?" Her friend's voice was resigned.

Kate spread her hands. "I can't, Liv, although I promise you I'll continue to keep your name out of it. For you, for Danny, for every person in the county who uses and loves this library, I have to try to stop this."

"Stop it?" Livvy looked thunderstruck. "How do you propose to do that, Kate?"

"I don't know yet. But I have enough clues to pick at that I know I can find out who's behind this. The question is, can I find out in time?"

Livvy clasped her hands tightly together on her desk and studied them for a long moment. Finally she said, "If you need my help, I'll do whatever I can. I've been an ostrich, but I'm not going to bury my head in the sand anymore. However," she warned, "I can't just stop packing in hopes that we'll pull this off. What if we don't?"

"I wouldn't want you to stop packing," Kate said and smiled at her friend, relief sweeping through her. "It would help me a lot to have you to bounce ideas off of. I'll keep digging. The first thing to do is to find out if I'm right, and if so, why the library is being torn down. Then we can plan how to stop it."

KATE TOLD LIVVY EVERYTHING she had learned. She began with the town-council meeting where the lawyer had spoken and the closing had first been decided upon. Then Livvy had received the threatening letter, after which Kate saw the article about Tosten Glass not running for another term.

"Color me suspicious," Kate told her friend, "but I can't figure out why that man wouldn't want to stay in a position of power. I just think there has to be some reason he isn't running again, and I can't help but wonder if it's related to the library closing."

"Just because he's not very likable doesn't mean he's crooked," Livvy pointed out.

"Yes, but then I went to the council meeting on Monday afternoon," Kate told her. Then she mentioned overhearing the inspectors in the library basement and suspecting that the property was being sold for renovation.

"The town-council meeting on Monday was interesting," Kate went on. "Council members started blabbing about things that happened in the closed-door session on Thursday, and Tosten got really angry. He said he's worried that the council could be sued for discussing the library issues publicly, but I wonder if that's really why he doesn't want it getting out. Also, Tosten and Ben Dean seemed amazingly unconcerned about what will happen to the library's contents after the move, while the others seemed to be worried about getting you open again. Ben might just be a curmudgeon. Or he might be involved. I couldn't get a good read on him."

Livvy exhaled softly. "You've been busy."

Kate nodded. "Then," she said, "you got the next threatening note. Makes you wonder who I was upsetting, doesn't it?"

Livvy nodded. "I begin to see why you're looking at Tosten."

"So I went to the mayor and asked to read the town-council minutes. He also gave me a copy of the budget to review. I glanced over it, and frankly, it's a complicated mess. I've never seen anything like it. I nearly took it to an accountant, but I don't want to spread this around any further."

"Maybe Danny could make some sense of it. Since he teaches a class of business math, he knows something about accounting. I'll call him when we're done here." Livvy sighed. "I need to talk to him anyway. It's time for me to stop keeping this from him."

"That would be great." Kate spoke again. "I found the name of the lawyer in the meeting minutes. He's Ellis Hayer from McMinnville."

"McMinnville. That's weird."

"That's what I thought. Oh, I almost forgot. Lawton has pictures of himself, Tosten, and one other kid, Gerald Foxfield, who moved away, on the wall in his office."

"Tosten again!"

Kate grinned. "Yes. Again. The mayor mentioned that Tosten has really changed and that all he thinks about is money these days. And guess what? The friend was from McMinnville. I'm not sure if it fits in or if it really is just coincidental, but it stuck in my head, and I keep wondering if it could be important."

"It does seem a little too coincidental, doesn't it?" Livvy agreed.

Kate continued her review, telling Livvy about her visits to the asbestos and radon companies, where she heard the word *demolition*. She explained about her conversation with Eli

Weston, her plan to see if demolition really was a possibility, and her engineered encounter with Tosten in the Mercantile, where he had inadvertently confirmed the plans before hastily backing off.

"I couldn't decide whether Ben Dean is involved, and Eva Mountjoy seemed shocked by the demolition news. Either she's a terrific actor or she really doesn't know anything. Or I'm completely wrong, and there is no demolition coming. I also talked to Ellis Hayer."

"You went to McMinnville?" Livvy said, her eyes wide.

Kate nodded. "I did get one interesting bit of information, even though Ellis would barely talk to me. He got so agitated that he slipped up and told me the library has never been owned by the town. Can that be possible?"

Livvy looked puzzled. "I've never heard that. How can that be?"

Kate shrugged. "I haven't gotten that far yet. But last night, Louisa Pellman came for dinner with her children, and she offered to do a title search for me since she works in the deeds office right now. She's going to get back to me." She took a deep breath. "So. Today I need to visit the historical society to see what I can learn about the library's history. I also want to talk to Earl Pennyweather about his memories of the library, and I need to visit the demolition company."

"What demolition company?"

Kate grinned. "I looked in the phone book, and there's only one listed in Harrington County. In fact, it's the only one for miles and miles around. I don't imagine there's enough of that type of work to support a lot of demo companies."

She went on. "I don't know what, if anything, they can tell me, but I need to try to shake something else loose. At the very least, I want to find out if they have a demolition date set yet."

"When do you want to get together with Danny to look over the budget paperwork?" Livvy reached for the phone.

Kate shrugged. "It's a busy day. How about sometime tomorrow? What works best for Danny?"

"I'll find out," Livvy promised. She made a quick telephone call to her husband. "How's four thirty sound?"

"Sounds fine." Kate nodded. "It'll be nice to have a fresh pair of eyes look over that budget. Shall I go to the house?"

Livvy shook her head. "Might as well meet here." To Kate's delight, her friend looked determined rather than defeated. "I'm not going to be intimidated anymore. If there's a way to save this library, we're going to do it!"

Kate felt tears rise. She leaned over the desk and gave Livvy a hug. "Oh, it's so good to have you back again. Every time I learned something, I wanted to tell you, but I couldn't."

"You can now," Livvy said firmly.

Kate nodded and smiled. "Okay. Upward and onward. I'm off to Pine Ridge."

KATE ARRIVED AT Green Acres Retirement Home shortly after breakfast was over and the residents were dressed and starting their day. She was anxious to talk to Earl Pennyweather.

Earl had started the local paper, the Copper Mill Chronicle, and he had run it for many years until his retirement, when he sold it to Marshall Owens. Despite the fact that it was early in the day, Earl looked as if he was dressed for a dinner party in a white jacket and bow tie and carrying a cane with an ornate brass handle. Today's tie was white with a pattern of tiny yellow chevrons, an appropriately sunny choice given that the heat index was still hovering near one hundred.

"Good morning, Earl," Kate said loudly.

"Kate Hanlon! Well, hello." His eyes twinkled. "You don't have to shout. I've got my hearing aids in."

Kate chuckled. "Sorry. How are you doing?" She took a seat close to his armchair.

"Real well, except for this heat," he said. "Feels like I'm walking through water when I go outside."

"I know what you mean," she said. She sat forward. "Earl, have you heard about what's happening at the library?"

"Heard it was closing," he said in a disapproving tone. "Don't know what those morons on the town council are thinking. Why are they closing it, and when will it reopen?"

"It won't," Kate said. "At least not there. A new location hasn't been determined. Everything's going into storage."

"What?" Earl sat up straighter. "That doesn't make sense."

"I know. Do you remember how the library got to be town property? Or who owned it before?"

Earl was silent. Kate could see the sharp brain turning her questions over and over. Finally he said, "I can't remember the name of the folks who owned it. But I do recall hearing they deeded it to the town before my time."

The news puzzled Kate. "Are you sure about that?"

Earl nodded. "Pretty certain. There wouldn't be any newspaper records in Copper Mill because those began with me, but there could have been a mention of it in the Pine Ridge paper. That was the first one in the county."

"The first what in the county?" demanded an aging voice.

Kate turned, although she already recognized the imperious person who had spoken. "Why, hello, Caroline. Hi, Renee."

Caroline Beauregard Johnston had been a resident of Green Acres until she broke her hip, after which she had moved in with her daughter, Renee Lambert.

"Hello, Kate." Caroline said it as if she were a queen granting an audience.

Behind her, Renee rolled her eyes. Her dog Kisses was tucked under her arm. "Mama, it's rude to eavesdrop on other people's conversations," she said, as if she didn't do the very same thing every chance she got. She turned to Kate and Earl. "We're here to visit some of her friends."

"It's not eavesdropping when you can hear him plain as day," Caroline said haughtily.

"Earl said the Pine Ridge newspaper was the first one in the county," Kate interjected hastily. "Caroline, perhaps you can help me. I'm trying to learn the name of the people who deeded the library to the town. It had been their home, but it was large enough to house an impressive collection. I'm sure it was before your time, but maybe you heard about it?"

Caroline leaned heavily on her cane as she turned to look at Renee. "I know I should remember the name of those folks. Let's see, I believe I was a teenager, maybe about sixteen?" Caroline was coy about her exact age; Kate only knew she was over ninety. "They moved away after they gave that building to the town. But I can't remember their names," she said again, sounding a bit frustrated.

"Was it donated to be used as a library?" Kate asked, hoping to jog the old lady's memory.

Caroline nodded. "Yes, indeed. But as I recall, they nearly changed their minds."

"Why?"

"They wanted to donate a whole bunch of books along with the building. They had so many books, it was a sin."

"How can it be a sin to have too many books?" Renee asked.

"Anyhow," Caroline went on, "some of the local folks had something against a book called *As I Lay Dying* that had been published a few years before."

"What was wrong with it?" Kate asked.

Caroline shrugged. "It had a good many nasty words in it."

"Nasty words?" Kate wasn't sure what Caroline might classify as a nasty word.

"Cussing," Renee qualified.

"Ah." Kate returned her attention to Caroline. "But obviously that blew over."

"Not right away," Caroline said. "The whole deal fell apart. It took a whole lot of fancy footwork by the mayor to get the mess straightened out. But after it was, they gave that building to the town."

"William Faulkner," Earl said. All three women looked at him, and he said, "I remember now. William Faulkner wrote *As I Lay Dying*."

Kate got out a pad and pen and scribbled down both details. She could see when the book had originally been published, and perhaps that would at least give her a time frame in which to search.

"You don't remember their last name though?"

Caroline looked at Earl, and both of them shook their heads. "They moved away years ago," Earl said.

Kate felt a prickle of intuition shiver down her spine. "Did they move to McMinnville?" she asked.

"That's it!" Caroline said. "The family moved to McMinnville after they donated the house."

Kate nearly asked if the family had been the Foxfields, but she didn't want to put the suggestion in their heads. Perhaps they would remember the name later.

Chapter Sixteen

Kate needed to visit the historical society, but she also needed to get pies made for the Faith Freezer program. Reluctantly, she headed home. She would return to Pine Ridge later.

At home again, she got out her rolling pin and a baking mat, as well as four aluminum pie pans. She tried to keep a supply of aluminum baking dishes so that she could take meals to parishioners and the Faith Freezer Program without making folks worry about getting a dish back to her.

She quickly used a fork to mix lard, flour, and a dash of salt into enough dough for four pie crusts. Dividing the dough into four even portions, she set it aside and sprinkled flour lightly over her baking mat. In no time at all, she had rolled out four pie crusts, reserving enough to make strips for the latticework on top, and folded them gently into the pie pans.

One of their parishioners had brought Paul a large bag of peaches on Sunday morning, right before Kate had returned home from her trip. She had been so busy, she hadn't gotten to them, but she had to use them today if she didn't want the peaches to spoil.

Kate forced herself to set aside her concerns about the library until she had measured her ingredients. She'd learned the hard way to pay close attention when she was combining the elements of a recipe.

First, she mixed together flour, sugar, and several spices in a small bowl and set it aside. Then she relaxed her vigilance and let her mind drift back to the library closing. With efficient motions, she peeled and sliced the peaches while she mulled over the next steps in her investigation. The most pressing order of business was to find out who had engaged Ellis Hayer's services, she decided as she sprinkled lemon juice over the peaches.

She brushed the pie crusts in the pans with beaten egg so they wouldn't get soggy later. So how could she narrow down her search? Ellis Hayer had told her the town didn't own—had never owned!—the library. If that was true, then the town council as a group wasn't responsible for the demolition. And that would mean the name of the person who had requested it would be on the demolition order. Or if not on the actual order, certainly someone at the company would know who was paying the tab.

Dividing the peaches among the pans, she lay peach slices in each pie tin, then poured some of the dry ingredients over the fruit and gently mixed it a bit. While she spread the mixture evenly over each pan, she dotted the tops with butter.

Then she rolled out the rest of the dough, which she cut into strips with a pastry wheel, leaving a pretty fluted edge. While she wove the strips together, working her way across the pie and folding all the edges under, she decided that she was making progress. She needed to continue to investigate as she had planned.

With a fork dipped in egg, she pressed the edges of the pie crust to seal them, then brushed the latticed tops with the remaining egg.

Popping the pies into her preheated oven, Kate set the timer for ten minutes so she wouldn't forget to reduce the heat.

While the pies were baking, Kate settled into her favorite rocking chair. She could work in her stained-glass studio, but she felt too unsettled to be creative. Rocking slowly, she stared into space as she reviewed everything she'd learned about the library since learning of the closing on Sunday.

The ten-minute warning buzzed. She got up and turned back the heat in the oven, then reset the timer for thirty minutes. She also covered the edges of each pie with strips of aluminum foil so the crust didn't brown too fast.

She returned to the living room and lay down on the couch, kicking off her sandals. True, she had slept long and well the night before, but she might just close her eyes for a teeny-tiny catnap . . .

Kate jolted awake when the oven timer buzzed rudely, interrupting a lovely nap. She sat up and ran a hand through her hair, dragging it back from her face as she rose and went to the kitchen. *Time to get back in gear, Kate,* she thought to herself.

She removed the pies from the oven, setting aside the aluminum strips. She could reuse those the next time she made pies. The peach pies were gorgeous, she thought, and they also smelled heavenly.

After grabbing a quick bite to eat and dashing off a note to Paul in case he beat her home—*Love you, but DO NOT touch my pies!*—she tidied up and headed back to Pine Ridge.

KATE'S FIRST STOP AFTER LUNCH was the Pine Ridge Historical Society. As she drove the short route from Copper Mill to the larger town, she mulled over what she had learned.

How odd, she thought, that the lawyer representing the mystery client hailed from McMinnville, and the family who donated the library to Copper Mill had moved there. Not to mention the mayor's childhood friend who had moved there as well and just happened to be a friend of Tosten's. That couldn't all be coincidence.

Gerald Foxfield. As Kate parked in front of the historical society, she decided that if what she was beginning to suspect was true, it was even more important to track down Gerald Foxfield and introduce herself.

The Harrington County Historical Society in Pine Ridge was housed in an old brick schoolhouse with the Harrington County Museum. As Kate entered, a woman said, "Hello, Kate. Welcome to the museum and historical society."

"Hello," Kate said.

As her eyes adjusted to the dimmer light, she recognized Miriam McLaughlin, the wife of the hospital's emergency-room doctor. She was a pleasant woman in her late thirties with dark hair and wide blue eyes. "How are you, Miriam?"

"Just fine, thanks," Miriam said, smiling. "Can I help you with something today?"

"I hope so. I'm trying to find out who owned the Copper Mill Public Library when it was a private home, and I need to confirm that it was donated to the town. I've heard that the original owners may have moved to McMinnville, but I have no other details."

"Let's see what we can do about that." Miriam came out from behind the counter. She motioned for Kate to follow her upstairs and then gestured to a door on the left. "Over here is the room with the records, old papers, journals, and other stuff."

"Do you have any thoughts on where I should look?" As they entered the room, Kate saw there was an enormous amount of material compiled.

"This section here is specific to Copper Mill," the woman told her. "The census records might be the fastest way to find out who lived there. Then you could check to see if that person was the owner. The census records are on computer now, so you could check by the address rather than by the name."

Kate immediately perked up. "Really? That would save a lot of time."

Miriam showed her to the lone computer in the room. "It's not new, fast, or fancy, but it's adequate for this kind of work. And it was free." She chuckled.

"That's the best kind," Kate said. She sat down and clicked on the program Miriam had indicated. It was created specifically for census searches and had a search field with several kinds of searches available. Kate typed in the address of the library and changed the parameter for the address.

The computer hummed steadily, and slo-o-o-wly the bar near the bottom of the screen indicated that information was being compiled. Minutes later, the screen changed, and Kate saw a list before her.

Eagerly, she perused the information. There were three names listed at that address, the first in the 1900 census. Then a new family was named in the 1910 census, followed by yet a third in the census of 1920.

Kate wanted to shout "Yes!" in triumph when she read the third name: the Charles W. Foxfield family. According to the 1920 census, Foxfield had a wife and six children. The Foxfields still lived at the address during the next census, completed a decade later.

Looking over her shoulder, Miriam pointed to the line for the next one, the 1940 census. "There's no one listed there. It became the Copper Mill Public Library sometime between 1930 and 1940."

WHILE KATE WAS IN PINE RIDGE, she wanted to make one more stop at the demolition company. It would have been nice to have gotten there earlier, but Monday and Tuesday both had evaporated in the heat of the many leads she was trying to pursue all at once.

The parking lot was loose gravel, and small puffs of dust squirted out from beneath her sandals as she walked to the door. *We need a day of steady, soaking rain*, she thought.

The company's office was a modular home that had been altered. What had once been the kitchen area was a small reception area with a desk. The counters held office equipment rather than appliances.

"Hi. Can I help you?" A young woman looked up from a computer monitor as Kate entered. She sported spiky deep burgundy hair gleaming with purple highlights.

"I don't know," Kate said.

The young woman lifted one eyebrow, and Kate saw a small silver stud at its far corner. A row of silver hoops marched down the outer edge of her left ear. Her fingernails were painted black, and she was dressed in black cargo-style pants with a black T-shirt. Still, the smile she flashed Kate was friendly and open.

"Wanna give it a shot?"

Kate had to chuckle. "I was wondering if I could see the paperwork on the Copper Mill library demolition, please."

The girl looked skeptical. "You'll have to leave your name, and I'll get back to you."

"Why?"

"Because those kinds of records are private unless the company president authorizes it. If you're the owner, of course, it's no big deal."

No big deal, Kate surmised. She shook her head. "I'm not. I don't even know who the owner is, which is why I had hoped to look at the demolition order."

The redhead looked regretful. "Sorry. I really can't let you see that. Dad would kill me."

Kate smiled. "That's all right. May I ask you another question?" At the girl's nod, Kate went on. "Are there federal, state, or local regulations for demolitions?"

"Oh yeah. Major. All three." She grinned. "It wouldn't be good to blow up a neighbor's place while knocking down the one beside it, you know?"

"It sure wouldn't," Kate said. "Do you think I could get a copy of those regulations?"

"Sure." The girl looked pleased that Kate's request was one she could fulfill. As she took down a binder and removed several sheets of paper, she said, "Dad's out of the office, but he'll be in tomorrow morning. You're welcome to stop by." She ran the pages through the copier and extended them to Kate. "This is the condensed version. We have a whole notebook full of bureaucratic language from the government, but this is what we usually give clients."

"Thank you." Kate accepted the papers and the information. "Perhaps I will. Have a good day."

As she walked back to her car, one strap of her handbag suddenly gave way. The bag fell to the gravel before Kate could catch it, and several items fell out.

Kate bent to gather everything up, examining the frayed ends of the strap with resignation. The bag was old, but it was one of her favorites, and she'd been trying to keep it as long as possible. The encounter with Eva Mountjoy in the library must have been the last straw.

Suddenly she froze when she saw what was in her hand. She held a white piece of copy paper folded into a small square. On one side, her first and last names were printed in blocky capital letters.

Slowly she unfolded the sheet of paper. It looked like the two Livvy had received, and Kate braced herself for the threat she was certain she was going to receive.

I know about the library. I don't want to see it get torn down. Look at Malcolm Dekker. Investigate the owner of the antique shop. Good luck.

Kate reread the note. Was it a joke? What about Malcolm Dekker? Was there something she had missed or could it be a bid to focus her attention on someone other than the real culprit? She hadn't thought that the funeral-home director was involved with Tosten after observing him at the council meeting. In fact, she hadn't thought Malcolm even liked Tosten very much. Malcolm was a very unique individual, but she couldn't imagine him plotting to tear down the library.

And what was this about the owner of the antique shop? Was the author of the note suggesting Eli Weston was involved in the plot to tear down the library? It sure sounded like it, although Kate couldn't imagine that could be true. Again, she wondered if it was just a ploy to distract her. Eli may have had his problems in the past, but he had suffered a terrible loss, recovered from it, and was now a dependable member of the church and the community. Wasn't he?

Kate got back into the Honda and headed toward home. As she drove, she thought about the note she had just found.

Who could have put it in her purse? She'd had her hand-bag with her all morning. Except . . . except for the incident when Eva had nearly knocked her down with the box, and it had hit the floor and scattered items everywhere.

Eva Mountjoy? Could it be? Not unless she already knew about the demolition. Kate had thought Eva's reaction had been honest when she'd told the woman why she suspected the building might be demolished. The note specifically men-tioned the library being "torn down," so how could Eva have authored it?

Perhaps she hadn't. Perhaps she had only been the mes-senger, instructed by someone else to deliver the note in some inconspicuous fashion.

Kate was so intent on her thoughts that she was unaware of the weather until a fat drop of rain splashed onto the windshield. She looked around.

To the west, in her rearview mirror, the sky was a deep purple. A flash of lightning split the sky. Kate couldn't prevent an involuntary squeak, and her breath came faster as panic began to rise.

Where could she go? She had to get off the road, and clearly, she didn't have a lot of time. Coming up on her right was a small empty building that once had been a branch bank on a wide-open paved lot. Quickly she pulled into the lot, then realized that the drive-through lane would provide a little cover, with the sturdy brick building on one side and a roof over her head.

It was already raining hard by the time she parked beside the drive-up window. She strained to see beyond the sheets of rain gusting sideways across the parking lot. Lightning flashed, and the whole world went white. Kate flinched.

To distract herself, she closed her eyes, leaned back against the headrest, and thought about all the things she wanted to do.

Number one: go back to the demo company and speak with the boss. In an ideal world, she'd learn who hired them. Who was the person behind the plot to tear down the library? She was beginning to suspect that Tosten Glass wasn't the lead character in this drama, but he still had to be involved somehow. He had known the building was going to be demolished. But what could his motive be?

Number two: find a copy of *As I Lay Dying*. She wasn't

sure what the book could tell her, but it must have caused a significant flap at the time. No pun intended, she thought to herself, chuckling.

Number three: meet with Danny the following afternoon to go over the town's unbelievably convoluted budget. Did everything add up? Was there a huge shortfall that might have necessitated selling the library? But if that were true, wouldn't the other board members have mentioned it? Or wouldn't Jennifer McCarthy have reported it in the paper?

Number four: get the deed information from Louisa. She needed to know exactly who owned the library after 1930, when it had clearly belonged to the Foxfields, and who held the deed now. The census had been able to tell her an approximate decade during which it passed from the Foxfields' hands, but it didn't show any new owners or occupants of the building. And subsequent census records only listed it as the Copper Mill Public Library, without specifying any owner, not even the town.

She paused, feeling a little overwhelmed as she reviewed all she had learned about the library closing since returning home. There was so much to do! Then she recalled that she'd promised to try to photograph the squirrels for Elspeth Getty. And finally, there was the note she had found. Even if Eva had put it in her handbag, she didn't think the woman had authored it. But Kate was at a loss as to who had.

Suddenly she realized that the storm had passed. It was still sprinkling lightly, but the sun was coming out. She mentally patted herself on the back for being able to successfully distract herself from her recently acquired wariness of storms.

Upward and onward, she thought as she turned the key in the ignition. Operation Save the Library was moving ahead at top speed.

A COUPLE HOURS after the brief storm that had done nothing to alleviate the steamy humidity, Paul felt about as hot, grimy, and tired as he could remember feeling in a very long time. He and several other men had been working on the roof under Drew Mears' supervision.

Drew was a stern taskmaster. Before a single man had been allowed on the roof their first day on the job, they all had learned safety techniques to reduce the risk that anyone on the roof would fall off, or that anyone on the ground could be injured by something sliding off the roof, like a hammer. They had learned to carry water and drink it liberally and to wear heavy work gloves to protect hands and fingers from hammers, utility knives, and sharp edges of metal.

They had spent a good part of the week prepping the roof for the actual shingling process, tearing off old shingles and rotting wood and attaching a whole new layer of plywood to the rafters. Several of the rafters had also needed to be replaced after the tornado damage was assessed.

They had nailed flashing, as the sheet metal was called in the roofing process, into place around the chimney and installed a drip edge, bending the metal down at the lower edge of the roofline.

Then Drew had taught them how to score shingles with a utility knife and bend them back and forth to break them in certain spots. He had overseen the laying of a starter course of shingles over a strip of felt, and then he had shown the teams how to lay row after row of shingles.

"Hey, Paul?" It was Jerry Cox, the newcomer to the project.

Paul turned, wiping sweat from his brow. "Yes?"

"Do you know how that whole library closing thing is going? I heard your wife might be looking into it."

Paul chuckled. "You could say that."

"What do you mean?" Jerry asked.

"She's been trying to check out every angle she can," Paul said, hammering in a nail and pulling another from the work apron he wore. Then he remembered Kate's concern for Livvy. Perhaps he shouldn't be broadcasting Kate's activities. So he added, "You know women, always making mountains out of molehills," with a silent apology to his astute wife.

"I see." Jerry returned to his own hammering.

The rest of the afternoon passed quickly, and the men knocked off work shortly before five.

"See you tomorrow, Paul," called Joe Tucker as he headed toward his own vehicle.

"See you then."

Paul headed homeward. When he found himself parked in his own driveway, he was vaguely surprised. He must have been on autopilot because he didn't remember a single moment of the drive.

The garage door was still up, and Kate was climbing out of the Honda inside the garage. She came to greet him, giving him a light kiss on the cheek.

"Sheesh. You look like I feel. Long day?"

Paul laughed. "And then some. Yours was the same?"

His wife nodded, and he realized her pretty brown eyes were deeply shadowed with fatigue. He knew she'd been working hard to try to keep the library from closing, but he hadn't realized just how hard. He supposed he'd been too preoccupied with his own project.

"Let's grab some dinner and tell each other war stories about our days," Kate suggested. "I have some gazpacho chilled in the fridge, and someone gave Millie a pan of corn bread today. She didn't want all of it, so she left some at our door with a note, since she hadn't seen you."

"Cold soup and corn bread," Paul said dreamily. "Already made. Sounds terrific."

Kate chuckled. "It does, doesn't it? Why don't we get cleaned up first? Dinner in ten minutes."

"I have to shower," Paul said, "or you won't let me near the food. Better make it fifteen."

A cool shower felt wonderful and did a lot to refresh him. By the time he joined Kate in the kitchen, she had the meal assembled on the table and had sliced a quarter of a seedless watermelon to go with the soup and corn bread.

"Thank you," he said. "I'll clean up the dishes."

Kate smiled. "You've done your share of taking care of me this week. We don't have to keep score."

After a brief prayer, he told her how the roofing project was proceeding.

THE NEXT MORNING, Kate had a pleasant Bible-study time and made blueberry pancakes for Paul. After dressing in a pair of pale blue-striped crop pants and a white sleeveless top, she added pretty blue glass earrings.

Kate tucked her small camera into her handbag. She hopped into the Honda and stopped by the old Bixby house next door, where the Faith Freezer Program was located. She dropped off the pies she had made the previous day before she turned the car toward Pine Ridge. She needed to visit the demolition company again and speak with the owner. Finding out for sure whether the library was to be demolished —and the name of the person who wanted it torn down—was her first priority.

Chapter Seventeen

When Kate stepped into the front office at the demo company, her young friend with the purple hair was standing at the counter, manning a copier with one hand while she slurped a McDonald's drink with the other.

"Oh, hey!" she said. "I told my dad about you yesterday. He's here now if you want to see him."

The young woman smiled, the same open, friendly smile from earlier. Kate thought it looked a bit incongruous coming from the tough-looking Goth girl. It just went to show, she thought, how deceiving first impressions could be.

"Yes, I'd like to talk to him," Kate told her, smiling.

"I'll go tell him." The young woman started off down a hallway, then turned around. "I'm Lissa, by the way."

"Kate Hanlon. Nice to meet you, Lissa."

Lissa was back in a moment, followed by a tall, slender man in chinos and a light blue dress shirt. He came toward Kate with a smile that told her immediately he was Lissa's father. They looked quite a bit alike.

"Hi. I'm Adam Crawford." He made a circling motion with his index finger, indicating the building around them. "Crawford Demolitions, you know?"

Kate introduced herself and extended a hand. "Thank you for speaking to me."

"Why don't you come back to my office?" he suggested.

He gestured for Kate to precede him to an office down the hall and then showed her to a comfortable chair across the desk from his own.

"So, you met Melissa," he said, smiling ruefully. "Not your typical receptionist."

"No indeed. But charming and capable," Kate said. "I like her a great deal."

"A lot of people are put off by the look," he said. "But I'm not going to fight with her about it. I just keep telling myself it'll pass."

Kate laughed. "Very wise. As the mother of three grown children, I can attest to that."

"So," Adam sat back, placing his elbows on the arms of his chair, and steepled his fingers in front of him, "you're here about the library demolition."

Kate's heart skipped a beat. Finally! Her hunch was confirmed. She forced herself to calmly nod. "I'm trying to learn who the current owner of the property is. It's been surprisingly difficult to track him down. All I've been able to find out so far is that the Foxfield family owned the property back in the 1920s."

Adam sighed. "It's always been my policy that our records remain confidential unless I have an order from a judge to divulge information. Saves a big hassle if the client knows he can trust you, you know?"

Kate nodded. "I can understand that. But this is such an unusual situation. The Copper Mill Public Library is a beloved institution in the community. It just doesn't seem right that it's being evicted and the building will be torn down with barely any notice."

"It's a great little place." Adam Crawford scrubbed his hands over his face. "We lived in Copper Mill when my kids were young, and we used the library a lot." His gaze grew unfocused and faraway. "We had a lot of great times at that library. My kids went to Story Hour every Saturday morning."

There was a moment of silence. Kate sensed the man was wading through a deep internal struggle.

Without speaking, he got to his feet and opened a file drawer behind him, withdrawing a simple manila folder and laying it on his desk. "I'm afraid I can't tell you the name of the owner, Kate."

Disappointment rushed through her. She'd hoped . . . but she respected his opinion. She started to rise and extend her hand, but he waved her back into her seat.

"I'm really sorry I can't *tell* you the name." He emphasized the word *tell* as he repeated his regret. "I have to go talk to Lissa for a few minutes," he continued. He tapped a conspicuous finger on the file he had gotten out, holding her gaze as he smiled. "Perhaps there's some other way you can find the name you need."

Kate cleared her throat. "Perhaps."

He started around his desk. "You take your time gathering your bag. I'll be in the front office." And with that, the owner of Crawford Demolitions strode out of his office, closing the door behind him.

He left the Copper Mill Public Library file on his desk right in front of Kate.

Her heart was pounding as she snatched up the file and flipped it open. She began to nod to herself as her gaze sped over the information. Gerald Foxfield. Just like the family who had donated the library to the town.

Perhaps a grandson, she thought, reviewing approximate ages in her head. Or a great-grandson.

Also on the paper was the date the demolition contract had been signed. Kate frowned as she glanced at the date. June 30? That couldn't be. The town-council meeting hadn't even occurred until last Thursday. What nerve! Foxfield must have been quite sure of his ability to shut down the library.

The second sheet contained all the regulation information Lissa had given her the previous afternoon, only in checklist form. Kate could see that everything was in order. All the steps had been marked off with the date they'd been completed. So there was no chance to use that to stop the demolition.

Her eyes widened, and her mouth fell open as she saw the date of demolition listed on the form. Monday! This coming Monday, the very same day that the library was to be vacated.

Kate knew from the things Livvy had said that they intended to complete the move on Sunday. But Monday!

Panic tightened a lump in her throat. How on earth was she going to stop this demolition before Monday?

Monday . . . Monday . . . Monday! It took Kate several

moments to calm herself enough to think past hideous visions of the library disappearing in a huge cloud of dust. Finally her mind began to take control again, and she shooed away the helpless feeling that gripped her. She could fix this, she told herself firmly. *One step at a time, Kate. Don't look at the big picture; it's too overwhelming. Just go one step at a time.*

At least now she had confirmed that Gerald Foxfield was indeed the owner. That was a giant step forward. A few more of those giant steps, and maybe, just maybe, she could find a way to keep the Copper Mill Public Library from being demolished.

On Monday, she thought again, still dazed by the discovery.

FIFTEEN MINUTES LATER, she arrived back at the library.

Livvy was working with the volunteers again, packing boxes and passing them to someone else to tape shut.

Kate caught her eye and tilted her head toward Livvy's office. "Let's go into your office for a minute."

Once in the office, Kate sat Livvy down behind the desk and told her friend what she had just discovered.

"Monday? The day after we finish the move?" Now Livvy was the one who was pale. "That's only four days away!"

Kate nodded. "I know."

Livvy began to hyperventilate, her voice rising until Kate took her shoulders and lightly shook her. "I know how you feel. I was doing this very same thing myself just a short while ago. But we don't have time for this, Livvy. We're going to stop the demolition, and right now, we need to concentrate on how to do that."

Livvy slumped in her chair. "Oh, Kate," she said in a

thready voice. "What a rock you are." She sat up and straightened her shoulders. "All right. We are going to stop this. Let's concentrate."

"All right. So this man," Kate said, "this Gerald Foxfield, supposedly owns this property. I've never met him, although I saw a picture of him as a kid in the mayor's office. Apparently they were friends way back when. I had never even heard the name before this week. Had you?"

Livvy hesitated. "Foxfield rings a bell. But I don't remember why." She shook her head. "How can it be true? If the town didn't own the library, how could it have stayed open for so many years?"

"One of two possibilities that I can see," Kate said. "One is that Foxfield didn't realize his family still owned the property. The other is that he knew but until recently had no reason or desire to claim it."

Livvy looked skeptical. "I hate to say bad things about human nature, but I think if he had known it, he would have let us know. My vote goes to the first theory."

"I'm thinking that too."

"So what's next?" Livvy made a fierce face. "If you figure this out in time to stop it, I'm going after Foxfield, or whoever is responsible. I'm going to make them read an entire dictionary— *backward!*"

Kate chuckled. "That's a pretty terrible punishment, for sure."

"You try it sometime," Livvy said. "See how long you last."

Kate thought about it. "You may have a point." Then she gestured to the packing going on all around them. "You're going to kill me, but I'd like to find a book titled *As I Lay Dying.*"

"By Faulkner," Livvy said promptly. "*That's* where I've heard the name Foxfield before." She beckoned Kate to follow her. "That section is packed, but it hasn't been moved yet. Each carton of books is labeled with the title, author, and Dewey number of the first and last book in it."

"So all we have to do is find it," Kate said with relief. "A piece of cake."

But as she followed Livvy back through the fiction stacks to an open area near the far end where bookcases had been moved to make space, she was confronted with a wall of boxes.

"Oh my," she said weakly. It was the first time she had seen all the boxes stacked in one spot like that.

Livvy grinned, the first time all week that Kate had seen her friend display any real amusement. "It's a little overwhelming at first glance."

"And second and third and so on." Kate shook her head as the realization struck her. Even if, by some miracle, she was able to figure out a way to keep the library from being demolished or taken away from the town, it was going to take even longer to put everything back than it had taken to dismantle it. How could this have happened?

"Livvy, there's something I don't understand. It seems odd to me that there's no record of who gifted the library to the town. That normally would be a big deal that would become part of a historical record, don't you think?"

"Oh, I can answer that," Livvy said. "Whoever donated this building wanted to remain anonymous. Everything in the documentation notes an anonymous donor, and I guess once the people who really did know the truth passed on, there wasn't anyone left who would remember the names." She paused.

"Ah." That had been bothering Kate. Now she understood why there were no plaques honoring the Foxfield family, if that was who the donors had been. "So the only way to find out is to check the deed. Rats."

"Why rats?" Livvy asked.

"Because if I go to the courthouse and do it myself, it will take half a day. You remember how slowly Mrs. Sedberry moves."

Livvy chuckled. "I do."

"Let's check these books before I do that," Kate said. "It will take less time if I can find it here."

"Okay. Let's get started," Livvy said. "I don't have a lot of time, but you're working so hard at finding answers for us that I have to do what I can." She started at one end. "Let me scan the boxes in the front. Hopefully it'll be here and we won't have to move an entire layer forward."

Kate stood back as Livvy quickly reviewed the information written on the top and front side of each carton. Unfortunately, Livvy stood back a few moments later and shook her head. "Not in these boxes."

"Okay." Kate sighed. "Tell me what to do."

The two women slid the whole first row of vertical stacks forward so that they could read the information on the boxes in the second row.

Livvy was almost to the end of the row when she said, "Bingo!"

"Great!" Kate heaved a sigh. "I wasn't looking forward to moving this whole row out of the way so we could get to the third one."

Livvy grabbed the top box off the stack she had indicated and set it aside. "It's the fourth box down."

Kate moved the second box, and Livvy moved the third. Once those boxes were out of the way, Livvy slid an X-Acto knife from her pocket and slit the tape holding the top flaps of the box together. "Cross your fingers. Maybe it'll be on the top."

It wasn't, but it wasn't too far down. As Livvy pulled out two copies of *As I Lay Dying*, Kate eagerly grabbed one and opened the flyleaf.

Nothing.

"Here," said Livvy. "There's a bookplate in this one. It reads, 'From the collection of Mr. and Mrs. Charles Willard Foxfield. May 27, 1934.' That makes sense. The library opened that year."

"Charles Willard Foxfield." Kate nodded. "That was the name of one of the owners I found in the census information at the historical society. So if the books were donated at the same time the library opened in 1934, and the Foxfield family owned the building in 1930 when the census was taken, it's likely that Charles Foxfield was the person who donated the building as a library."

"So we have to find his descendants," Livvy said. "Does Gerald Foxfield, or any of his relatives, still live in Harrington County?"

"Not as far as I know," Kate said. "I couldn't find any in the telephone book. Gerald Foxfield was listed as the owner of this property on the demolition order, but I haven't been able to turn up anything on him."

"Maybe he doesn't live around here anymore," Livvy said. "He could have hired a local lawyer and the demolition company without coming to Harrington County."

"True." Kate let the thought roll around in her brain for a moment. "I don't know, Livvy. I just have this feeling that he's around somewhere."

"If he is, you'll find him," her friend predicted as the two of them bent to the task of replacing the books and the cartons back in the order in which they had found them.

"Something else happened to me." Kate straightened and rubbed her arthritic knee, which was protesting the heavy lifting. She couldn't imagine how Livvy must be feeling after nearly a week of this.

"What?" Livvy straightened too and stretched her arms high over her head.

"I found an anonymous note in my handbag yesterday afternoon."

"What?" Livvy dropped her arms quickly. "Who sent it?"

Kate chuckled. "If I knew that, it wouldn't be anonymous."

Livvy had to laugh. "I withdraw the question. What did it say?"

Kate explained about the strap on the handbag breaking and paraphrased the contents of the missive, mentioning both Malcolm Dekker and Eli Weston.

"I think," she went on, "that it must have been placed in there while I was here, because there was no way for anyone to get to my handbag during the rest of the morning."

"You're sure it occurred then?" Livvy asked. "Could the note have been in your purse longer, and you overlooked it until everything spilled out?"

"I can't imagine—" Kate began. Then she stopped. "Yes. It could have."

Chapter Eighteen

Kate blew out a frustrated breath. "It could have been put in there at any time, I suppose. But I know it wasn't there Tuesday morning, because I switched handbags."

"Have you switched handbags since then?"

"No," she said slowly. "But I can't think of a single time my handbag was unattended yesterday or the day before. I made about a million stops on Tuesday, but the only times it wasn't on my shoulder or in my lap was when I stopped at Joshua Parsons' on my way home. I believe it lay on the kitchen table for about ten minutes while we visited."

Livvy grinned. "I can't quite imagine Old Man Parsons stuffing an anonymous note in your purse." Then her face grew serious. "But someone, somehow, must have managed it."

"Well, Louisa Pellman and her children came to dinner Tuesday evening, and Eva Mountjoy and I had a little collision here yesterday morning while she was helping with the move. Those are the only other two I can think of, and neither of them seems the type to be involved in something like this."

"What happened with Eva?" Livvy asked.

Kate shrugged. "She was carrying boxes, and we bumped into one another. My bag flew out of my hands and spilled, and she helped me pick up everything."

Livvy's eyebrows rose. "Giving her opportunity, if not motive."

"Yes, but when I told her about the demolition, she seemed genuinely shocked. It just doesn't feel right to me. She could be in league with Gerald Foxfield. Or Tosten Glass, if he's involved in this somehow as I suspect, but I don't see Eva being responsible for that note."

"Have you investigated Tosten very much?"

Kate hesitated. "No. I didn't want to tip him off any more than I already have, in case it might impact you. He's the only one who might suspect how diligently I'm pursuing this. I suppose I figured it might be better to go around him than through him, if possible."

"But have you thought about why he might be involved?"

Kate shrugged. "What are the basic reasons people do un-kind or illegal things? Greed, passion, power, peer pressure, opportunity . . ."

"Lack of moral or social values," Livvy added. "I'm sure there are more, but that certainly covers the big ones." She cleared her throat. "According to Danny, who heard it from Tosten's sister who teaches at the high school, Tosten lost his shirt recently when the stock market crashed."

Kate said, "Well, isn't that interesting." Then she shook her head. "But he definitely isn't the person who put that note in my purse. I didn't even see him yesterday or today. I did see him Tuesday, but he didn't have any opportunity to slip something into my handbag."

"He could have paid someone to put it there for him," Livvy mused.

"Eva's recently divorced," Kate said. "I wonder what her financial situation is like."

"Not good," Livvy said immediately. "Renee told me her husband made off with quite a few of their joint assets when he left her. She sold that big house they lived in and moved into a much more modest place here in town."

"So for her to be involved, it would be likely that she would benefit financially."

"And Louisa?"

"She brought her children over for dinner Tuesday evening. My handbag was on the coat tree in the foyer the whole time. She did have the opportunity, I suppose, but what motive would she have?"

"She's also recently divorced," Livvy said. "Although from what I hear, getting her ex-husband out of the picture is a good thing. I don't believe he even has unsupervised visitation with the children."

Livvy's comment jarred loose a memory, and suddenly Kate was afraid she might be able to answer her own question. Paul had mentioned the possibility of her children being placed in foster care when Louisa had gotten pneumonia earlier in the year. What lengths would the woman go to in order to keep her family together under one roof?

The problem with that theory was that Louisa's custody was in no jeopardy that Kate was aware of. And she suspected she would know if that were the case by now from either Jeremy or Louisa. No, Kate just couldn't see how Louisa and the library demolition could be connected. Was it possible it could benefit Louisa in some other way? The notion seemed like quite a stretch.

PAUL CAME HOME FOR LUNCH AGAIN. Today, his truck was already there when Kate pulled into the driveway. She left her car outside, running a hand over the dented hood as she walked past it into the house. She couldn't wait to get those dings from the hailstorm fixed. Not only were they unsightly, but she was worried about rust damage.

Paul was slicing tomatoes when she walked into the kitchen. A neat pile of thinly sliced cucumbers was already stacked to one side.

"Uh-oh. I guess I know what you're hungry for," Kate said with a laugh.

"Is this okay? I had a hankering for those tomato-cucumber sandwiches you make, Katie."

She smiled and kissed his cheek. "What an excellent idea. Nice cool sandwiches, with the added bonus that we use some of this never-ending stream of produce our wonderful parishioners bring us. Which reminds me, would you run out to the garage and grab the sack of green beans along the far wall? Old Man Parsons insisted I take them the other day, and I forgot to bring them in yesterday."

"Yum." Paul was already headed toward the door that led into the garage.

He was barely through the door when the telephone rang. Kate picked up the receiver in the kitchen. "Hello?"

There was only silence on the other end.

Could she hear someone breathing? "Hello?" Goose bumps prickled over her skin. "Is someone there?"

"Stop investigating the library demolition. Or you'll be sorry." The voice was a harsh whisper, gravel against sandpaper, and the menace in the clipped words was palpable enough to make her swallow.

"Who is this?" she demanded. But the only answer she got was a dial tone. Her mystery caller had hung up.

As Kate stood there with the receiver in her hand, Paul came back in with the bag of beans. "Sorry," he said, "I picked up the wrong bag first." Then he noticed the look on her face. "What's wrong?"

"I just got a threatening phone call," she told him.

Paul dropped the sack of beans. "What did they say?"

Kate described the call. As she talked, she buttered slices of wheat bread and then spread a thin layer of cream cheese over half of them: two for Paul and one for her. She covered the cream cheese with a layer of cucumbers and ground a bit of pepper over them. Then she added a layer of sliced tomatoes and very lightly salted them before covering each with a second slice of bread.

"I don't like this," Paul said. "That's a serious threat."

"Maybe." It *had* been scary, but . . . "At least I know I'm getting somewhere with this investigation. Apparently I'm making someone nervous."

"Apparently," Paul said in a dry tone. Then his voice grew serious again. "If it happens again, promise me you'll tell Sheriff Roberts."

"I promise." Efficiently cutting the sandwiches into quarters, she transferred them onto a plate and covered them with plastic wrap, then she placed them in the refrigerator. In thirty minutes, they would be cool and delicious.

While she was waiting, she took a bowl into the living room, sat down in her rocker, and snapped the beans Paul had brought in. Paul waved a newspaper at her from his seat on the couch. "Hey, we're famous."

"Oh?"

"This is today's *Chronicle*. We got a mention in the tornado article. More than a mention, actually. Three paragraphs and a couple of quotes."

"Woo-hoo. I'll clip it and send it to the kids."

"Not until we've called each of them and explained that we were nearly caught in a tornado, but we're not hurt."

"Excellent plan."

LIVVY'S HUSBAND, DANNY, was waiting for Livvy and Kate at the circulation desk at four thirty. He waved as he saw them walking toward him.

"I didn't get time to eat lunch, so I asked Danny if we could all go get something to eat at the diner while he looks at the budget," Livvy said.

By unspoken agreement, the three of them chatted about general topics on the short walk east along Main Street and then north on Smith Street to the Country Diner at the corner where Smith met Hamilton. It was a pleasant summer afternoon, despite the heat. Kids whizzed by on bicycles, other pedestrians greeted them as they passed, and young mothers chased toddlers on the Town Green.

The diner was a popular spot all day long. Even before the supper rush began, there was a decent crowd. It was calm and cool inside, although sunlight battered the blue gingham curtains at the windows.

LuAnne Matthews was waitressing. Her red hair looked as if it came straight from a bottle, and her fifties-style eyeglasses swung from a jeweled chain around her neck. She greeted Kate, Livvy, and Danny as she showed them to a quiet booth near the back of the restaurant, then fished an order pad and pencil out of the white apron wrapped around her ample frame.

"Y'all ready to order?"

Livvy nodded. "I'd like a tuna melt on rye with swiss cheese, whatever the vegetable is—"

"Baby carrots," LuAnne inserted.

Livvy nodded. "And a piece of that apple pie. Carbs, protein, dairy, vegetable, and fruit."

LuAnne laughed. "And what would ya like to drink? We have fresh-squeezed lemonade." She winked. "Loretta was annoyed with the produce delivery today, so she took it out on the lemons."

Livvy grinned. "Lemonade sounds delicious, especially in this heat."

"Just lemonade for me," Kate requested. "I'm eating dinner with Paul at home."

"I'll have lemonade too," Danny said. "And I'd like the pork chops with mashed potatoes and the vegetable. No pie for me. I'm watching my figure."

Kate and Livvy both groaned as he chuckled.

"Three lemonades and two suppers comin' right up," the waitress sang out as she hustled back toward the kitchen.

Livvy heaved a deep sigh. "Oh, what a week this has been. If I've had one any worse, I can't remember when."

Kate made a soft sound of sympathy. "I'm so sorry I wasn't here when all this started."

"What could you have done?" Livvy asked. Then she mimed smacking herself in the forehead. "Oh, wait, I forgot who I was talking to."

Sitting beside his wife, Danny grinned. He looked at Kate and said, "Thank you for all the work you're putting into this. Livvy finally told me what was going on." He shook his head, looking appalled and bewildered. "It's hard to believe the town council would let this happen."

"The council doesn't know yet, unless Eva has told them," Kate pointed out. "I haven't told them, and I'm quite certain Tosten Glass hasn't. And even when they do find out, they may not feel they have a choice if it turns out the property really is owned by someone else, and that's what it's looking like right now."

He sighed. "This is crazy."

"I know." Kate opened her handbag and pulled out the copy of the town budget Lawton had made for her. "Here's the budget. I glanced over it and didn't see anything out of place, but I'd like your opinion. It's pretty confusing."

Danny took the budget and began to read it. After a moment, he looked up. "I'm not an accountant by any means, but this looks awfully complex for a small town's budget." He fell silent as he became absorbed in going through the figures.

LuAnne returned with their lemonade. As she tossed a couple of straws on the table and departed, Kate's eye was caught by a tall man coming in the door. His red hair made him hard to overlook.

"There's Carey Carver," she said.

Livvy turned around. "Indeed it is."

"I'll be back." Kate slid out of the booth. She hurried across the diner, offering her hand as she reached the man who had just folded his long frame into a chair at a small table near the front of the diner.

"Mr. Carver? Kate Hanlon. I attended the council meeting the other day."

"Of course," he said, shaking her hand. He grinned. "You shook up our fearless leader a little bit."

"Did I?" Kate knew he was referring to Tosten. "It wasn't my intention to upset anyone."

Carey shrugged. "Lots of things upset him. I wouldn't pay him too much mind."

It was the perfect opportunity.

"Mr. Carver," Kate said, keeping her voice low. "Have you heard anything about the disposition of the library after the contents are moved?"

Carver frowned. "No." He cleared his throat. "This is awkward. Tosten warned us not to discuss the particulars with anyone. I believe you heard that we fear a lawsuit."

Kate nodded. "Yes, but I have discovered the building is going to be demolished."

"Demolished?" Carey Carver gave a visible start. "What?"

Kate nodded. "Today I found out that the demolition is scheduled to take place on Monday."

"Monday!" Carey fell back in his chair, clearly perplexed by this news.

"You didn't know?" she said, even though it was obvious

that he didn't. Apparently Eva had been serious about not discussing the situation. "Wasn't the town council responsible for hiring the demolition company?" She already knew the council had nothing to do with the demolition order, but she wanted to see how the tall man reacted.

"No, no. That's not right. We didn't hire anyone to tear down that building." Carver sounded genuinely distressed. "Why, it's a historical landmark."

Chapter Nineteen

I n that instant, Kate became certain the red-haired man hadn't been told about the planned demolition.

"I wonder who did hire someone to tear it down," she said, fishing again. Even though she had seen the demolition orders and knew Gerald Foxfield was named as the owner, she didn't know if his name was known to any of the other council members. Tosten, she assumed, knew exactly who he was, although she doubted she'd ever get him to admit it face-to-face.

"Gerald Foxfield," Carey said. "He's the guy who owns the property. He came to that closed meeting we had."

"I've heard his name mentioned before," Kate said carefully.

"We weren't supposed to talk about it," Carey said, bitterness evident in his tone, "but I never signed up for anything like this. I'm going to call Tosten as soon as I leave here."

Coming from the man she'd pegged as the wishy-washiest person on the council, Kate was surprised by his declaration.

"I'm going to call Chalmers and the others too. I want to find out who knew about this and if it's true." Carey stood up. "Tell LuAnne I'm sorry, but I don't have time for lunch."

Kate wished him luck, then returned to her booth as Carey rushed out the door.

"What on earth did you say to him?" Livvy asked, looking after the departing council member.

"I told him about the demolition," Kate said. "He wasn't happy. I'm confident that he knew nothing about it. He's planning to contact the rest of the council. I hope he follows through."

Livvy nodded. "He's not the most . . . forceful of personalities. But if Carey said he would do it, he will. He graduated with me." She grinned. "We called him 'Matchstick' because he always stuck out in a crowd, being so tall and skinny and having that bright red hair."

Kate laughed. "It sort of fits, doesn't it?"

"If Carey didn't know, I wonder if the rest of the council does," Livvy mused.

"I already spoke to Eva and Ben Dean," Kate told her, "and unless she was acting, I'm pretty certain Eva didn't know. Ben was harder to read."

Livvy snorted. "That doesn't surprise me."

"But it would surprise me if he was involved," Danny said, raising his head from the budget. "Ben isn't a very subtle person, and I wouldn't trust him with an important secret."

LuAnne returned then with Danny and Livvy's supper platters, which she slid in front of each of them. "Anything else?" she drawled.

They all shook their heads. "Thanks," Livvy told her. "I think we're good."

As LuAnne walked away, Livvy picked up her knife and cut her sandwich into quarters. Then she pointed the knife at Kate.

"While we eat, you have to promise me we won't talk about anything to do with the library," Livvy said.

"I promise," Kate said promptly. It would be a wonderful relief to give the topic a short rest. "Want to hear about my trip?"

"Oh! I practically forgot. Yes. Every detail. Especially New York. Next time you go up there, I want to go along. I'm dying to see a Broadway show."

Danny set aside the budget and began to dig into his meal. "Oh yes," he deadpanned, "I'm just dying to see a Broadway show."

Kate laughed as Livvy socked her husband in the shoulder. "A little culture would be good for you," she told him.

Dinner was enjoyable. Kate regaled her friends with stories about her trip. Danny had gone back to perusing the town budget, and he barely looked up, periodically running the fingers of one hand through his dark curls. At one point, he pulled out a calculator and began punching in some numbers.

Beneath the facade of her carefree demeanor, Kate continued to worry about what was happening to the library. It was becoming clear to her that the demolition had been kept very quiet so it could be accomplished before many people knew about it or could organize to stop it.

Finally Danny pushed away the budget papers and sat back, running his fingers through his dark hair again. "This budget appears to be in order, Kate. The library is right on track with spending projections for the fiscal year." He grimaced. "Or at least it was before they hired movers and had to restore storm-damaged books."

"Thanks, Danny." Kate collected the papers and put them in her bag. Another dead end.

Was it too late to stop the mysterious Gerald Foxfield from tearing down their library?

KATE WAS THOROUGHLY frustrated. She had talked with Paul, Livvy, and Danny about Malcolm Dekker. But she had yet to find the slightest shred of evidence that would point to his involvement in the library demolition.

Malcolm was considered more than a little strange, although everyone agreed that he was an excellent funeral director, efficient and unobtrusive. He was well liked enough to have been elected to the town council, Kate mused, although his ability to cut through the fat and get to the meat of a matter, as well as his capable manner, probably had a lot to do with that. He was considered a doer in the community.

Malcolm had lived in Copper Mill all his life and took over the funeral home when his father passed. It was generally agreed that he was a far better funeral director than his father had been.

But Kate couldn't see how any of those things might fit with the profile of a man trying to have the library torn down. As far as anyone knew, Malcolm's finances were in order, although she knew that appearances could be deceptive where money was concerned.

Eli Weston was a similar story in that she couldn't find anything problematic in his lifestyle or his history that would lead her to believe that he was involved in this for some reason. His antique business was thriving, despite the economy, and he was a regular volunteer with the Faith Freezer Program.

When Paul and Kate had first arrived in town, Eli had been a sad and troubled man. His fiancée had died after battling cancer, and in his grief and anger at God, Eli had accidentally burned down Faith Briar Church. But Eli had healed, Kate thought. If she had a group of favorite folks in town, Eli would be among them. How could he possibly be involved in the demolition scheme?

AFTER LEAVING DANNY AND LIVVY, Kate opened the door of her home. It felt as though she hadn't been there in a very long time.

Paul came out of his office. "Hi, honey. Long day?"

"Unbelievably so." Kate walked into the living room and collapsed on the couch, kicking off her sandals. "I feel just like I did when I was pregnant—so exhausted I'm loopy. Remember how tired I always was during those early months?"

Paul smiled. "I sure do. Have you gotten anything ready for supper yet? If not, I could make us some soup and sandwiches."

"Oh, that would be wonderful."

While Paul made the meal, Kate set the table and got drinks. She told him about the note in her handbag. Then, feeling that since she now had solid proof, she told Paul about the intended demolition and her shock when she saw the date on the demolition order.

He was as stunned as Livvy. When he had gotten over the surprise, he said, "Your name is on everyone's lips these days. Even the guys on the job site want to know what you're up to."

Kate sent him a sleepy smile as they finished their meal. "Oh?"

"Jerry Cox asked me yesterday about what you were doing. He's the new volunteer I told you about from McMinnville."

Kate's eyes flew wide, and she sat up abruptly, her hair flying. "*McMinnville?* You didn't tell me he was from McMinnville."

"I didn't?" Paul frowned.

"I would have remembered that," she said. "He's the one who said he knew Louisa, the one she didn't seem to remember right away."

Paul nodded.

Kate felt as if she were just on the edge of discovering something new and important. "Would it be all right," she asked, "if I were to visit your job site tomorrow?"

Paul nodded. "Sure. Do you want to meet Jerry?"

"I certainly do. But Paul?"

"Yes?"

"Do me a favor and don't mention to anyone that I'm coming."

KATE RETURNED TO THE LIBRARY on Friday morning. As she pulled into the parking lot, she spotted Clifton Beasley, an elderly man whom she often saw kibitzing with his cronies in front of the Mercantile. Clifton waved as Kate got out of her car and came toward him. He told her he'd come down to see what the fuss was with the library, and he had something to give her that he had left in his car.

"Ida Mae sent this along," he said, opening the door of his Buick and reaching onto the passenger seat.

As he slowly straightened, Kate could see that he had a

book in his hands. It was spiral-bound in creaky, red plastic and had a folksy cover with a hand-drawn picture of Copper Mill Creek's best-known set of little waterfalls on it. Emblazoned on the cover were the words *Copper Mill Chronicle: Best-loved Recipes.*

"What's this?" Kate asked, delighted. She immediately opened the book and began to flip through it.

Clifton harrumphed. "The town paper used to publish these cookbooks every once in a while. Ida Mae wanted you to have this," he said. "She thought you'd enjoy some of the recipes. We been using some of them for years and years."

"Clifton, I can't take Ida Mae's recipe book," Kate said, touched by the gesture. She tried to hand it back to him.

"Yes, you can," Clifton insisted. "She can't use it anymore because of her health." Ida Mae had heart trouble and exertion of any kind was troublesome for her. "If you really have to thank her, make one of the pies in that book. You do make excellent pies, Mrs. Hanlon."

Kate hugged the book to her as she stretched up and pecked him on the cheek. "Thank you. You tell Ida Mae I'm honored, and I promise to bring her a pie."

"Oh boy." Clifton smacked his lips, and Kate laughed. Clifton was especially fond of Kate's pies and even claimed they helped his bursitis.

Then something occurred to her. "Clifton, do you know Malcolm Dekker?"

Clifton snorted. "Of course. I've known him since he was a little kid. His father and I used to bowl duckpins together years ago."

"As you probably know, he's on the town council now,"

Kate said casually. "I guess he's one of the people making decisions about what's going to happen to our library."

"Malcolm keeps the town council and that windbag of a president in line," Clifton said, grinning. He squinted at her. "The library's in good hands. Malcolm's an odd duck sometimes, but he's got a heart of gold."

His turn of phrase reminded her of the photo in Lawton Briddle's office of Briddle, Tosten Glass, and Gerald Foxfield panning for gold and the mayor's statement about Glass' interest in gold.

Her own interest piqued, Kate said, "Hey, that reminds me. Have you ever heard anyone talk about finding gold around here?"

Clifton nodded. "That's what they say, although I never saw any."

Kate was ready to ask him who "they" were, but she was instantly diverted by the sight of a car down the street. It was moving at a slow crawl, but as her gaze met that of the driver through the window, the car sped up and moved off down the street at a much brisker pace.

"Clifton! Do you know that car?" She tried to fix the driver's features in her mind, but it was very sunny outside, and the interior of the car had been in shadow. All she knew for certain was that it was a man with short, darkish hair.

"Hoo-wee! I haven't seen a car like that in forever. What a beauty." The old fellow shook his head. "No, Kate, I didn't get much of a look at the driver. But from what I could see, I didn't recognize him. Or the car either, for that matter. Never seen it around here before."

Kate had. It was the same white-topped, pale blue

Cadillac in near-mint condition that had been parked along the street in front of Louisa Pellman's parents' house on Monday.

LOUISA CAME WALKING into the library not long after Kate arrived. Jeremy trotted at her side.

The moment the boy saw Kate, he broke away and came running to her. "Mom says you want to take pictures of the squirrels today, and I should help! I brought some peanuts so I could help get them to come out."

"I'm counting on it," Kate told him with a smile. She gestured toward the door, where Jeremy was already glancing longingly. "Go ahead. I have to talk to your mother for a moment, and then I'll be out."

Jeremy rushed back out the door. "Cool!"

"I want to thank you again for dinner the other night," Louisa began as she drew near. "And I got the title information I promised you." She tapped a folder she was carrying. She was wearing a slim indigo skirt and an ivory blouse, and she looked chic and slender. She also looked even more tired than she had earlier in the week, Kate thought, observing the dark circles beneath the young mother's eyes.

"That's great," Kate said as Louisa handed her the file. "I can't tell you how much I appreciate it."

"I couldn't make copies of all of the deeds," Louisa said quickly. "Just the current owner. So I just wrote down all the information from the older titles. I hope that's all right."

"That'll be fine," Kate assured her. "Thanks again." She hesitated. "By the way, do you know who drives a light blue Cadillac around town?"

Louisa stared at her. "N-no. I don't think so."

"But the car was parked in front of your mother's house when I dropped Jeremy off the other night."

"Oh!" Louisa said, suddenly animated. "That car. That's just a friend of my mom's. I don't really know his name."

Jeremy had told Kate that the blue Cadillac belonged to Louisa's friend, not a friend of her mother's. But the young woman was looking agitated, and Kate realized that the time to ask probing questions was *not* in the library lobby.

"Well..." She grinned and held up the camera she had taken out of her handbag. "I guess I'm headed outside with your son on a squirrel photo op."

Louisa's anxious expression eased. "He's totally obsessed with animals," she said, smiling a little.

Kate chuckled. "There are many worse things he could be obsessed with. Count your blessings."

Louisa nodded, her smile fading. "I do. Every single day."

As Louisa turned away, Kate eagerly opened the file the young woman had brought her.

The first name on the list was the person who must have had the house built. The first deed was drawn up in 1897. It had been sold to a different family in 1903, and that family lived there until 1916. Then the property had been purchased by Gerald Foxfield's ancestor Charles. That meshed with the information she had gotten from the census documents at the historical society.

It was there that the records showed property information that the census had not. According to this information, the property had stayed in the Foxfield family, rather than being donated to the town, as Livvy had assumed. The building passed to a second Foxfield in 1976 and then to a third in 2006 at which time it had passed to yet another member of the family: Gerald Foxfield. But according to what Kate had learned about the town, the library was deeded to the town by an anonymous donor in 1934. Kate recalled that she and Livvy had concluded Charles W. Foxfield was likely the anonymous donor.

So Gerald Foxfield had recently inherited the property, although it appeared he hadn't inherited his ancestors' benevolence. Disappointment swamped her. Now that she'd confirmed that the man really did have a legal claim to the property, she suspected it would be much more difficult to refuse his right to dispose of the property as he wished.

Chapter Twenty

"Hey, Mrs. Hanlon! Come on, there's a squirrel out here." Jeremy had pushed back through the lobby doors, his voice jarring her from her unpleasant thoughts.

"I'm coming," she said, moving toward him.

The two of them walked to a shady spot and took seats on the grass beneath a tree.

"Jeremy," Kate said casually, "Remember when your mom said you notice details?"

Jeremy nodded. "If you watched the squirrels more, you'd notice how different they look from gray squirrels or red squirrels."

Kate smiled. He certainly was single-minded. "Do you remember the blue car in front of your grandmother's house the night I dropped you off?" She tried to keep her tone casual. "Whose car was that?"

Jeremy nodded his head. "Some man." Clearly he had little interest in the topic.

"A friend of your grandma's?" she asked.

"No. He's mom's friend . . . I guess." The child's voice lowered. "But he talks kinda mean to her, like my daddy did."

Kate's heart went out to the boy. "I'd like to talk to him. Do you think he'll be coming back to your grandma's house?" Jeremy shrugged. "I dunno." Then his face lit up. "Oh! Oh! There's one." He pointed. "Get your camera, quick."

True to the boy's claim, there was a squirrel moving near the corner of the building's foundation. Quickly she dug for the camera she had placed in her handbag, thankful for the timely distraction.

When she found the camera, she debated about how to get the best photographs. If she moved much closer, she might scare the squirrel into hiding again. But she was so far away . . . She settled for using the zoom function on her little point-and-shoot camera to bring the squirrel as close as possible. Elspeth could try to enlarge the photos if she desired.

She shot about a dozen photographs, giving a silent cheer when a second squirrel came out and joined the first. Finally she put her camera away and went inside, leaving Jeremy to his observations.

After taking time to upload her photos and send them to Elspeth, Kate went to Livvy to get her work assignment for the morning. She hoped to work on Jeremy's sun catcher in the afternoon after her visit to Paul's work site.

Paul called midmorning. "Hello, wife," he said when she answered her cell phone. "Would you like to join me for lunch today?"

"Hello, husband. I'd love to." Kate smiled, her heart warming at the thought of spending time with the man she loved.

"I . . . ah . . . thought we could go out to the Smokeshack," he told her.

The invitation made her laugh. "Any excuse to go out for barbecue," she teased. Then she said, "That's fine as long as you don't make me eat outside in this heat."

"We'll take it home," Paul promised.

"All right. How about I come pick you up?"

"That would be fine," he said.

"Remember," she cautioned him, "don't mention that I'm coming to the site, okay?"

After saying good-bye, Kate headed back downstairs to get more boxes and saw Renee and Caroline coming into the library.

Renee looked around, spotting Kate immediately. "This is just devastating," she said. "I can't believe the library is closing."

Kate nodded. If Renee only knew!

Caroline sank down in a folding chair near Kate and fanned herself with a large picture book from the top of a stack of boxes. "My stars, it's hot out there," she said.

Kate nodded. "It certainly is." She sat back on her heels. "I found the name of that family you were talking about."

"Well, what is it?" Caroline demanded. "I still can't pull it out of these old, musty files." She tapped her head to indicate her brain.

"Does Foxfield ring a bell?"

"Foxfield!" Caroline exclaimed. "That was it!"

"When the Foxfields moved to McMinnville," Kate said, "do you remember anything about where they may have lived? I'm trying to locate a descendant, Gerald Foxfield, to ask him a few questions, but he's not easy to find."

"Did you check the telephone book?" Renee wanted to know.

Kate took a deep breath. "Yes. And I checked several Internet sources, but there's no listing for him."

"My mama used to play bridge with Mrs. Foxfield," Caroline said. "And I recall we went to tea at their house once after they moved." She thought for a moment. "It was a big yellow house, and I recall playing Gold Miner down in the kitchen until the cook kicked us out."

"Gold Miner?" Kate couldn't help but find that an interesting statement, given the photo she'd seen on the mayor's wall.

"There was a placer of gold found here years ago." Caroline's eyes took on a faraway and unfocused look as she reminisced. "We did love to pretend. I believe the Foxfield home was on . . . Maple Avenue." She nodded her head, short and decisive. "Yes, it was on Maple, although I don't remember the number."

"On Maple. Thank you, Caroline!" Kate was elated. Even without a number, that brought her a lot closer to locating Gerald than she'd been before. "I believe I'm going to take another little trip to McMinnville," she said.

"Oh, I'm sorry I can't go with you," Renee said as if Kate had invited her. "But I simply must bathe Kisses this afternoon. Isn't that right, my sweet Little Umpkins," she cooed to the tiny dog, who was snuggled in her arms.

"Oh well," Kate said, doing her best to sound regretful. "I suppose I'll have to do it alone." She turned and said farewell to Caroline, who was preparing to take her leave.

BEFORE SHE WENT ON any more excursions, Kate needed to finish the work she'd promised Livvy she would do. There were a few books still upstairs in the room that had been water damaged. She trudged up the steps and filled a small box, returning to the first floor to add it to a stack for the movers.

As she went back for a second box, she decided not to mention anything more about Foxfield, Tosten Glass, or the demolition to Livvy, who was looking increasingly frazzled. She appeared to have given up any hope that the library could be saved since her guarded optimism the day before. Kate was becoming a little discouraged herself, and she didn't want to get Livvy's hopes up.

Kate climbed the stairs to the historical room again for one last load. The broken window was still covered up, but no repair had been done. What was the point until they knew what was going to happen to the building? Kate took a seat at a small table that had been left in the room with two chairs. All of the other furniture had been moved, except for several bookcases that still held books.

When she sat down, she saw the glitter of glass beneath one of the bookcases. It probably hadn't been visible from a standing position, and Morty must have missed it when he cleaned up after the storm. She rose and went over to the shelf, carefully getting down on her knees to pick up the glass. It was a rather large piece, and she was glad she had seen it. A mover picking up the bookcase could have hurt himself. As she withdrew the glass, something else caught her eye.

There was a book under there too, way back against the

wall. She never would have seen it if she hadn't noticed the glass.

Kate disposed of the glass in a metal trash can and then returned to get the book. It was old, she saw as she withdrew it and held it up to the light. Perhaps it had been on the shelf beneath the window that had gotten damaged by the storm. It looked as if it had been knocked underneath this other bookcase, which had kept it dry when other books on the floor had gotten wet. She thought she'd better give it to Livvy so it could be packed with other things from the proper time period.

It was titled *"Entering the Twentieth Century: A Celebration of Copper Mill History."* She sank into a chair, ready for a short break as she leafed through the tome. It appeared to be a collection of photographs and articles written about the festivities celebrating the town's history during the summer of 1900. It appeared there had been quite a few events dedicated to portraying the town's history as it moved into a new century.

Kate smiled over an Independence Day parade in which female participants were identified by their husbands' names: Mrs. David Tabler, Mrs. Robert Nutting.

Then another photograph caught her eye. It was a float in the same parade, drawn by two horses and festooned with bunting and other period decorations. The title of the float was printed beneath the photograph: Prospecting for Gold. Kate peered more closely at the old black-and-white photograph. Sure enough, there was a man kneeling beside a slightly raised streamed filled with tumbling rock, and he seemed to be panning for gold with some kind of large, flat basin. Behind him was a rough wooden hut with a pair of long johns pegged on a length of rope that served as a clothesline.

A little thrill went through her. Caroline obviously had known what she was talking about. Gold mining had been a part of Copper Mill's history.

Clutching the book, Kate went downstairs.

"Livvy? I'd like to borrow this book. I found it beneath one of the shelves in the history room."

Livvy waved a tired hand. "Take it."

"Shall I sign it out?"

Livvy gestured around her, her posture defeated. "Where? Everything down here is just about packed. I have no way to record it other than to write it on an index card and hope it doesn't get lost." She blew a strand of hair out of her face. "Take it. If I can't trust you to return it, I'm in even bigger trouble than I thought."

Kate gave her friend a hug. "Thank you. I'll be back later."

Livvy didn't even ask where Kate was going, an omission that saddened Kate. It was as if Livvy had given up.

Lord, she prayed, *be with Livvy during this trying time. Fill her with your spirit, surround her with your love. Remind her— and me—to believe in miracles. After all, the gift of eternal life you promise us rose from the very worst time imaginable, the willing surrender of your Son on the cross. That's the greatest miracle of all.*

As Kate took her car keys from her handbag, she thought, *And Lord? If you could send a little of that my way, I'd really appreciate it. Amen.*

KATE DROVE OUT to Louisa Pellman's home, where she knew Paul and his team were taking their turn working on the roof today. As she neared the house, she realized her hands were shaking.

Well, of course. The last time she'd been there, she and Paul had nearly been caught in a tornado. She decided to forgive herself for a small case of nerves.

She left the car running when she got out. No sense letting it get hot inside when she and Paul would be leaving in minutes. She walked around to the back of the house, wondering where all the men's cars were.

She got her answer the moment she rounded the house. There were five or six vehicles parked back there. They apparently had driven the whole way back, where the driveway wound around to a detached garage. She saw Paul's truck and a motley assortment of other vehicles, mostly SUVs and trucks.

But there was one vehicle that stood out like a sore thumb. She couldn't say she was entirely surprised, after Paul had told her last evening that his co-worker had been asking about her. She'd had her suspicions about exactly who Jerry Cox was.

Still, it was a shock to see the white-topped, blue Cadillac parked right beside Paul's truck, large as life.

"Hello there." The voice belonged to her husband.

The men were on the ground, wiping their hands and clothes off before they broke for lunch.

"Hello," she called, waving and walking toward them.

Just then, a dark-haired fellow at the back of the group

snapped his head up. Their eyes met for a fleeting instant, then he turned away and walked quickly toward his car.

"Hey, Jerry," she heard Sam say. "What's up? I thought you were coming with us."

Jerry ignored Sam and leaped into the Cadillac. He gunned the engine, backed up, threw it into gear, and took off down the driveway.

Chapter Twenty-One

W hat the dickens was that about?" Joe Tucker said.

Sam laughed. "You must've done something to scare him silly, Kate." All the men guffawed at this jest. All except for Paul, who was watching Kate carefully.

He walked toward her, calling over his shoulder, "See you in an hour, fellas," as he took her elbow and turned her back toward the Honda.

Kate slipped into the passenger seat while Paul held the door, then she waited as he rounded the car and took the driver's seat. Gratefully, she angled her head up, letting the cool air blow her hair back from her face.

"Ah, that feels good," Paul murmured. He draped an arm over the back of the seat and turned to look at her, eyebrows raised. "Was that about what I think it was about?"

Kate grinned. "I don't know. What do you think it was about?"

"I think," he said slowly, moving down the driveway, "that Jerry Cox is connected to your library demolition, and he knows you figured it out. That's why you didn't want him to know you were coming. You knew he'd recognize you and react that way."

"Well, perhaps not *exactly* that way." Kate hesitated. "You're right, sort of."

"Sort of?"

"I believe," she said, "his real name is not Jerry Cox."

Paul's eyebrows threatened to climb right up his forehead to his hairline.

"That man is Gerald Foxfield."

Paul was nodding slowly. "It makes sense," he said to himself. "It makes perfect sense. But wait, didn't Louisa tell us she knew Jerry Cox?"

Kate nodded. "I believe she's been helping him."

Paul's whole face fell. "Are you sure? She seems like such a nice young woman. And she's such a good mother."

"I think it's possible that he's coercing her somehow," Kate said. "I just have to figure out how. And I have to figure out why he's doing this."

"Does Livvy know?"

Kate shook her head. "She's so stressed that I don't think I can talk to her about this much now. I'm too afraid I won't be able to find a way to stop the demolition, and I don't want to get her hopes up."

There was a dejected silence for a moment. Then Kate roused herself. "So, tell me what you did this morning after I left."

"I finished my sermon."

Kate turned in her seat. "Oh good! Congratulations." It was only Friday. She could recall many times when he'd still be polishing his words on Saturday evening, or even early on Sunday morning.

Paul took one hand off the wheel to point his index finger up toward the sky. "Don't congratulate me; I'm just the conduit for deepening folks' faith. You know what the apostle Matthew wrote about moving mountains."

Kate thought for a moment. "Chapter 17, verse 20, right?" When Paul nodded, she quoted, "If you have faith as small as a mustard seed, you can say to this mountain, 'Move from here to there' and it will move. Nothing shall be impossible for you."

"That's it." Paul beamed, his enthusiasm for God's Word evident in his expression. "Nothing's impossible. All we need is faith."

They ordered an excellent lunch of barbeque and coleslaw from the Smokeshack and took it home. Kate added some sliced honeydew melon she had picked up from a local farm and two small pieces of boysenberry cobbler for dessert.

"Boysenberries." Paul sighed the word. "I love boysenberries." He took a bite, eyes closed. "This is heavenly."

"It's a new recipe," Kate said. "I know you like boysenberry pie, so I thought you'd enjoy this."

"There are many reasons I adore you," Paul said, "but your boysenberry cobbler might be in my new top ten."

As Kate made the drive to McMinnville that afternoon, she thought about the best way to track down Gerald Foxfield. Before she had left Copper Mill, she'd driven by Louisa Pellman's mother's home. No blue Cadillac had been anywhere in sight.

So what now? She couldn't come up with a better idea

than knocking on the doors of Maple Avenue residents, asking questions and hoping to get lucky. So in the end, that was exactly what she did.

She started on the third block. On the first and second blocks, the houses were small, no more than two stories with attic dormers. On the third block, the homes were on larger lots, spread out beneath lovely old trees. The houses themselves were sprawling brick homes of three full stories, with attached garages and carriage houses. In some cases, she could see a glimpse of a guest house or a pool in the back.

She pulled into the driveway of the first one she came to, coming to a halt in the circle in front of the house. She got out of her car and knocked on the door, but though she could hear what sounded like a large dog barking somewhere in the depths of the house, no one came to the door.

No one came to the door at the second home or at the third either. She was beginning to get discouraged.

At the fourth house, she finally found someone home. After she rang the bell, which pealed with a stately gong, she could hear footsteps slowly approaching.

The door opened, and an old man—probably in his nineties —with wavy silver hair peered out. He was smartly dressed in khaki trousers, a white shirt, and a blue-and-tan-striped bow tie, and he leaned heavily on a walker.

"Hello. May I help you?" he said in a surprisingly strong, courteous voice.

"I hope so." Kate smiled and held out her hand. "I'm Kate Hanlon from Copper Mill. I'm trying to locate a family that once lived in this neighborhood—the Foxfields. Have you ever met them or heard of them?"

"I'm Eldan Powers." The old man smiled as he took her hand, and Kate was careful not to apply too much pressure to his fragile hand. "Please come in, Kate. I'd be happy to tell you what I can about the Foxfields."

Kate's heart leaped. He had said it so casually, as if her request was quite ordinary. "That would be wonderful," she said in a heartfelt tone.

"Would you please follow me?" He turned and walked across the wide foyer to a sitting room through a wide arched doorway.

Kate followed her host, marveling at the lovely old home. It had dark, polished woods; hardwood floors covered with oriental rugs that looked very old and very costly; and what certainly had to be custom drapes at windows that spanned two stories in some places.

The parlor was beautifully appointed in shades of dusky blue and cream. An ivory baby-grand piano stood near the back of the room. Mr. Powers waved Kate into a brocade wing chair near an unlit fireplace. The house, despite its age, was pleasantly cooled by central air.

"Thank you for seeing me." Kate smiled at the dapper old gentleman.

He returned her smile as he took a seat in an identical chair on the other side of a pretty piecrust table. "Thank *you*," he said. "I enjoy guests. Now how can I help you?"

"Might I ask how long you've lived in this house, Mr. Powers?"

He smiled. "I was born in this house, and I expect I may die here too. It's been a good life and a good home."

Kate was intrigued. "Really? You were born right here?"

"Right upstairs in the master bedroom in the very same bed," he said. "Different mattress, though."

Kate laughed.

"But you didn't come to talk about me. You have questions about the Foxfields."

"Just one. I'm trying to locate a descendant of Charles Foxfield. The family would have moved here in the 1920s, I think."

Mr. Powers was already nodding. "Two fifteen. They lived at 215 Maple. Charles and Deenie Foxfield. They had six children. Their oldest son, Willard, was a little older than me. He moved back in after his daddy passed and lived there until he died. He was ninety-six years old."

"Gracious," Kate said. "You must miss him."

The old man nodded, the twinkle in his eye dimming slightly. "We were friends for a long time. He was a good man," he added quietly.

"I'm sorry for your loss," Kate said. It felt like an inadequate sentiment, since this man also may have outlived a wife, siblings, and even his own children.

"Thank you." Mr. Powers nodded graciously before he went on. "His son sold the place before there was even grass on Willard's grave." His lip curled just the tiniest bit. "Not much like his granddaddy or his daddy, that one."

"Is that one's name Gerald?" Kate was almost afraid to hope.

He nodded. "It is."

"Did he ever marry?" She was quite curious about Gerald after everything she had learned.

He snorted. "No. Never found a woman that could stomach him, I guess."

Kate struggled not to laugh at his obvious disdain. "That bad?"

"That bad," he agreed. "Rude, ungracious, downright unfriendly. Why do you want to find him?"

Kate slumped back in her chair. "I'd like to ask him some questions about the Copper Mill Public Library," she said. "I understand his grandfather donated the house to be used as a library."

Mr. Powers nodded. "I believe that's correct. But you'll have to confirm it with Gerald."

"I'd like to, but I haven't been able to talk to him about it."

"I don't know where he moved to," the old man told her. "Rumor is he had to sell the family home to pay off gambling debts. I believe he stayed in the area, but I can't swear to that."

"Oh, he's in the area," Kate said with a sniff. "I saw him this morning. Unfortunately, he saw me first and decided not to stick around."

Kate spent a few more minutes talking with the personable Mr. Powers. She resolved to return and visit with him one day when she had more time.

After she had thanked him for his assistance, Kate returned to her car. She drove to the McMinnville library on the main street through town, mostly because she couldn't think of another more useful way to find Foxfield. She considered stopping at the post office, but she decided she would save that as a last-ditch effort, since it was illegal for postal employees to reveal information about addresses.

THE LIBRARIAN at the Magness Community Library in McMinnville couldn't have been more different from Livvy.

Under five feet tall, she was so heavyset that she huffed and puffed when she walked. Her hair was steel gray, and she wore tiny bifocal lenses perched down on the very tip of a considerably prominent nose as she peered over them at Kate.

The one way in which she resembled Kate's friend was the sweet smile with which she greeted patrons.

"Welcome to our library," she said to Kate when Kate introduced herself. "I've seen you here before, haven't I?"

Kate nodded. "I'm from Copper Mill."

"Oh! Do you know Olivia Jenner, the librarian there? What a delightful lady. I've spoken with her at several conferences."

Kate chuckled. "She's one of my best friends. She is a gem, isn't she?"

"Indeed she is. How can I help you, Kate?"

"I'm trying to find someone from your area. Is there a computer I could use to do some searching?"

"Of course." The librarian waddled off, beckoning to Kate to follow. "All of our records are on electronic files. You may have some success doing a search that way."

She showed Kate to a small computer lab and helped her find the proper program. After showing her how to use it, the librarian left her to her task.

Kate searched the obituaries and found the one for Charles Foxfield. His address had been listed as 215 Maple Avenue in McMinnville.

He was survived by six children and nine grandchildren. The grandchildren's names weren't mentioned, but the eldest son was named Willard. That, she recalled, was the son Mr. Powers had mentioned who had inherited the house.

Kate did another search for Willard Foxfield and came up

with his obituary. The article had noted that Willard was survived by one son, Gerald, and—oh, God bless small-town
newspapers!—gave the address, which was *not* the Maple
Avenue house.

Kate thanked the librarian, asked for directions to the
address she had found, and rushed back to her Honda.

When she finally found Gerald Foxfield's house, she was
shocked. It was a modest Cape Cod on a very small lot, but
it wasn't the size of the property that disturbed her. It was
the air of neglect and disrepute that surrounded the poor little home: peeling paint, missing shingles, grass long enough
to hide any number of wild creatures. The shrubbery around
the front door was so overgrown that the door was partially
hidden. Compared to the elegant homes Kate had seen on
Maple Avenue a short while before, the condition of the
house indicated that Gerald Foxfield had suffered some kind
of serious reversal of fortune.

There was a weather-beaten garage with sagging boards at
the back of the driveway, but no cars in the drive. At the sight,
Kate's heart beat faster. She had a suspicion about Gerald
Foxfield, and she wondered if her intuition would prove true.

Don't get your hopes up, Kate, she cautioned herself. *You
don't even know for sure that the man lives here.*

Stepping over clumps of dandelion that had grown up
through cracks in the concrete sidewalk, Kate approached
the front door. There was a half-moon of glass above the tar-
nished brass knocker, but it was so clouded and dirty that she
couldn't see a thing, and she doubted anyone inside could see
out.

She pressed a finger to the doorbell, but there was no sound that she could hear. She pressed it again, then picked up the knocker and gave several hefty raps against the door. She repeated the process twice more before she finally acknowledged that no one was coming to the door. Walking around the side of the house, she approached the garage. It had a sturdy silver padlock on the door that looked newer than anything else she'd seen on the property.

Her mouth went dry as she peeked through the row of windows at the top of the garage door by standing on her tiptoes. Surprisingly, these windows looked cleaner than the one at the top of the front door.

Inside, indirect sunlight filtered through a window on each side. It illuminated the interior enough for Kate to see a vehicle parked in each space. On the left was some kind of old truck. Really old. Kate had seen Model Ts before, and this one looked even older. It might be a Model A, although she couldn't be sure. The one thing she was sure of was that it had been taken care of. The exterior gleamed and the headlamps sparkled as if they were new.

On the right was a pale blue Cadillac.

Chapter Twenty-Two

Unlike the truck, the Cadillac appeared to have been driven recently. It was a lovely vehicle.

As lovely as she remembered. Kate had now seen the Caddy in front of Louisa's mother's house, downtown cruising past the library, and today at Paul's work site, where it had been driven away in haste by Jerry Cox.

And Jerry Cox, she was certain, was the elusive Gerald Foxfield.

THE MINUTES SEEMED TO CRAWL BY as Kate strategically placed her car on the street outside Gerald Foxfield's home. She called Paul to let him know where she was while she waited for Foxfield. She had water, which she rationed and drank at regular intervals, knowing how quickly the heat could get to her. The sky was looking a little peculiar, as if rain was on the way. Unbidden, thoughts of Sunday evening's brush with the tornado crept into her thoughts. It had been one of the most frightening events of her life, and she had no desire to repeat it. She kept a wary eye on the sky, sending up a prayer that a storm wouldn't break out while she was on the road.

She thought about the two antique vehicles. If they did indeed belong to Gerald Foxfield, she wondered why he hadn't sold them if money was such a problem. On the other hand, perhaps these were the two items he most valued, and he was sacrificing other things to hang on to them. She recalled what Mr. Powers had said about Gerald spending his inheritance.

Just before five o'clock, her patience was rewarded when a black Ford truck pulled into the driveway. Kate got out of her car as the driver of the truck stopped along the sidewalk at the back of the house.

A dark-haired man with a sprinkle of silver at his temples got out of the truck. It was the first good look she'd gotten at him. He was physically fit, although not any taller than Paul's not-quite-six-feet.

His face was thunderous. "You're on private property, lady."

"Mr. Foxfield, I believe you already know who I am," Kate said, refusing to acknowledge the little quiver in her stomach. "I'd like to talk to you about the demolition of the library."

Foxfield glared at her. "Why?"

"You supposedly own the property."

"I do own the property." His voice became even more aggressive, and he took a step toward her.

Kate steeled herself not to step back. She ignored the statement. "The residents of Copper Mill are going to be very upset that their library is going to be torn down, Mr. Foxfield. Surely there is some way we can avoid that—"

"There's nothing you can do," he said so fast he nearly

tripped over the words. There was almost a sneer in his tone. "I own that land. It's been in my family for years."

"So how could the library have been in operation all these years if it wasn't the town's property?" She didn't understand how such a thing could have occurred.

"It was a mistake," he said. "Someone fouled up when the deed was being registered. I discovered it after my father died, and I have no interest in hanging on to a useless piece of property."

"Like the home your family lived in on Maple Avenue for more than eighty years?" Kate couldn't help feeling upset at his attitude. "You don't appear to have much respect for history, Mr. Foxfield."

"It's not a crime," he said.

Kate ignored his belligerence. "How did you discover it?"

"Excuse me?" Her question had thrown him.

"How did you discover that you owned the library?" Kate pressed.

He glared at her. "Not that it's any of your business, but after my father died, I had all his properties surveyed so I could sell them. In his safe-deposit box was an old deed that he must have overlooked for years. It showed that my family owned that land free and clear. My grandfather might have intended to donate it to the town, but the actual deed transfer never took place."

Kate couldn't believe he was giving her so much information. "Don't you feel uncomfortable about kicking the library out, especially when it was your grandfather's intent to donate it to Copper Mill? The library doesn't have a place to move to, and the town will suffer. Many people won't have computer access, and there won't be any books or other valuable resources for them to check out. How can you do this?" She took a deep breath. "You just said yourself that your grandfather's intent was to give the property to the town. How can you completely disregard your ancestor's wishes?"

Gerald Foxfield made a rude noise. "My ancestor's wishes don't hold a lot of weight with me, lady. The man's dead and buried. I'm a whole lot more concerned about my income stream."

Her suspicions were confirmed. "So that's why you're rushing the library out?"

"Rushing?" he said contemptuously. "I gave 'em a whole week to pack up and move. I was within my rights to get 'em out of there immediately."

The rumor of apartments being built downtown rang clearly in Kate's head. "You're tearing it down to build apartments, aren't you?"

For the first time, she saw unease in Foxfield's unfriendly demeanor. "Where'd you hear that?"

Kate smiled grimly. "The rumor mill. Although from your expression, I'm pretty certain there's a lot more than rumor to it."

"If I'm building on the property, it's none of your business," he snarled. "Now get off my land."

Kate didn't budge. "You're the one who wrote those threatening notes to Olivia Jenner and the note leading me on a wildgoose chase, aren't you? And you made the threatening phone call too, didn't you?"

Foxfield paused, his brow furrowed. "What? I didn't write any notes. You have no business coming here and harassing me. Get off my property now, or I'll call the cops."

Kate turned and began to walk back to her car. "That won't be necessary. You've given me all the information I need to know."

"What information?" he shouted after her. "That library's coming down on Monday. There's nothing you can do to stop it."

Kate didn't acknowledge that she'd even heard him as she steamed back to the Honda. "We'll see about that," she muttered beneath her breath. "There's always something that can be done. The key is finding it in time."

KATE'S HANDS WERE SHAKING and her heart was pounding as she drove away from Gerald Foxfield's home. What an odious man!

That library's coming down on Monday echoed over and over in her head. She'd heard the truth from Gerald's own lips. Now, how could she stop the demolition? A wave of despair swept over her. Who was she to think she could stop something like this single-handedly? Particularly something that was happening legally?

But if Foxfield really thought he could steamroll right over the town council, he would have publicly gone ahead with his demolition plans, wouldn't he? He wouldn't have bothered keeping it a secret if he didn't have some concerns about the townsfolk's ability to thwart him.

And despite his contention that he hadn't threatened either her or Livvy, she had to assume that he was indeed responsible for that. Why bother unless he was worried that they might be able to stop him somehow? Then she remembered her Bible study from that very morning, a verse from

Isaiah that talked about putting her trust in the Lord. That was what she'd been leaving out of this quest, she realized. She had been depending on herself instead of depending on Christ.

As she drove, she began to pray. She prayed for patience and for the wisdom to discern her path. Was saving the library really what God wanted from her? She'd thought about this and worried over it several times. But each time she came back to a conviction that she was indeed following the path the Lord had set before her. The Copper Mill Public Library provided so much to so many people.

She thought of Livvy, face glowing as she taught a young person—or an older person—how to use a search engine. Her friend truly loved her job. Kate thought of Jeremy Pellman, patiently lying in the grass watching his squirrels. What would happen to the squirrels if the library was demolished? She thought of Morty Robertson, for whom the library was a way to give worth and meaning to retirement, and of so many others who wandered in and out in the course of a week, reaping the fruits of the town's investment in literacy and learning.

And that thought segued into yet another. How and why had the town council poured so much money into the library over the years when they didn't own the building? How had a mistake of this magnitude been made? Land ownership was very serious business.

Suddenly her heart sank as she recalled how she had gotten her information about the library deeds: Louisa Pellman. Based on where Kate had seen the blue Cadillac, she was certain Louisa was connected to Gerald Foxfield somehow. And if that was true, Kate couldn't trust the information Louisa had given her, not even the photocopy of the current deed.

She needed to get to the deeds office and check out the deeds herself as soon as she could. But the next day was Saturday, and all the public buildings were closed.

To distract herself from her mounting worry, she thought about the earlier encounter with Renee and Caroline, and Caroline's mention of gold. Was it true? From the library book she'd seen, it appeared that gold had been found in Copper Mill "back in the day," as the kids in the youth group said.

Then a new thought occurred to her. Foxfield had looked anxious, uncertain, when she had mentioned building apartments on the site. She remembered the picture on the mayor's wall. Lawton Briddle was a good man, if a bit set in his ways. Tosten Glass, however, was someone she could picture being involved in this scheme.

Yet another thought intruded, sparked by the memory of the picture of three young boys. According to Lawton Briddle, Tosten Glass was convinced at the time that he was close to finding gold. Had Gerald Foxfield heard and believed those childhood stories as well?

Surely the slim possibility of finding gold couldn't have anything to do with Foxfield's determination to tear down the library. Or could it?

It was pretty far out there as theories went. But Kate's intuition told her not to discount the idea. She was going to have to talk to someone about gold.

AT HOME THAT EVENING, Kate flipped through the phone book and looked up the number of Pine Ridge Community College. Did they have classes on Friday evenings? It couldn't hurt to try.

She was mildly surprised when a receptionist answered the telephone. Apparently, all after-hours calls were transferred to the library, which was open until eleven.

"I'd like to speak to someone who might know something about gold mining," she said.

The receptionist said, "Maybe the geology department? Hold on, and I'll transfer you if there's someone there. If they don't have the answer, maybe they can tell you who might."

Kate heard a few moments of soft classical music before a new voice said, "Pine Ridge Community College, geology department."

When Kate explained what she was seeking, the woman said, "Oh, I'm sure Dr. Wilde could answer your questions. He has a PhD in Geology of the Appalachians, and he knows a tremendous amount about the local area." She told Kate the professor would be in his office from nine till noon the following morning.

Kate resolved to be on his doorstep at nine on the dot.

KATE WENT INTO their home office, bypassing her studio to check her e-mail on the computer. She had hoped to complete the squirrel sun catcher for Jeremy's birthday, but the past few days had been such a whirlwind of chasing clues that she hadn't been able to spend much time at all in the studio. She sighed as she told herself that keeping the library intact and in its present location—with its resident squirrel population safe—was the best birthday gift she could give Jeremy.

The thought made her smile as she sat down at the computer. Although the Internet connection was much slower than the library computers, it was fine for e-mail.

She had the usual assortment of e-mails from people coordinating church events and projects, a few advertisements that were easily deleted, and one message from egetty@hcwc.org that she didn't recognize for a moment. Then she realized it was from Elspeth Getty, the director of the Harrington County Wildlife Center. Elspeth wrote that she had sent the squirrel photos Kate had taken to an expert who thought it was possible the tiny rodents might be a previously unknown subspecies of flying squirrel.

After typing a quick reply and shutting down her e-mail program, Kate went to the living room, where Paul was watching the backs of his eyelids while a nature show played on television. She chuckled, and his eyes slowly opened and focused on her.

"Good program, isn't it," she teased.

"Excellent," he said, straightening. "Couldn't you see how much I was enjoying it?"

She laughed out loud as she took a seat beside him on the couch. "Indulge me for a few minutes," she said as he turned his palm up and she laced her fingers through his.

"Indulging," he said. "What's up?"

"I'm getting desperate," she admitted. "There has to be some way to save the library, but I haven't found it yet. Now I'm thinking outside the box. These are long-shot possibilities, I admit, but I have two scenarios I'm going to pursue, in addition to checking out the deeds more closely first thing Monday morning."

"How outside the box are you thinking?" Paul asked.

"Think flying squirrels and gold," she told him.

"Together? This I can't wait to hear."

"Not together, smarty," she said, elbowing him gently. "Squirrels first. I just got an e-mail from that wildlife place where I took Jeremy's injured squirrel. She sent those photos I took to a flying-squirrel expert who thinks it's possible that they might be a new subspecies."

Paul's eyes opened wider, and he sat up straighter. "So you're wondering if they could be classified as an endangered species."

"Exactly. If they are, could that save the library? It wouldn't resolve the ownership problem, but at least it might keep the building from being demolished."

Paul ran a hand through his hair. "If you're asking my opinion, I'd have to say that's a serious long shot."

"Yes, but maybe an injunction could prevent the demolition until further study is done and a determination is made," she said. "I know there's something funny going on with Gerald Foxfield. I just need time to prove it."

Paul sighed. "I suppose it's a possibility, but you'd have to work awfully fast. What's the other scenario?"

"I'm not exactly sure," she admitted. "But something Caroline Johnston said to me is sticking in my head, and I can't help thinking it could have something to do with Foxfield's interest in the library."

"What is it?"

"Gold. Caroline said that there used to be gold prospecting in Copper Mill. I found an old book that appeared to substantiate it."

"But what does that have to do with the library?"

"I have no clue," she said in frustration. "But I don't have time to pursue a whole lot else, so I'm going to look into it.

What if there is gold beneath the town? Even the possibility of that could make people awfully greedy. You should have seen Gerald Foxfield's family home, Paul. It's practically a mansion in a beautiful established neighborhood with other old estate homes. Mature trees, spacious lots, carriage houses, the whole works. According to a neighbor, Foxfield sold the house soon after his father passed away to pay off gambling debts. When I finally found him, his current residence is a small and very poorly maintained Cape Cod in a less-than-stellar neighborhood. The only signs of wealth I saw were two antique cars hidden away in a garage."

"So Jerry—Foxfield—has fallen on hard times, you're saying, and wants to . . . what? Find gold?" Paul looked skeptical. "That sounds pretty far-fetched, Kate."

"I know," she said, "but without anything else to consider, it's at least a possibility."

Chapter Twenty-Three

Before nine the following morning, Kate drove to Pine Ridge and headed for the community college. The whole way there, she mulled over her theories. Gold had been found in Copper Mill at least once, it appeared. How was that relevant to what was happening today? Or was she imagining that her intuition was leading her this way because she was so desperate for any lead?

The campus of Pine Ridge Community College was a lovely rolling expanse of green lawn beneath large shade trees. It was tranquil now in the midst of the summer break. Kate knew there were summer classes, but the main parking lot held only a handful of cars.

She walked to a large campus map displayed on a corner and identified the sciences building. It was a handsome brick structure with shallow concrete steps. Pulling open one of the white double doors, she went to one wall that held a directory. Dr. Wilde's office was number 227 on the second floor. A wide set of stairs mounted to a second-floor lounge. Off the lounge were several hallways with numbers prominently displayed. She saw 210–230 and moments later was standing in front of 227.

The door was slightly ajar. Kate rapped on the door frame and heard a deep bass voice say, "Come in."

She pushed open the door to reveal a typical professor's office, crammed with bookshelves, two visitors' chairs, and an enormous wooden desk in front of a window. A tall man in a casual knit shirt and pants stood and extended a hand. He looked to be about the age of her son, Andrew.

"Hello. Devon Wilde. Are you a student?"

Kate shook her head. "I'm Kate Hanlon. I'm visiting from Copper Mill, and I was hoping you could answer some questions for me."

"Shoot." Dr. Wilde waited until Kate sat, and then he resumed his seat. He looked more like a golfer than a professor, she thought, although the mountains of paperwork around him certainly gave evidence of his occupation.

"I recently learned that there once was gold found in Copper Mill," she said. "I understand you know a lot about the Appalachians, and I was hoping you might be able to tell me more about it."

Dr. Wilde smiled. "You might be sorry you asked, but I'll try to keep it brief. How much do you know about gold as it occurs in nature?"

Kate shook her head. "Other than the fact that miners panned for it, very little."

"All right. Crash course. Gold is found, like other precious metals, in host rock. As that rock weathers, it frees the gold, which falls or is washed down among other rock, often in streambeds or alluvial formations." He must have noted

Kate's lack of comprehension because he added, "An alluvial fan is an area where a fast-moving stream of water fans out across a wider, flatter area."

Kate nodded. "Got it."

"Gold is nineteen times heavier than water," Wilde went on, "so much of the time, it doesn't move far from the source rock, the host rock. Without going into detail, I'll just say that as the water erodes the gold, smaller nuggets and flakes break off and move downstream. If you find gold flakes in a stream, you need to move upstream to find the bigger stuff. Gold has been found in the southern Appalachians for well over a hundred and fifty years now. In 1829, articles detailing the discovery of gold in northern Georgia caused thousands of miners to rush into the area. Ultimately, their presence hastened the removal of the Cherokee Indians. In the winter of 1837 and 1838, the Cherokee were forced on a march west to Oklahoma, during which more than a third of them died."

"The Trail of Tears," Kate murmured.

"Right." Wilde pointed a finger at her as if he were shooting. "I digress. There are some major fault lines running through the Appalachians. Where there are faults, the upheaval of rock brings formations to the surface, and in our case, an old fault line practically right under Copper Mill left deposits of several minerals close to the surface. In the mid-1800s, copper was found, giving the town its name. But what most people don't know is that for a short time during the 1860s, the discovery of gold in three key sites around the town caused a mini gold rush."

"Where were the sites?" Kate asked.

"Two were along what is now Main Street," Wilde said.

"One where the library stands, and the other farther east near the creek. The third site is south of town, also near the creek."

"But the library isn't near water," Kate said, "so how was gold found there?"

"At that time, there was a small tributary of Copper Mill Creek that ran west of the current creek. It dried up after a huge storm sent a flash flood down the creek and shifted a big boulder."

"So the gold was found while there still was a stream there?" Kate asked.

Wilde shook his head. "No. It was private property owned by a prominent local man named Severn. Mr. Severn owned the land, and he refused to prospect for gold. The Severn family eventually sold it just before the turn of the century, and a house was built on the property in 1897. Several nuggets of gold were found when they dug the foundation for the house, presumably deposited there before the stream was diverted."

Dr. Wilde paused to take a breath. "The house was sold two more times—in 1903 and 1916. In 1916, it was purchased by a fellow who lived there with his family until 1934, when he donated the home to the town of Copper Mill for the purpose of becoming a library. The family made the donation anonymously, but at that time, everyone knew the man who donated the house was named—"

"Foxfield," Kate inserted.

Wilde looked surprised. "You've been doing your homework, I see."

Kate smiled. "Only a tiny bit."

"The Foxfields were already landowners in the area in

1934. They amassed a small fortune by establishing a toll road through the town. In 1928, Foxfield built a carriage house to the north of the home. When he did so, the workers uncovered several more gold nuggets."

"And those were also in the path of the original stream-bed?" Kate asked, leaning forward.

"Right," Wilde said. "As I said, the Foxfields were already wealthy, but they became significantly more so after the find. Once the initial excitement died down, little more was heard about gold in Copper Mill. Every once in a while, an enterprising person finds a flake of gold in the creek." He paused. "Does that help, or shall I continue?"

Kate glanced at her watch. "I'm finding this quite fascinating, but I'm on a tight schedule." She rose, extending her hand and shaking Wilde's. "Thank you so much for your time and the geology lesson."

Wilde laughed. "Oh, if only my students were half so enthusiastic."

"One last question," Kate said. "Do you think there's still gold to be found?"

Wilde smiled. "It's almost a certainty that there's more gold beneath Copper Mill, especially if one were to follow the original mineral formation beneath the library."

"That," said Kate, "is exactly what I wanted to know."

"Good luck prospecting."

She laughed. "Prospecting is what I'm hoping to *prevent*."

LIVVY HAD A SLIP OF PAPER in her hand, which she handed to Kate. "I'm a messenger now. Someone from the Tennessee Wildlife Resources Agency called. He tried you at home, and

Paul gave him this number. I guess you didn't have your cell phone with you?"

Kate shook her head.

"He wants to talk to you about the squirrels," Livvy went on. "His home number is on there too, in case you aren't able to get back to him during the day."

Kate glanced at the note. His home number? The man must have wanted to talk to her pretty badly.

Livvy cleared her throat. "The demolition team was here today. Some of the volunteers recognized the head of the company and put two and two together, and now there are a lot of upset and anxious people running around here."

"What did Mr. Crawford say?" Kate asked.

"He was horribly apologetic. I actually felt bad for the man." Livvy swallowed. "They're set up for a one o'clock start on Monday."

"And does everyone know that?"

Livvy nodded. "There was no way to keep it a secret any longer." Her eyes were dark with worry. "I hope no one thinks it's my fault the word got out."

"They couldn't possibly blame you," Kate reassured her. "Crawford Demolitions coming in here in broad daylight sort of blows the secrecy wide open." She put her arm around her friend's shoulder and squeezed. "How are you doing?"

"We're doing well with the packing. We should be able to have everything out by Sunday evening, and then I'll do a walk-through on Monday to be sure nothing was missed." Her voice caught.

Kate said, "Oh, Livvy," but her friend held up a warning hand.

"Don't," she said. "Unless you can tell me you've found a way to stop the demolition, don't offer me sympathy. I'm having enough trouble holding it together."

What Livvy didn't say was that there would be plenty of time for sadness and tears the following week when there was only a gaping hole on Main Street between Sweetwater and Smith.

AT HOME, KATE LISTLESSLY put together a turkey sandwich and sliced some peaches into a bowl. There wasn't much more she could do today, she thought, frustrated. Offices were closed on Saturday and Sunday.

Then she remembered the note with the phone numbers of the wildlife guy on it that Livvy had given her. Going to her handbag, which she had tossed on the coat tree in the entry, she fished out the information. She went into the office and got the cordless phone, then dialed the office number. As she'd expected, she got an answering machine. By now it was Saturday afternoon, and she hadn't thought the man would still be in his office. She dialed again, trying the home number, and was pleased when a masculine voice answered.

"This is Kate Hanlon," she said, going on to explain who she was and listen as the wildlife expert introduced himself as well.

"Elspeth Getty forwarded your photographs and descriptive information to me," he said. "I found them intriguing, so I took the liberty of sending them along to several other squirrel people."

"Squirrel people." Maybe it was because she was so tired that she found it so amusing.

The wildlife expert laughed as well. "As opposed to bobcat

people or hawk people. I guess we're a weird bunch. Anyway, I wanted to tell you that the general consensus is that these are a new subspecies that is significantly different from other flying-squirrel populations."

"The Northern and Southern flying squirrels," Kate said, recalling her research.

"Exactly. If you looked them up, you're probably aware that these little guys look different from those."

"We thought maybe they were babies at first," Kate told him. "But the more we saw of them, the more we thought they might be something unusual."

"Very unusual," he told her. "No one has documented this particular squirrel anywhere else but in that one location. It seems likely that there are additional populations, but finding them may take time. And the chances that there are very, very few of them are high."

Kate perked up. A small sliver of hope worked its way through her. "You mean they might be endangered?"

"They might be," he agreed. "I'll leave that to someone farther up the food chain to decide, although I registered all of your documentation—excellent job, by the way."

"Thank you." Kate swallowed. "Are you aware that the building in which they appear to be living is scheduled for demolition on Monday?"

"What? This Monday?" The man sounded shocked. "That's terrible."

"I know. For more reasons than one." She sighed. "Is there any chance of having them designated endangered immediately?"

"Not one," the fellow said, his tone somber. "The whole

process takes a lot of time and money and ultimately has to be decided by the US Fish and Wildlife Service. It may help if I send this information on to the Center for Biological Diversity, but not by Monday. The best we could hope for is a temporary injunction to give researchers time to study them and make a recommendation to the USFW. And I have to warn you that it's extremely difficult to get a judge to issue an injunction."

"So whom do I contact at the Center for...what?" Kate felt a surge of renewed energy. Maybe today was Saturday, but that didn't mean she had to sit back and do nothing all weekend.

"The Center for Biological Diversity. You don't have to do anything. I already sent this to them as well." He chuckled. "I guess I got a little excited." He went on. "The only thing I need to do is confirm your contact information, because they'll want to talk to you when they see this. I'll be sure they understand the need for speed."

Kate gave him her full name, her address, her home and cell numbers, the library's number, and Paul's e-mail address as well as hers. Just in case.

She thought again about the next problem looming. Should she ask Louisa about Foxfield? She wanted to, but she was afraid that Louisa would immediately contact Gerald. And she didn't want him alerted that she planned to look at the deeds for herself. Her suspicions about exactly what those deeds said grew.

Kate marched to the kitchen, where a pad and a pen lay on the counter near the telephone. In great big letters, she wrote *COURTHOUSE* across a sheet. That had to be her priority Monday morning.

SHE SPENT THE AFTERNOON in her studio working on Jeremy's sun catcher. It wouldn't be done by his birthday, but it wouldn't be too far past it either, if she worked steadily. The photos she had taken for the wildlife people turned out to be a blessing for her, allowing her to closely copy the little creatures' appearance. It wasn't highly complicated. The biggest issue was choosing the right pieces of glass.

Fortunately, she'd recently purchased an assortment of colored glass that had a dark opal gray kokomo in it that would be perfect for the animal's coat, and once she had the pattern worked out to her satisfaction, she began the process of cutting her glass.

At suppertime, she assembled the fixings for tacos and turned on the oven to bake the shells, which Paul preferred crispy. There was melon left over from the previous night, and she set that out as well.

Checking her watch, she saw that Paul would be home any minute. He'd been working harder on that roofing project than he'd worked on anything in years. The sheer physical strength and endurance required was staggering.

The phone rang. Absently she picked up the one in the kitchen and greeted the caller.

"This is Gerald Foxfield. Lady," began the rough male voice, "I'm only going to say this one time. You need to stay out of my business."

"You mean the business of the town of Copper Mill?"

"It's *my* property," he said, "and I can do what I want with it. Stop digging into my property records. I've already called my lawyer—"

"Ellis Hayer," Kate recalled. "A very pleasant young man."

Her lack of agitation seemed to inflame him more. "My lawyer will be contacting you!" he told her just before he hung up on her.

Kate replaced the receiver. How odd. She had assumed the creepy caller before was Gerald. But if *that* was Gerald, who had the scary voice been just now? She rubbed her arms, more unnerved than she liked by the unknown voice.

Chapter Twenty-Four

After the pressures of the week, it felt wonderful to have a leisurely breakfast and go to church on Sunday. It was definitely cooler today, and people looked happier and more energetic as they congregated in the sunshine outside the little white church.

When Kate arrived, she went to prepare for the service with the choir. She wasn't surprised, but she was saddened when Livvy didn't join her in the alto section. As she looked at the congregation from her vantage point in the choir, she saw that Danny, James, and Justin were in church. But no Livvy. Just like the previous Sunday.

As the service began, she did her best to slide her worries into a drawer, which she closed for the duration of the service. She might have to give it a shove to keep it closed, but she intended to do her best. This was her time to give praise and thanks to God for the many blessings in her life.

The opening hymn was "A Mighty Fortress Is Our God." Kate loved the song. The familiar melody and lyrics were comforting, taking her back to the church of her childhood. She had sat with her father during services, watching her mother sing in the choir, and she blinked back tears as she realized that she was following in her mother's footsteps. Did people ever get over missing their mothers? She couldn't imagine it.

Singing the hymn today, Kate was struck by some of the lyrics, which seemed especially appropriate to the dilemma the library faced:

> *A mighty fortress is our God, a bulwark never failing;*
> *Our helper He amid the flood of mortal ills prevailing.*

God *was* a bulwark, whom she had failed to lean on during the hectic discoveries of the week. Oh, she had taken time for her daily Bible study, and she'd offered a few fleeting prayers here and there, but she hadn't done a very good job of living her faith. It was a very human failing to forget to put God before all else, and Kate acknowledged that she had indeed done exactly that.

> *Did we in our own strength confide, our striving would*
> *be losing;*
> *Were not the right Man on our side, the Man of God's*
> *own choosing;*
> *Dost ask who that may be? Christ Jesus, it is He.*

Well, she thought, that told it like it was. She had been trying to rely on her own strength, forgetting that right beside her was her Savior, ready to carry her load and walk with her. Ready to carry *her* if need be.

The choir sang an anthem right before Paul's sermon, and

then her husband took his place at the simple wooden pulpit. In a ringing voice, he declared, "'God is our refuge and strength, an ever-present help in trouble.' Psalm 46:1."

He let that statement hang in the air for a moment. Then he said, "And you had better believe that when Kate and I were lying in a ditch listening to a tornado roar over our heads last Sunday night, I was awfully glad to know that." He said it with a self-deprecating humor that lightened the impact of his words and made many in the congregation smile as heads nodded.

As her husband continued to deliver his sermon, Kate felt that he had designed it especially for her, encouraging her not to give up the struggle she'd been in all week, reminding her that the Lord was with her, even when she forgot about him.

It warmed her and gave her the courage and strength she needed to get up the next morning and fight as she never had before to save the Copper Mill Public Library.

AFTER LUNCH, Kate headed for the kitchen. A parishioner had given her a bag of blueberries, and she wanted to use most of them for a contribution to the Faith Freezer Program. She had seen a recipe for blueberry pound cake in the cookbook Ida Mae Beasley had given her. It looked tasty, and she thought it might be a nice change from blueberry pie. But she'd promised the Beasleys a pie, so she whipped that up first, using a familiar recipe she had made for years.

The blueberry pound cake was actually a simple recipe in which blueberries dredged in flour were folded into a butter and sugar pound cake batter and baked in a tube or Bundt pan dusted with confectioner's sugar. She owned two fluted Bundt pans and a classic straight-sided tube pan that she occasionally used when she made angel food cake. It was a good thing she had all three, because the quart-and-a-half of blueberries she still had left after she made the muffins were exactly equal to the three pints she needed for three cakes.

As she mixed, dredged, and folded, she thought about the library dilemma. In one week, she'd gone from knowing nothing about the proposed library closure to learning that it was going to be demolished, and from there, ultimately to the name of the property owner who intended to demolish it. She also suspected that Louisa Pellman was helping Gerald Foxfield somehow in his bid to demolish the building. And Tosten Glass, although she hadn't figured out how he fit in yet, unless she could find a connection between the library demolition and the discovery of gold in town.

Oh, it was no use. All she was going to be able to do was obsess about the library. She might as well go down there and help Livvy with the final evacuation of the contents of the building.

After she finished with her baking, she explained to Paul where she would be. It took only moments to reach her destination. As she walked in, she was shocked by how sad and lonely the empty rooms looked. Almost everything had been moved out, and there were large places on the floor where the carpet was darker because it had spent years beneath shelves and furniture. It was like someone had disappeared and left only fingerprints behind.

"Hey." Livvy appeared in the doorway of her office. It was clear that she had been weeping. "What are you up to?"

Kate gestured to the empty room. "I came to see if you needed any more help, but . . ."

Livvy shook her head. "Everything is out. Everything." Her voice dropped to a whisper.

A youthful voice calling "Mrs. Hanlon! Mrs. Hanlon!" made Kate turn around again, dragging her arm across her eyes to dash away the tears that had collected.

"Hi, Jeremy." She looked over the boy's head. "Is your mother here with you?"

He shook his head. "My grandma dropped me off and said she'd pick me up in a couple of hours. Mrs. Hanlon, what's going to happen to our squirrels when they tear down the building?" The boy had tears in his eyes.

Kate put a hand on his shoulder. "I don't know, Jeremy. I've talked to some wildlife people about them, but I just don't know." Somehow she wasn't surprised at Louisa's absence. The woman had to know Kate had some hard questions for her.

"Maybe we could trap them," he suggested, "and take them somewhere safe."

"That's a good idea." Kate hugged him. She couldn't imagine much success with that method between now and Monday, not to mention that they had no idea how many squirrels there were to start with. "I can call the wildlife people back and ask them how to do that. Maybe they can get us some traps and tell us the best way to get them out of the walls."

Jeremy nodded in agreement, pleading in his eyes.

"I have to go," she said, squeezing his shoulder again. "I'm still looking for ways to keep this library from being torn down. And I'll still be looking tomorrow morning if that's what it takes. I'm not giving up."

"Me either," he said stoutly, making her smile for the first time since she'd arrived at the library. "I'm going outside now and watch to see if I can figure out a way to catch them."

When the child was gone, she turned back to Livvy. Surely there had to be something she could do to further her investigation, even if offices were closed. Sunday was a day of rest, but her brain refused to rest. Maybe she needed to spend some time in prayer. Perhaps an answer would come from a wiser source than she.

Then she thought of the Center for Biological Diversity. She wished she'd thought to get the number of someone from that center. She would have liked to have spoken to them herself, to impress on them the desperate race against the clock in which she was engaged. It had sounded as if that organization was capable of taking a more activist stance than a government facility, and it might be of more immediate assistance. Then she remembered that she still had the number of the first wildlife expert who had contacted her. He would have a number for her, she thought, already reaching for her cell phone.

"I have to go," she told her friend, giving her a hug. "I know it's a very long shot, but I'm still trying to talk to people about getting an injunction to study these squirrels."

Livvy tried to smile. "Thank you, Kate. I know you've done everything possible. I'll see you tomorrow."

"I'll be here at one, if not before," Kate promised.

Twenty minutes later, she was home again, speaking with a representative of the Center for Biological Diversity. The man already had a file with her photographs that he had received from the wildlife agency. The last fellow with whom Kate had spoken apparently had attached a "Red Alert" Post-it note to the file to let the CBD know that time was of the essence. Still, the man was aghast when he realized that the building where the squirrels lived truly was to be demolished the next day.

"I can make some calls right now," he said. "Let me see what our attorneys can do. I'll be in touch."

When Kate hung up the phone, Paul was standing in the kitchen, grinning. "If that library can be saved," Paul said, "I have absolute faith that, somehow, you and the Lord will pull it off."

Kate smiled at him, although she still felt terribly worried. "I guess we'll know this time tomorrow, won't we?"

"We will," her husband said. He took her hands. "Let's pray."

After a few moments of listening to her husband's comforting dialogue with God, Kate wandered back to her studio again while Paul went out to weed. Although she hadn't thought she could do it, Jeremy's squirrel sun catcher would be done by Tuesday if she worked on it some more today and Monday, and she was quite satisfied with the way the piece was going. She was not satisfied at the thought of how she was going to get the gift to the child when his mother was probably trying desperately to avoid Kate.

Unfortunately, now her mind was careening in about a dozen directions as the next day's demolition looked more likely by the minute. Lack of concentration could be a deadly error, both for her and for the piece she was creating, so she put away her tools and went to find Paul.

"How do you feel about a Sunday drive?"

"Where to?"

"Pie deliveries," Kate said. She needed to get out of the house again. Worrying herself sick until the next morning wasn't going to help anyone.

It was a pleasant day for a drive, and having Paul accompany her made the trip more relaxing and fun.

They dropped off a pie for Clifton and Ida, and another for Joshua Parsons, and stayed a bit at each home to visit. On the way back, they stopped at a little antiques shop that Kate had been eyeing and checked out a gorgeous walnut Victorian settee with a needlepoint cover in unbelievably good condition. Unfortunately, the price was just as unbelievable.

"Besides," said Kate, "we downsized for a reason. No sense in filling our home up again."

When they returned home, the message light on their answering machine was blinking. Kate punched the button and listened to the man from the Center for Biological Diversity. He invited her to a meeting he had set up with a federal official from the US Fish and Wildlife Service at nine the next morning in front of the library. He asked Kate to return the call only if the time did not suit. She would make it suit, she decided, although she still needed to fit in a trip to the courthouse to check out the library deed for herself.

"Yes!" She pumped her fist in the air and hopped up and down. "Progress at last." But almost immediately, she calmed herself. "I can't get too excited about this," she told Paul. "It's very likely that it'll be too late to save the library using the squirrel method."

"So why are you meeting them?" he wanted to know.

"Because as long as that building is standing, I have hope," she said. "And because even if it doesn't help the library, these animals still may be an endangered species, and I have to do everything I can to protect them. If we can't stop the demolition, we need to try to save the squirrels at least. I'm hoping the wildlife experts will have some thoughts on how to trap them quickly."

"And if you can't stop the demolition tomorrow," Paul asked, "will you feel that you tried your very best to save it?"

Kate was quiet for a moment. "I believe I will," she said quietly. "But it will be difficult to accept."

As she walked toward the kitchen to start dinner, something struck her. She'd been so down in the dumps about wasting time because it was Sunday, and as it turned out, it had been a productive day after all.

"Thank you, Lord," she murmured. "You provide even when I doubt."

Chapter Twenty-Five

At nine o'clock Monday morning, Kate walked toward the library after parking her car along Main Street. She was very conscious that in a mere four hours, the library would be demolished, and her heart was heavy.

She sat down on a bench near the front door and bowed her head. *Lord God,* she prayed, *I know it's a big deal, asking you to work a miracle here this morning. But you are a God of miracles, after all. I ask you to bless this special structure and keep it safe. Keep it open and available to the citizens of the community. Stay the hand of those who would destroy it, and replace greed with charitable intentions in their hearts. Amen.*

A dark car with government plates pulled into a space along the street, and a man in a conservative dark suit got out.

"Hello," he said. "I'm meeting Kate Hanlon here."

"That would be me," she said, smiling as she offered him her hand.

"Troy Silhouse," he told her as he returned the handshake. "US Fish and Wildlife Service. All information about species protection goes through our department."

Another car pulled up, and a second man hurried toward them. "Gordie Connaly, Center for Biological Diversity," he said, introducing himself to Kate. He grinned as he gave the USFW man a hearty handshake. "Troy and I are already acquainted. Let's talk about these squirrels. Has your office reviewed the information we sent?"

Troy nodded. "It's the opinion of my office," he said, "that further study is needed. There's a significant chance that these squirrels may represent a new subspecies of flying squirrel that's undocumented."

"Woo-hoo!" Gordie clapped his hands. "Now we're cookin'!"

Troy didn't look as thrilled. "Even if I'm in time today, this building ultimately is coming down, right? It would be incredibly difficult to move an entire population of animals to a new location, provided we can even learn enough about them in time to make relocation a possibility."

There was a heavy silence.

Finally, Kate said, "I'm working on saving the building."

Both men looked sharply at her.

"Permanently?" Troy asked in a skeptical tone.

"There is a possibility," she said, "that this demolition may be halted for good. I just need time to figure out how to prevent it."

"When will you know?" Troy asked.

It was a reasonable question. Kate took a deep breath. "I hope to have an answer this morning." And if the deeds at the courthouse showed what she suspected they did, there would be no need to close the library ever again.

Both men looked surprised. "That," said Gordie, "would be extraordinarily good timing."

The quiet understatement made all three of them grin.

"So." Gordie rubbed his hands together. "What's our P of A?"

Kate looked at him blankly.

"Plan of action," Troy translated. "The fact that I understand him means we've worked together too many times."

Kate chuckled. She liked both of these men immensely. If nothing else, they gave her badly needed hope this morning.

"I've got some plans to pursue to try to prevent this," she said.

Troy pointed at Gordie. "Then you and I need to put our heads together and see which judges we want to approach with this. After that, we can come back here and observe for a while, maybe see some of these squirrels for ourselves."

Kate directed them to the Country Diner and wished them luck. Just as she turned to go back to her car, she saw Livvy coming toward her. Every line of her friend's posture radiated dejection.

"Hi," Kate said softly, putting an arm around Livvy's waist. Together they turned to look at the library.

Livvy sniffed, holding a tissue to the corner of one eye to absorb the tear gathering there. "Everything's out. Tosten Glass is meeting me here in a few minutes to do the final walk-through. Yesterday I went through alone and said good-bye." Her voice caught. "I just can't believe this." As she started to cry, she turned and buried her face against Kate's shoulder.

Kate's own eyes were brimming now. She had to bite her tongue in the most literal sense to keep from blurting out the attempts she was still making to save the building. She just couldn't tell Livvy her plans. What if she encouraged Livvy to hope and then things fell through?

She hugged Livvy once more and stepped back. "All right," she said, dashing away tears. "I have some places I have to go this morning, but I'll meet you here at one o'clock. Whatever happens, we'll face it together, okay?"

"Okay. Together," Livvy repeated.

They shared a brief bracing smile, and then Kate turned toward the Honda. She had to get busy right this very minute.

KATE DROVE TO PINE RIDGE and parked on the town square close to the Harrington County Courthouse. The place was hopping on Monday morning, she discovered.

Kate loved the old courthouse. On the National Register of Historic Places, it was a graceful antebellum treasure that had been used as a Union hospital during and after the campaign of 1863, when Union forces crossed the Tennessee River southwest of Chattanooga, running the Confederate army out of the city.

Kate walked up the wide marble steps to the main entrance and stepped into the expansive foyer. Deputies strode down hallways, people stood around nervously waiting for their court appointments, and other folks rushed in and out of all of the offices that kept the county government functioning smoothly.

Heading down a back stairway to the basement level, Kate followed a long corridor to the deeds office. On the door was a sign that read Register of Deeds. She opened the door with its frosted windowpane and walked into the tiny office, hoping that she was on the right track.

Kate filled out a request form before approaching the registrar at the desk.

"Hi, Mrs. Sedberry. I'd like to see the deed for the Copper Mill Public Library," she said.

In a slow, methodical manner, Eleanor Sedberry straightened the already perfectly aligned edges of the calendar blotter on her metal desk. She held out a liver-spotted hand. "Let me see your paperwork."

Kate handed over the form she had just filled out. Mrs. Sedberry adjusted her glasses and glanced at it.

"I'll be back in a minute," the woman said, shuffling around the counter and out the door.

Kate knew it would take the older woman more than a minute to find the files, so she settled in a chair for the long wait. The county deeds were housed in a large storeroom on the same floor, but getting there required a meandering trip down a confusing maze of corridors.

Kate looked down and realized that her hands were shaking. What if she was wrong about the notion she'd been considering? *Dear Lord*, she prayed, *if I was wrong about this, give me the strength to be a comfort to Livvy.*

After what seemed like an eternity, the moment of truth arrived. Mrs. Sedberry shuffled back through the door toward Kate, an ancient-looking file folder in her gnarled hands.

"This is it. You can look at it, and I can make you copies, but it can't leave this room."

Kate hesitated for a moment. The contents of this file could be the difference in whether the town of Copper Mill lost its library today. Slowly she flipped open the file. The pages inside were firmly fastened in place and obviously hadn't been removed in some time. The document on top was the current deed. Kate's heart began to pound as she read it.

Just then, the door opened and a clerk came in. Kate glanced up. The clerk was Louisa Pellman.

Louisa saw Kate, and her gaze flew to the file folder Kate was reading.

Kate tapped the file and said quietly, "It's the library deed."

Louisa's face crumpled, and she began to cry.

A FEW MOMENTS LATER, Kate walked up the stairs from the Register of Deeds office with Louisa at her side. She followed signs to the sheriff's office, reaching it from an inside door rather than the side entrance she normally used.

Rosalie Merriman, the sheriff's receptionist, looked up from her monitor. "Hi, Kate. What are you doing over here?"

Kate gestured to the person who had come into the room with her. "We need to speak with Sheriff Roberts, Rosalie."

Rosalie assessed Kate's grave demeanor instantly. She pushed her chair away from her desk and rose. "He's in the office today. Let me see if he's available."

A moment later, Sheriff Alan Roberts came up the hallway to shake hands with Kate. A stocky man with a Santa Claus belly, Roberts had shrewd brown eyes that were evaluating Kate and her guest carefully. Although he wasn't fond of civilian involvement in his investigations, he had found Kate to be helpful on a number of occasions.

"Good morning, Kate. How can I help you today?"

"We need five minutes of your time," Kate told him.

"Sure thing." He led the way back to his office and held the door wide so the two women could precede him. "I thought you'd be over at the library consoling Livvy today," he said, shaking his head. "Heck of a thing, tearing down that great old building."

"Actually," Kate said, "that's what we'd like to talk to you about."

PAUL AND HIS WORK CREW had been shingling Louisa Pellman's roof all morning. Minus "Jerry Cox," of course. The man, whom Paul now knew was really Gerald Foxfield, hadn't shown up since the day Kate had appeared at the job site. At noon, Paul called a halt to the work.

"Today is the day of the library demolition," he said. "One o'clock. I'd like to be there, so let's knock off for a while. Can we meet back here at three?"

"I'm going with you," Eli said. "I have to see it with my own eyes to believe it."

"Me too," Sam said. In the end, Joe Tucker and Carl Wilson, the remaining two crew members, decided they'd go along too, and everyone piled into Sam's SUV.

KATE DROVE BACK to Copper Mill with Louisa in the passenger seat. She followed the sheriff's cruiser, which led the way. Tears trickled silently down the young woman's face from time to time.

Finally Kate said, "Why, Louisa? Why would you do this?"

"Gerald threatened me. That's why he was at my mother's house the day you saw his blue Caddy. He saw my picture in the paper after it was in that article, and he saw that I worked at the courthouse. He told me if I didn't help him falsify the deed to the library, he'd see to it that I lost full custody of the kids." She began to sob harder. "He's my husband's cousin, and he said he'd testify that I had . . . neglected and abused my kids. He said my ex-husband would get them."

"How could he do that?" Kate asked. "It's not that easy to prove neglect, and I can't imagine that he could prove abuse without any physical evidence. Your children certainly wouldn't have testified to that."

Louisa looked horrified. "That was exactly why I couldn't take that chance. I would never let them be put on a witness stand. Their father doesn't really want them. He just wants to use them to control me. And he's hurt Jeremy before." Her voice grew quieter. "I'm afraid he'd hurt them, just like he hurt me."

Kate thought about the dark circles beneath the young woman's eyes. Guilt was the reason she hadn't been sleeping, Kate was certain. Louisa's children were so well behaved that Kate hadn't been able to imagine them giving her that much to worry about.

Louisa rushed on, words pouring out like a waterfall now that the floodgates were open. "When Gerald started asking me questions about what you were doing, I did tell him that Mr. and Mrs. Jenner weren't involved. I didn't want him to do those terrible things he threatened them with."

"How did you know about them?"

"I was the one who had to slip the notes into her office after Mr. Glass wrote them. I read them. And the same with the one in your purse."

"*Mr. Glass* wrote them?" That was a new revelation. Kate had already realized that Louisa had placed the note in her handbag the night the Pellmans had come to dinner. It hadn't been Eva Mountjoy or anyone else.

"I hated deceiving you," Louisa said miserably. "You and Pastor Hanlon have been so kind to us. You've been so wonderful with Jeremy . . . and we love the library too. He's been terribly upset about the demolition." She buried her face in her hands. "I'm a horrible person." Then her head snapped up, and her whole body twisted to face Kate. "If they put me in jail, will you take my children? Will you help me keep my ex-husband from taking custody? I'm not kidding about him being violent. He'll hurt them. I know he will."

Chapter Twenty-Six

Kate took one hand off the wheel and clasped it over Louisa's clenched fist. "I'll do everything I can," she said soothingly. "But I can't imagine that you're going to jail. You were coerced into wrongdoing."

"I should have gone to the police," Louisa whispered. "But Gerald said he had friends in the county police force. I was just so afraid . . ."

Kate's heart ached for the frightened young mother. Her mouth tightened. Gerald Foxfield certainly had known every button to push to use Louisa's fears to his advantage.

She glanced at her watch. Twelve fifty. She was conscious of her heartbeat racing. They were barely going to make it.

SAM GORMAN DROVE PAUL and the rest of their roofing crew into town and parked along Smith Street. Sam couldn't get very close to the library because Main had been blocked off with sawhorses between Smith and Sweetwater, so the five men got out and walked two blocks to where a crowd had gathered. There were still thirty minutes to go before the scheduled demolition, but word seemed to have spread quickly.

There were expandable steel barricades of yellow and black creating a barrier around the library. Signs attached to the barricades read: WARNING! Restricted Area. Authorized Personnel Only. No one could get closer than the middle of Main Street. A crew from Crawford Demolitions had already maneuvered several machines into position in front of the library. Paul recognized a backhoe, a small Bobcat, a larger bulldozer, and a wrecking ball, and there were several more machines of varying sizes and shapes. Two large trucks waited, presumably to carry away debris. The crew and machine operators stood around, some smoking in a desultory fashion, never making eye contact with the crowd.

The crowd was oddly silent. Depression hovered like fog. But at ten till one, young Jeremy Pellman sped down the street on his bike, slid right under the barricade without stopping, and screeched to a halt in front of the library.

"Hey, kid, you can't be over here," called one of the crew members.

"I have to check on the squirrels." Jeremy darted past the men and knelt by a hole in the corner of the library foundation. "You're going to kill them all," he accused the men.

"Huh? What squirrels?" said one of the workers.

"There's a whole family of squirrels in here," Jeremy said to him, pointing toward the exterior wall of the library.

One of the other men, looking sympathetic, said, "They'll run, kid, when they hear all the noise."

"No, they won't." Normally a sweet, mellow kid, Jeremy

looked rebellious, a determined expression Paul had never seen before on his young face.

"Jeremy," Paul called, putting authority into his voice. "Come over here."

The boy hesitated and then leaned his bike against the ground and came slowly toward Paul. He ducked under the barrier to stand at Paul's side.

"I'm sorry, son," Paul said, placing an arm around his shoulders. "I wish there was something I could do." Where was Kate? He couldn't believe she would miss this. Livvy, who stood at the front center of the crowd with Danny on one side and her sons on the other, looked terribly vulnerable and alone, despite her family's presence, and the library employees ranged around them.

Five minutes before the hour, a tall man in coveralls and a yellow hard hat walked around from the side of the building, followed by two other men with clipboards and small tools.

"Fire 'em up, fellas," he called.

The demolition crew stretched and put out their cigarettes. One climbed into the cab of the bulldozer.

Just then, Jeremy broke away from Paul's side. "No!" the boy cried. "You can't tear down our library."

Before Paul could stop him, Jeremy ducked beneath the barrier and ran through the equipment to the door of the library. He turned around and faced the crowd defiantly, then slowly and deliberately sat down on the ground. Paul could see his lower lip trembling, and his heart ached for the boy.

The worker in the bulldozer swung out of his seat and hung in the doorway of the cab. Paul appreciated the action;

it ensured that there was no chance of a machine starting while the child was in harm's way.

"Hey, son," called the man in the coveralls, clearly the head of the operation. "I'm really sorry, but you can't stay there. This is a demolition site. I don't like it any better than you do, but I have a job to do."

The man leaned down to lift Jeremy to his feet but froze when a raspy voice that sounded strained to its limits called, "Don't you lay a hand on that boy or I'll have you arrested for assault!"

The crowd gasped. A moment later, Paul saw a bleached-blonde in a sea of pink clothing and high heels tottering toward the library. He was stunned to recognize Renee Lambert, who was carrying an oversized tote bag with Kisses' tiny head poking out of it.

She glanced around, held out the tote, and ordered, "Morty, come and take my precious baby. I don't want him to get hurt."

Morty Robertson ducked beneath the barricade and silently took the large tote Renee carried, then walked back to the barricade, cradling the tote with Renee's Chihuahua inside.

Renee said, "I cannot believe I'm about to do this," then she slowly lowered herself to the ground beside Jeremy.

The boy grinned at her and gave her a thumbs-up. Paul choked back an inappropriate burst of laughter at the expression on Renee's face. He wasn't sure whether she had meant she couldn't believe she was about to protest, or if she'd simply meant she couldn't believe she was going to sit down on the ground.

A third person ducked the barricade and ran up to sit on

the other side of Renee. It was a young woman in black with a mop of purple hair and a lot of silver jewelry.

The crew chief in the coveralls stared at her for a minute and said, "Melissa!"

"Relax, Dad," the young woman said. "It's the right thing to do."

Livvy eased under the barricade next. She ran forward, knelt and kissed Jeremy on the cheek, and sat down beside him.

Father Lucas stepped up next. He caught Paul's eye, grinned, and shrugged as he seated himself. "Peaceful, non-violent solutions," he said. "What better way than to lead by example?"

More people followed Father Lucas: Dot Bagley, who needed help from the priest to lower her plump body to the ground; Fish, the mail carrier; Jeff Turner; the oldest Rowland brother, Mike; and Ronda from the beauty salon. Paul recognized Eva Mountjoy and Carey Carver from the town council as well.

And many more! People Paul never would have expected to see rally in defense of the library came forward to position themselves in front of the building. When he saw his own secretary walk forward, Paul shook his head in disbelief.

Millie waved at him and yelled, "Get up here." Paul promptly ducked beneath the barrier and joined her, and the other four men who had come to town with him followed. Soon it began to look like there were more people in the group of seated protesters than there were standing behind the barricade.

Morty Robertson tapped the crew chief on the arm. When

the man turned to him, Morty said, "Would you mind holding this for me?" and before the man could protest, Morty shifted the tote containing Kisses into the fellow's arms, ducked beneath the barricades, and joined the protesters. The construction workers began to laugh.

After a moment of stunned silence, the crew chief began to chuckle too. He called to his men, "Knock off, guys. Go get some coffee. We can't do anything until these people are cleared."

He looked back at Jeremy Pellman and winked before he leaned against one of the silent machines, carefully holding Kisses. Slowly the demolition team dispersed, and Paul saw a few of them still grinning and giving the protesters a thumbs-up. It warmed his heart to realize that even this rough-and-tough group of construction workers regretted the destruction of a valuable community institution.

Everyone cheered as the crew walked away. But as it grew quiet again, a strident voice could be heard. Paul turned to see who it was. He recognized the fellow instantly; after all, Paul had worked with him.

Gerald Foxfield was doing the shouting. Beside him, Tosten Glass, the council president, stood with his hands on his hips. A younger blond fellow stood slightly behind Foxfield with his arms folded. He looked as if he'd rather be anywhere else. Paul suspected it was the lawyer Kate had spoken to earlier in the week. Straw? No, hay. Hayer.

Paul's heart sank. What trick did Foxfield have up his sleeve that he'd needed to bring his lawyer?

Chapter Twenty-Seven

It was five after one. Kate's heart was in her throat. *Please, Lord, don't let us be too late*, she prayed as she ran toward the library with Louisa and her two conservationist friends who had met her when she parked. They'd been forced to park a distance away. Kate hadn't expected the size of the crowd that apparently had turned out.

As the women, Gordie, and Troy hurried toward the library, Kate realized she didn't hear anything that sounded like demolition going on. Surely they would be able to hear a machine tearing down walls, wouldn't they?

Sheriff Roberts passed them, the flashing lights on his official SUV clearing a path through the people clogging the street as he inched closer to the scene. As she drew near the barricade, Kate saw Gerald Foxfield, the lawyer Ellis Hayer, and town-council president Tosten Glass huddled together. Foxfield was shouting and gesticulating at the library, where Kate could see a bunch of demolition equipment and—

Protesters?

She looked closer, and her mouth fell open. She stopped running to stare, her chest heaving as she caught her breath.

"What's wrong?" The two men behind her nearly ran her down.

She pointed. "Th-that's my husband!" *And my friend and —and half the town*, she realized. They were all calmly seated in front of the library.

Gordie began to laugh. "Wow. This town is amazing."

Jeremy yelled, "Mom! Come join us," and Louisa, after scrubbing the tears from her face, ducked beneath the barricade and headed toward her son.

Troy was smiling too. "Is that Foxfield?" he murmured to Kate, indicating the ranting and raving man. When she nodded, he said, "Showtime." He moved ahead of Kate and Gordie, heading for Gerald.

Livvy scrambled up from the ground and ran to meet them. Paul also got up and came toward the group.

"What's going on?" Livvy asked Kate. For the first time since Kate had come home from her trip, there was hope and animation in Livvy's face.

"Just watch," Kate said, grinning as she took Livvy by the elbow and drew her along with them.

Paul followed, and when Kate came to a halt in front of Gerald Foxfield, Paul rested his hands on her shoulders in a supportive, protective gesture. Thankful for his presence, she briefly leaned back against him.

Sheriff Roberts joined them. He hadn't been able to get as close to the scene as he might have liked, and he was still breathing hard after the rush from his SUV.

As the group stood in front of Foxfield, Kate took a

moment to whisper to the sheriff what Louisa had told her about the threats Gerald had made.

Then Troy extended a hand, forcing Gerald to do the same. "Mr. Foxfield. I'm Troy Silhouse, from the US Fish and Wildlife Service. This is my colleague, Gordon Connaly, who's with the Center for Biological Diversity." Troy reached into the breast pocket of his snappy suit. "This is an injunction from Harrington County Judge, the Honorable Emmett Barger, who has issued a temporary restraining order against any persons or agencies attempting to commence the demolition of the Copper Mill Public Library in Copper Mill, Tennessee." He slipped it into Foxfield's hand while the man stood looking at him in disbelief.

Tosten Glass said, "Why, that's preposterous!"

Ellis Hayer, Gerald's lawyer, had been standing a pace behind him. He stepped forward and took the injunction from Foxfield's frozen hand, opening it and scanning its contents.

"This is in order," he said to Gerald. "You can't do anything with the library until the status of . . . a population of *squirrels* is determined?" His voice rose in disbelief, and he looked at Silhouse for confirmation.

Troy nodded. "If you wish to contest it," he said, "there's a number you can call to set up a meeting with Judge Barger and my office."

"You can't do this!" Gerald said. His face contorted with fury.

"I assure you I can," Silhouse told him. "The USFW is a bureau of the Department of the Interior, which I'm sure you are aware is a branch of the federal government and, as such, has the power to delay projects undertaken in unseemly haste until their impact on the environment can be measured."

Kate had to stifle a grin at the stilted official language she was sure Tony had used on purpose.

Gerald angled his body and took a step toward Kate. His fists were clenched and his head lowered as if he was about to charge. "This is all your fault," he bellowed. "You meddling—"

Sheriff Roberts stepped in front of Kate as Paul's hands began to draw her backward. "Mr. Foxfield," he said, "you are under arrest for forging a document pertaining to the ownership of the Copper Mill Public Library and for attempting to perpetrate blackmail."

"What?" Gerald's face turned deep purple. "I didn't do any such—"

"We have copies of the original deed, stating that Charles Foxfield donated the property to the town of Copper Mill for the establishment of a public library," Kate said. She watched with interest as Tosten Glass began to sidle away from Foxfield. "In addition, Louisa Pellman has told us about your scheme to claim ownership of the library and demolish it in order to search for gold and ultimately turn it into an apartment complex. She also told us that you forced her to plant blackmail notes in Mrs. Jenner's office. You also had her plant a note in my purse attempting to cast aspersions on Malcolm Dekker and Eli Weston. Louisa has agreed to testify to all of that."

Gerald looked at Louisa with loathing. "You stupid girl. I knew you were going to be a problem."

"What?" Ellis Hayer looked ill. The attorney's color had drained away beneath his tan, and he regarded his client with disbelief. "You forged the deed to the library that you showed me?" His voice rose. "The one I took to the council? You don't own this property?"

"That's correct," Kate said.

Gerald started to bellow something, but Sheriff Roberts spun him around and expertly cuffed his wrists behind his back before Foxfield could move. Efficiently, Roberts began to frog-march the resisting man to his SUV, where Deputy Skip Spencer waited to help load the prisoner.

"He forged the deed," Ellis Hayer said again in disbelief. "Why would he do that?"

"Personal gain," Kate told the lawyer and the others assembled. "His family was quite wealthy, but it appears that Gerald Foxfield squandered the fortune after his father passed away. He lost nearly everything."

Paul gave a low whistle behind her and several sets of eyebrows shot up.

"But why our library?" Livvy asked.

"The library was donated to the town by Gerald Foxfield's grandfather in the 1930s," Kate told them all. "I think Gerald cooked up the fake deed plot to claim he owned it for two reasons. First, if he demolished the library, he could build multiunit apartments in its place. Second, there was once a vein of gold discovered in a streambed that ran through here. Foxfield had some crazy idea that he was going to find gold, I believe."

"But what about zoning requirements and building codes?" Livvy said. "He couldn't just excavate or build there willy-nilly without the proper permits."

"Oh, I believe he thought he wouldn't have any trouble

getting the permits he needed," Kate said. She turned to the council president, who had stepped back even farther in an attempt to distance himself from the trouble. "Isn't that right, Tosten?"

"I don't know what you're talking about," Glass bluffed. "When that man came to the council with a copy of the deed and Foxfield's demands, we had no way of knowing it was a false document. We only did what we had to do, legally speaking."

"And Gerald Foxfield will testify that you had nothing to do with it?" Kate countered. "That he didn't bribe you to push his requests through with the promise of sharing his future wealth?"

Glass wilted visibly, the pugnacious expression on his face fading. "Everyone knows that man's a liar," he said.

"Then why did Foxfield hire the demolition company on June 30, before the council had even learned about the supposed deed problem? A person might think that Foxfield knew someone on the council who was going to smooth the way."

Glass hesitated. It was only a fraction of a second, but everyone watching him caught the flare of panic in his eyes. "You're crazy. You'll never prove it." He sneered at Kate.

Suddenly she realized who had made the threatening phone call on Thursday. Tosten sounded hoarse and desperate—much as he had on the phone.

"When your telephone records are subpoenaed, and we can prove you made a phone call to my home threatening me if I didn't stop investigating the library demolition," Kate told him, "we will."

Sheriff Roberts had returned from his SUV, where Deputy Spencer was keeping watch over Gerald Foxfield.

"All right," he said, "then let's get started. Mr. Glass, I suggest you call your attorney, because if you aren't telling the truth, you are going to face some conspiracy and attempted blackmail charges, at the very least."

"You're wrong," Glass said desperately. "All of you." He turned and forced a path through the curious onlookers who had gathered. Sheriff Roberts followed close behind him, pulling out a second set of handcuffs.

There was a brief silence in the wake of Glass' departure, broken by loud, angry protests as Sheriff Roberts began to read him his rights. For the first time, Kate noticed council member Ben Dean standing near the back of the crowd. Dean looked as stunned and betrayed as many others in the crowd. She had suspected him at one point, but it appeared that he was truly just a fiscal conservative who didn't appreciate the value of the library.

Ellis Hayer cleared his throat. "Please give my apologies to the citizens of this community," he said to Kate. "I thought the deed was legal."

"So did the town-council members the first time they saw a copy of it," Kate said. "Apology accepted."

Hayer turned and walked away. The crowd was dispersing now that the drama was over, and as word spread, the protesters were climbing to their feet. People could be heard asking it if was safe to leave their places.

Troy and Gordie smiled at each other and shook hands, and then each offered a hand to Kate.

"Your efforts were both heroic and astonishing," Gordie said to Kate.

"Oh, it wasn't me." Kate blushed and smiled as she pointed heavenward. "I'm just one of several instruments. Jeremy, come here," she called, spotting the youngster approaching with Louisa at his side. "I want to introduce you to the boy who discovered these squirrels," she told the men.

After the introductions were made, Paul opened his arms and hugged her. "You *are* astonishing," he told her. "I'm so proud of you, Katie. I thank God for sharing you with me every day."

Tears stung Kate's eyes, and she kissed her husband right there in the middle of Main Street. "I love you," she told him. Then she remembered what he'd been doing that morning. "Why are you here? I thought you'd be working on Louisa's roof."

"None of us wanted to miss this," he said. "When we thought the library was coming down, I thought moral support might be needed. As it turned out, we were able to lend a little more than just moral support."

Kate laughed, thinking of all the people who had stepped in front of those machines to stage a sit-down protest.

Over Paul's shoulder, she caught sight of Livvy. Her friend was surrounded by Danny and their boys and a dozen other library workers and volunteers. Louisa Pellman had moved to her side, and Livvy had her arm around Louisa's shoulders, patting her as she wept. But as Kate's eyes met Livvy's, Livvy grinned and beckoned.

"We'll talk later," Kate said to Paul. "Right now I have to go celebrate with Livvy!" And she flew off to her friend.

Livvy met her halfway, and they threw themselves into each other's arms as their families and friends beamed.

"Oh, Kate," Livvy said, hugging her so tightly that Kate squeaked and gasped for breath, "if not for you, this horrible event would have had a very different outcome. How can I ever thank you? I gave up, you know. When I should have been trusting God and supporting you, I was throwing in the towel and bracing myself for the worst."

"It's understandable," Kate said. "It's called self-protection. You had to prepare yourself for the worst so you could function afterward. If the demolition had occurred, everyone would have been looking to you for leadership."

Livvy closed her eyes for a moment. "I still can't believe it isn't going to happen!"

Kate took her by the shoulders and gently squeezed. "It *isn't* going to happen," she said. Then she shook her head. "Although we've got a huge task ahead of us putting everything back."

"I don't care!" Livvy laughed, sounding giddy and just the teeniest bit hysterical. "It needed a good cleaning anyway. And maybe new carpet and some paint while we're at it!"

Kate and the volunteers gathered around and laughed. Renee had retrieved Kisses from Adam Crawford, who was directing his men as they got ready to take the demolition equipment away.

Renee said, "And we'll all help, Livvy. I can direct the restoration of the historical room for you."

Livvy smiled and patted Renee on the shoulder. "Thank you," she said. "I'll decide how to handle it all in a little while."

Behind Renee, Morty rolled his eyes.

Paul joined Kate. "We have an awful lot to be thankful for here today," he said. "Would anyone care to pray with me for a moment?"

"Excellent idea," said Father Lucas. He extended his hands to those on either side of him, and within minutes, a huge circle had formed in front of the library, hands clasped tightly together.

Paul pitched his voice loudly so that everyone could hear. "Dear Lord," he began, "we thank you for this glorious day. We thank you for your divine intervention in the form of all the people who worked to save this library—"

"Especially Mrs. Hanlon," piped up Jeremy.

Everyone chuckled, and Paul said, "Especially Mrs. Hanlon. And also Jeremy Pellman, who was brave enough to stage a peaceful protest to save his squirrels." He continued to pray, ultimately inviting everyone to join in saying the Lord's Prayer together.

As they prayed, Kate opened her eyes a tiny bit. Beneath her lashes, she peeked around, thanking God for this special little town.

About the Author

A BEST-SELLING AUTHOR with multiple awards to her credit, Anne Marie Rodgers has more than three dozen novels of inspirational and romance fiction in print. She has been honored by Washington Romance Writers with the chapter's highest volunteer award for outstanding chapter service. Anne Marie enjoys needlework, singing with her church choir and Nittany Lions' sporting events at her home in State College, Pennsylvania. She and her family have raised guide dog puppies, and she has worked in animal rescue for many years. After Hurricane Katrina, she volunteered at the Humane Society of Louisiana. Anne Marie currently volunteers at a wildlife rehabilitation center.

A Note from the Editors

GUIDEPOSTS, a nonprofit organization, touches millions of lives every day through products and services that inspire, encourage and uplift. Our magazines, books, prayer network and outreach programs help people connect their faith-filled values to their daily lives. To learn more, visit www.guideposts.com or www.guidepostsfoundation.org.